GRETCHEN McNEIL

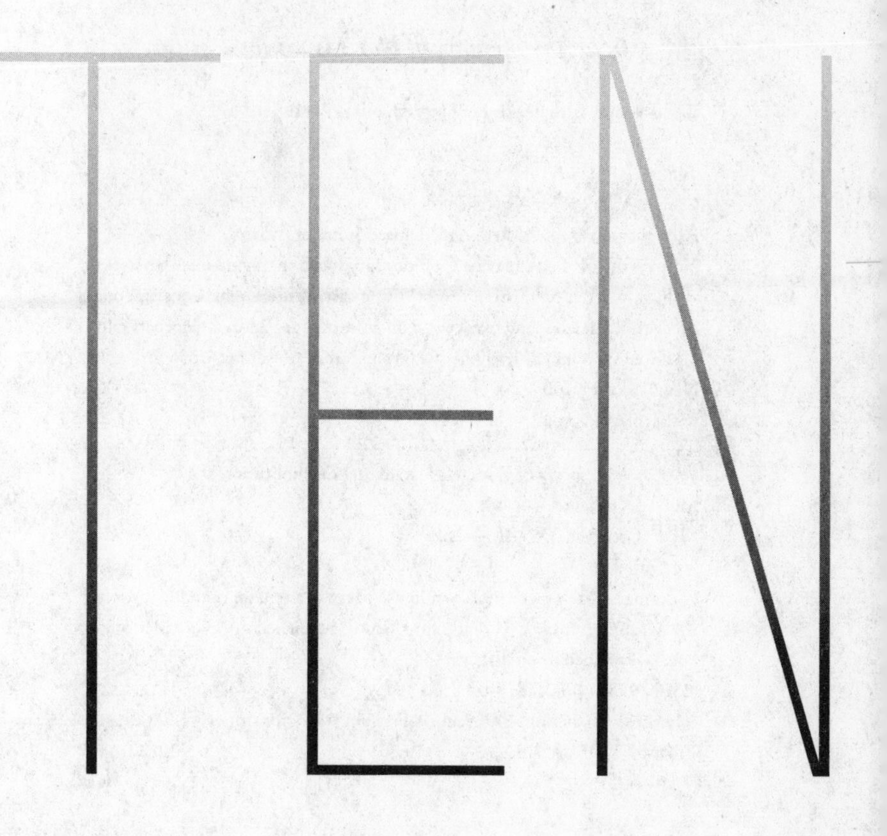

Balzer + Bray
An Imprint of HarperCollins*Publishers*

In loving memory of Doris Godinez-Phillips

Balzer + Bray is an imprint of HarperCollins Publishers.

Ten

www.epicreads.com

Library of Congress Cataloging-in-Publication Data
McNeil, Gretchen.
Ten / Gretchen McNeil. — 1st ed.
p. cm.
Summary: "Ten teens head to a house party at a remote island mansion off the Washington coast . . . only for them to be picked off by a killer one by one."—Provided by publisher.
ISBN 978-0-06-211879-0
[1. Murder—Fiction. 2. Revenge—Fiction. 3. Horror stories.] I. Title.
PZ7.M4787952Te 2012 2012014342
[Fic]—dc23 CIP
AC

Typography by Torborg Davern
20 PC/LSCH 20 19 18 17 16 15 14 13
❖
First paperback edition, 2013

AND THEIR DOOM COMES SWIFTLY.

ONE

MINNIE'S FACE WAS DEATHLY PALE. SHE STARED straight ahead, eyes fixed on the back of the stained cloth seat, and bit her bottom lip so hard that Meg was afraid she would draw blood. She'd never seen Minnie this seasick.

"Mins, are you okay?"

Minnie dug her fingernails into the seat cushion. "I'm fine."

"You're turning green."

The ferry rolled to the left as a particularly large swell hit them from starboard and Minnie clamped both hands over her mouth. For one tenuous moment, Meg was convinced her best friend was going to hurl right there in the passenger cabin, but as the boat slowly righted itself, Minnie relaxed.

"I'm fine," she repeated, lowering her hands.

"Uh-huh."

Meg rifled through her backpack and pulled out a plastic grocery bag, which Minnie absently took from her outstretched hand. "You don't think it'll be much longer, do you?"

Meg leaned against the cushion and propped her feet up on

the facing row of seats. "I think we're almost there."

"Promise?"

Meg sighed. "I can't promise when the ferry will arrive, Mins. But according to the schedule, we're almost there, okay?"

"Fine!" Minnie snapped.

Meg recognized the sharpness in Minnie's voice. It usually signaled a rapid change in Minnie's mood, which happened all too frequently these days, especially when she stopped taking her antidepressants.

Instead of asking about her meds, which would just lead to an argument, Meg tried to get Minnie to think about something else.

"Remember when your parents invited me to Friday Harbor?" Meg said. It had been the summer before high school, the first time Meg had been invited on vacation with Minnie's family.

A hint of a smile broke the corner of Minnie's mouth. "You were *so* sick."

"Right?"

"You puked all over the bathroom in that ferry."

Meg laughed. "I thought your mom was going to throw me overboard."

"Me too." Minnie giggled.

Not one of Meg's favorite memories, but maybe it would keep Minnie's mind off her churning stomach. "And you weren't sick at all. So I'm sure you'll be fine 'til we get to Henry Island."

Minnie shook her head. "But that was *summer*. When the water's *calm*." Minnie gestured toward the double-paned window. "Not like this."

"Good point."

Meg gazed outside. The rain had died down for the moment—erratic water trails no longer zipped diagonally across the pane—but the wind, if anything, had intensified. It howled past the cabin, whipping from ahead, then slamming into the sides of the ferry with a force that seemed almost supernatural.

Minnie leaned her head against Meg's shoulder. "Maybe we shouldn't have come."

Meg couldn't suppress a laugh. "It's a bit late for that."

"I know, but . . ."

"But what? This party is all you've talked about since we got the invites on Tuesday. I haven't seen you this excited about anything since your dad gave you an Amex card for your birthday."

Minnie sat up straight. "Jessica Lawrence invited us to her house party. That's not an invitation you turn down, but . . ." She sighed deeply. "I don't know. It's not like we're friends."

"You used to be," Meg said without thinking.

"Well, that was before—" Minnie stopped herself, but Meg knew what she was going to say: *before you*. "That was a long time ago," Minnie said instead.

The unspoken words hung in the air like stale cigarette smoke. Meg had been the reason for Minnie's fall from grace in the greater Seattle junior high social scene. They both knew it, but it was a touchy subject and one they rarely discussed. Minnie turned her head to the window and stared out into the darkening afternoon, and Meg instantly regretted even alluding to her friend's former closeness with Jessica.

To distract herself, Meg pulled a copy of the Facebook invite out of her backpack and read it over for the bazillionth time.

Shhh! Don't Spread the Word!

WHAT: Epic house party

WHEN: Presidents' Day weekend

WHERE: White Rock House on Henry Island

WHY: Because if you miss this party you'll regret it forever

Fully stocked house all to ourselves for three days. Like spring break in February! We've got special ferries set up and everything!!!!

But keep it quiet. We don't want just anybody showing up. Can't wait to see you there!

—Jess

Meg never felt comfortable at those kinds of parties; most of the time she just wanted to disappear into the wallpaper and pray that no one noticed her. But Minnie had been so excited. It was like an olive branch from the popular crowd. Meg couldn't say no.

With any luck, she could find some quiet time alone, maybe wander the beaches by herself, find an isolated spot with her journal or her laptop and get some writing done.

A gust blasted the side of the ferry, rattling the cabin window. Meg sighed. Or maybe write in an isolated spot indoors? Like a broom closet or something? Stupid storm.

"Hey, I don't want you spending the whole weekend in front of your laptop," Minnie said from out of the blue.

Meg started. Was she really that predictable? "Um, okay."

The plastic bag rustled as Minnie tightened her grip. "You're going to have fun this weekend if it kills me."

Meg bit her lip. "I have plenty of fun."

"You're kidding, right?"

Now it was Meg's turn to be annoyed. "Mins, what are you talking about?"

Minnie sighed dramatically. "You *used* to be fun. Remember? We'd *do* crazy stuff. Now you're like . . ."

Meg shifted in her seat. "Like what?"

"Like boring."

"I'm not boring."

Minnie snorted.

"Besides, we could've had fun at home. And not, you know, lied to our parents and gone to a house party on an island in the middle of nowhere."

Minnie threw up her hands. "It's not the middle of nowhere. Half of Seattle has summer homes on the San Juan Islands. And we were *not* going to tell our parents." Minnie finished with an emphatic nod of her head. "Especially not after that body was found in Everett this morning. Daddy would never have let me go."

Meg shuddered. She'd seen the report on the news, the charred remains of a body found in the locker room of their rival school, Mariner High. It was a gruesome murder and so far the body hadn't been identified.

"The last thing I need this weekend," Minnie continued, "is

Daddy dropping in to check up on me. That would ruin everything."

"Yeah, I guess you're right." Despite the remoteness of the island, Meg couldn't help but agree that Minnie's dad showing up at the party wasn't out of the realm of possibility.

Minnie placed her hand over Meg's and squeezed. "Look, we're going to have fun this weekend. We need it. Okay?"

Meg forced a smile. Minnie was right. There had been such a strain between them the last few months. First Meg's acceptance at UCLA, which Minnie interpreted as Meg abandoning her, then Minnie's struggles with her new medications. And of course the Homecoming night debacle . . .

Stop it, Meg said to herself. She needed to put that night out of her mind. It was over and done. And in a few months she'd never see him again anyway.

Without warning, the dull roar of the engines diminished and Meg felt the ferry slow. A second later, a scruffy-faced deckhand in an orange rain slicker shoved his head inside the cabin. "Henry Island. We'll be docked in a few."

Minnie sprang to her feet. "Finally!" She pulled her overnight wheelie and two small shoulder bags out of the luggage bin, then threw on her coat, glancing over her shoulder as she bounded out on deck. "Try to remember this is a party. Party equals fun."

Meg sighed. Party equals fun. Woo hoo. Yay. Party.

With a deep breath, Meg shouldered her backpack and followed Minnie out on deck.

TWO

THE AIR WAS DAMP WITH THE KIND OF COLD meatiness that signaled the approach of another storm. Wind whipped at Meg's hair, loosening strands from her ponytail. She tucked a few of them behind her ear as her eyes adjusted to the dusk.

Dull lights glowed in the distance across the bay. Roche Harbor, on the back side of San Juan Island. It looked closer than she'd imagined, and it was comforting to know that a decently populated town was just across the bay.

Meg shook her head. Why was she so skittish? She needed to loosen up. Secret house party hosted by the most popular girl in school? People would kill for an invite. So what if her parents didn't know where she was? That was the fun of it, right?

Minnie stood beside the scruffy-faced deckhand, staring down the side of the ferry as it bobbed up and down in the water.

"We have to climb down?" she asked.

"Sorry, miss. Weather's too rough," he said. "Gotta use the ladder."

Minnie glanced at her wholly inappropriate kitten-heel slingbacks. "But . . ."

"Just take them off," Meg said, trying to keep the "I told you so" tone out of her voice.

"Don't worry, miss." The deckhand nodded down to his mate on the dock. "Branson'll catch you if you fall."

Minnie leaned over the rail and looked down at Branson, the portly, middle-aged crewman. Her eyes grew wide and she turned to Meg. "How—"

"You'll be fine," Meg said. "I promise." It was what Minnie needed to hear, even if it wasn't true.

Minnie sighed and slid out of her heels, leaving them on the deck, and purposefully climbed over the side of the boat. "Okay. If you promise."

Meg shook her head as Minnie disappeared over the side, then picked up the discarded heels and shoved them in her backpack. This was why she was going away to college. She needed, for once in her life, to put herself first.

Meg watched the deckhand nonchalantly toss their luggage overboard with the kind of disinterested yet fluid motion that signaled a well-known routine. Branson caught each bag with the same easy flow, depositing it on the dock and swinging around just in time to catch the next one. There was something simultaneously cool and creepy about their unspoken luggage dance, fascinating in its choreography and yet ever so slightly disturbing in the mindless, dronelike way in which it was executed.

"Your turn, miss," the deckhand said, snapping Meg from her thoughts.

"Oh, right." She swung herself onto the ladder. As she started to climb down, the boat heaved and the deckhand grabbed Meg's arm to steady her.

"Thanks," she said, clutching the top rung of the ladder with both hands.

"You sure you'll be okay?" he asked. His hand still gripped her arm.

"Yeah. Short ladder. I'll be fine."

He cocked his head. "No, on the island."

Meg squinted up at his worn, lined face. "Yeah, why not?"

The deckhand paused, then craned his neck to look over toward the northern part of the island. "Nothing," he said at last.

Um, okay.

The ferry's engines fired up again as Meg climbed down the side. "We'll be back Monday to pick you up," the deckhand shouted just as her feet touched the dock. "Be careful."

Be careful? It was a weekend party full of hookups and beer bongs. Other than mono and dehydration, what did she need to be careful of?

Weirder and weirder.

As soon as Meg was clear of the ladder, Branson untied the line and, without a word, scrambled up the side of the boat.

Meg watched wistfully as he swung his body onto the pitching deck and disappeared behind the bulwark as the boat eased away from the island.

She half wished she could join them.

"Now what?" Minnie said. She stood barefoot, twirling a strand of her white-blonde hair.

Good question. Meg reluctantly pulled her attention away from the departing ferry and scanned the dock.

It was a rough, weather-beaten construction that jutted fifty yards out from the beach. Broken planks of moldering wood dotted the path to shore like little landmines, and the swells of water, even in the protected bay, seemed dangerously close to swamping the decaying pier.

Onshore, a forest of Douglas firs towered above the beach, silhouetted against the gray clouds that crowded the darkening sky. Meg thought she caught a glimpse of lights beyond the fringe of trees, but she wasn't quite sure. She couldn't see much in the gathering dusk, and with the moon and stars obscured by storm clouds, it was about to get extremely dark on Henry Island.

As the sound of the ferry's engines faded into the distance, Meg felt suddenly isolated. Other than the dull rumble of water and wind, she couldn't hear a thing, and there were no signs of life on the distant beach. Meg shivered. They were alone in the middle of nowhere, their only contact with the outside world retreating into the night.

Meg yanked her cell phone out of her jeans pocket. She desperately wanted to call someone—anyone—and tell them where they were.

"What are you doing?" Minnie asked.

Meg sheltered the screen of her phone from the ocean spray. "Nothing. Just wanted to see if we had a signal."

"Do *not* call your parents."

"I'm not!" Meg lied. Not that it mattered. She spun around, waving her phone slowly back and forth. The result was the same. "There's no signal anyway."

"Good!" Minnie snatched the phone out of her hand and shoved it in Meg's backpack, retrieving her shoes in the process. She grinned and linked her arm through Meg's. "It's more fun this way. Like we're stranded for three glorious days."

Glorious was not the word that immediately sprang into Meg's mind. "Sure, Mins. Whatever you—"

"Hello down there!"

Meg and Minnie turned sharply. Two figures appeared at the end of the dock, moving quickly toward them. Both were tall and wrapped up in heavy coats. In the muted light, Meg couldn't see their faces, but one of them seemed oddly familiar.

"Meg!"

Meg's stomach lurched. She knew that voice.

Minnie recognized it at the same time. She clapped her hands and squealed. "Oh my *God*!"

Meg felt all the warmth drain from her body.

It was T. J. Fletcher.

THREE

IT HAD BEEN MONTHS SINCE MEG AND T.J. HAD spoken a word to each other. Not since Homecoming. They didn't have any classes together that semester, and since Minnie had broken up with T.J.'s best friend, they never saw each other. Their friendship was over.

Not that everyone and their mom didn't know every detail of T.J.'s life. Meg had heard the rumors: the football scholarship to U-Dub, the string of girlfriends, the wild parties. Minnie talked about him incessantly, obsessively. Although that part was normal. She'd been in love with T.J. since freshman year, even going so far as to date his best friend, Gunner, after T.J. rejected her. So in the weeks after Homecoming, when merely hearing his name made Meg cringe, she had to listen to Minnie go on and on about how amazing he was. . . .

Minnie had no idea that Meg was in love with him too.

Which is why Meg needed to control herself, keep her emotions in check. One look at T.J.'s smiling face, his gorgeous dark brown skin, and prominent dimples, and it would be like one of those cartoon moments where the French skunk's heart pounds so fiercely it literally leaps out of his chest for everyone to see. She couldn't let that happen. No one could know how she really felt. Not Minnie. And especially not T.J.

"Glad you made it," T.J. yelled as he strode down the dock.

Meg tried—and failed—to prevent the hot flush from creeping to her face. She prayed Minnie didn't notice. *He doesn't like you*, she told herself. *He's still mad at you.*

Luckily Minnie only had eyes for T.J. "T.J.!" she squealed. She padded toward him, a slingback dangling from each hand. "We didn't know you'd be here."

No, they didn't. Because there was no way in hell Meg would have come if she'd known T.J. was on the guest list.

The second figure followed T.J. down the dock. At first Meg thought it was Gunner, but the figure was too tall, too lanky. Someone new.

"I was afraid you guys had missed the ferry," T.J. said, slightly out of breath. He wore a beanie cap pulled down low over his ears, covering his closely shaved head, and a peacoat buttoned up to his chin.

"You knew we were coming?" Minnie threw her hands—shoes and all—around his neck and practically launched herself into his arms.

T.J. gave Minnie a combination brosive chest bump and back pound, then side-stepped her entirely and moved to Meg's side. "Of course I knew you'd be here."

Meg's heart thumped so loudly she was convinced everyone

within a two-mile radius could hear it. She dropped her eyes to the warped wooden dock to hide her confusion. "Yeah," she said. "Um, you too."

"Hi." The other guy stood right behind them. "You must be Minnie."

He was just as tall as T.J., but thin and lithe where T.J. was muscular and athletic. His vivid blue eyes sparkled as he grinned at Minnie, the ends just crinkling by his temples, which gave his face a puppyish expression. More striking, he had a shock of hair almost as white-blond as Minnie's. Blonde and blonder.

Minnie cocked her head. "How did you know who I was?"

"I heard you'd be the pretty blonde one." Blondie winked.

Meg desperately fought the urge to roll her eyes at the nacho-cheesiness of his line, but it was like crack for Minnie.

"Oh!" Minnie cooed. She glanced at T.J. "Did you tell him that?"

"Um . . ." T.J.'s eyes darted to the retreating ferry. "Is it just the two of you?" he said, changing the subject.

"Yep," Meg said. "Were you expecting someone else?"

T.J. shook his head. "We got a call from Mr. Lawrence earlier saying Jessica was going to try to make the last ferry. Apparently she and a bunch of friends got stuck at some school thing today, so they'll join us tomorrow."

"Cheerleading," Blondie piped in. "Last-minute practice."

Now he had Minnie's full attention. "You're friends with Jessica?"

"Er," he said, flashing a boyish smile. "Something like that."

So Blondie was Jessica's new boy toy? Interesting.

"Sorry," T.J. said, slapping Blondie on the back. "I should have introduced you. This is Ben."

"No worries, dude." Ben's blue eyes landed on Meg. There was something kind of easy and comfortable about him that she immediately liked. "You must be Meg?"

"Yep," Meg said. She shifted her feet, suddenly conscious that a house full of strangers must have been discussing her if Ben knew who both she and Minnie were.

"M and M?" Ben laughed. "That's adorable."

Minnie grabbed Meg's hand, her attention fixed on Ben. "Besties since we met in the seventh grade."

Ben continued to smile at Minnie. "Can I carry your bags?" he asked.

"Ooh," Minnie said, glancing at T.J. "A gentleman."

T.J. ignored her, and while Ben shouldered Minnie's bags, T.J. gently tugged on the sleeve of Meg's coat. "This way."

T.J. hurried down the dock, his long strides putting easy distance between them and Minnie and Ben. Meg scrambled to keep up with him. Part of her wanted to stay behind with Minnie, avoiding alone time with T.J. at all costs. But there was something else spurring her on. In that moment when she saw T.J. smile at her, Meg realized how much she'd missed him.

They walked in silence, though Meg's mind raced. Should she say something? Bring up what happened on Homecoming night? Try to explain why she bailed on him and beg forgiveness? She wanted to, desperately. But instead she didn't say a word. As usual.

She wished it was September and she was already at college in LA away from all this, from everyone who knew her. Somewhere she could start over and not feel like such an awkward spaz all the time.

T.J. trudged steadily in front of her. As they approached the tree line, she caught their familiar scent—all piney and Christmasy—over the briny sea air and the stench of rotten seaweed wafting up from the beach. Meg took a deep breath. Those two smells, Christmas and the salty sea, were what home smelled like.

The dock itself extended well onto the island and disappeared into the trees, but instead of following it, T.J. deftly leaped down to the beach. He turned to help her just as Meg jumped into the sand. Her momentum pushed her forward into T.J., who put his hands on her waist to brace her. They stood there in the wet sand for a moment; T.J.'s hands never left her waist. It felt so comfortable to be that close to him again, as if there had never been a rift between them. She'd missed him so much. . . .

Minnie's high-pitched giggle rang out as she and Ben approached the end of the dock. Meg shook herself, then broke free from T.J.'s embrace and hurried across the tightly packed sand. *You have to get over him.*

She paused halfway down the beach. Through the trees a house was visible. It seemed as if every light in the two-story vacation home was on, and Meg could hear laughter and music, which swelled and ebbed on the wind.

"They've been partying since the sun went down," said T.J., at her shoulder.

"That's not White Rock House?" Meg asked.

T.J. shook his head. "The Taylors live there. Lawrence Point is at the tip of the island."

"How do you know?"

"I've been here a few times," T.J. said with a shrug.

Oh. Duh, Meg. *When he was dating Jessica's best friend.*

"It's kind of nice," T.J. barreled on. "To know there's another party happening nearby. Don't you think?"

"I guess." Actually, it *was* nice. Somehow knowing that a house full of people was close by put some of her nervousness at ease.

"Come on." T.J. nudged her and Meg followed him past the house. The trees thinned and a narrow strip of land lay ahead, illuminated by the soft orange glow of the Taylors' interior lights. The isthmus protruded from the main island, maybe twenty feet wide and barely four feet above the waterline, with Lawrence Point looming in the distance. The blanched carcasses of dozens of stripped tree trunks littered the isthmus like a giant game of pick-up sticks.

A severed strip of land, besieged on all sides by a hostile sea. Meg felt as if she'd reached the end of the world.

A giant wave crashed onto the eastern shore, completely washing over the tiny land bridge. Meg's eyes grew wide. "We have to cross that?"

"Yeah, there's a path down the middle." T.J. pointed into the semidarkness.

Meg didn't see anything at first, until the receding waves exposed what looked like a rickety handrailing. "Is that a bridge?"

"Kinda," T.J. said. "More like a raised platform, a footbridge to keep you above the water."

Another wave washed over the isthmus, fiercer this time, and Meg and T.J. had to retreat several steps to keep from getting wet. The wave submerged the footbridge completely, leaving only a few inches of the handrail visible above the churning surf. The water retreated, gurgling playfully as it withdrew to either side of the isthmus, taunting them almost, to test their luck.

"There's no other way to get to the house?"

"Nope," T.J. said. "But it's not too bad. We all made a break for it between waves."

"Easy when you could actually see them."

T.J. shoved his hands deep into the pockets of his coat. His face was serious, the dancing smile and dimples gone. "Are you being hostile on purpose?"

"I . . . ," she faltered. "I didn't realize . . ."

"Yes, you did. I know you, Meg Pritchard. You don't say anything unless you mean it."

Meg winced. That was true, the flip side being that she didn't say half of what she wanted to.

"Look," T.J. said in the face of Meg's silence. "I just don't want this weekend to be awkward for either of us. We used to be friends, remember? We used to have fun."

There was that word again. *Fun*. Had she really lost that side of her? No, she was sure she could be that girl again, the girl that laughed and joked with the one guy on the planet with whom she felt she could be completely herself.

"We *are* friends," she said. "And we'll have fun this weekend. I promise." *Even if I die trying.*

T.J. arched his brow. "Yeah?"

Meg eyed the footbridge. The white foam of a retreating wave sparkled in the dim light. The timing was perfect.

A grin stole across her face. "Yeah. Starting now." She spun on her heel and took off running across the isthmus.

FOUR

MEG'S BACKPACK THUMPED AGAINST HER HIP AS she ran. She didn't even look at the ocean to see if a rogue wave might be gathering to wash her out to sea. She honestly didn't care. She was so elated T.J. still wanted to be friends with her that death at the hands of a merciless current seemed a small price to pay.

He hadn't spoken to her since Homecoming. The whole thing had been a perfect storm of not awesome. The image of Minnie's face when she'd confronted Meg was imprinted on her brain. Eyes rimmed red from crying, mascara running in jagged black trails down her face, sunken cheeks, pinched jaw. *You're going to Homecoming with T.J.?*

Minnie had flown into a crying rage. She grabbed Meg's shoulders so fiercely she left five-pointed bruises on each side. *You're going to Homecoming with T.J.?* She spat the words out, her fingernails digging through the thin cotton of Meg's T-shirt and her eyes dashing back and forth across Meg's face. This wasn't her friend, this wasn't the person she'd known for years. She'd been replaced by someone irrational and crazy. It was one of the scariest things Meg had ever seen.

She'd been determined to tell Minnie the truth but there, in the moment, confronted with Minnie's pain, she just couldn't do it. Their friendship was more important to her than a boy.

No. No, of course not. Why would he want to go with me?

Then she'd texted T.J. to say she couldn't go. Not even a call. It was the coward's way out, but she knew if she faced him in person, her resolve would crumble.

And that was that.

Meg forced the painful memory from her mind as she reached the far side of the isthmus, where the footbridge gave way to a sturdy outcropping of rock. The point rose before her, tall and massive, and slightly out of place. Stone steps led up from the beach. Hewn into to the stark granite of the island, each step was polished flat and smooth—probably more a result of the elements than of foot traffic, Meg guessed as she hurried up them—and cut a gray path up the side of the forested hill.

"Meg, slow down!" T.J. hustled up the steps behind her.

"What, can't catch me, Mr. Football?" Meg said with a laugh. She was surprised how easy it was to slip back into flirt mode with T.J. Like she'd never left it. She bolted the last few steps and emerged in a clearing at the top of the hill, T.J. right on her heels.

"Damn, you're fast," he panted. "Didn't think a writer would have that in her."

"Har har," Meg said, wrinkling her nose. She couldn't keep from smiling, though.

"Hell of a climb." T.J. pointed behind Meg. "But worth it, don't you think?"

Meg turned and caught her breath.

White Rock House rose before them. A cross between a lighthouse and a Creole mansion, it stood like a shining whitewashed beacon in the middle of nowhere. A covered patio with a wrought-iron balustrade stretched across the front entrance and disappeared around the eastern corner, and the peaked gables on both the second and third floors hunched forward over the windows, guarding them, perhaps, from the onslaught of Mother Nature. A huge four-story tower emerged from the middle of the house looking like it didn't actually belong to the gabled façade at all.

Meg's eye caught something glistening on the side of the house. She squinted and realized the entire ground floor was covered with an appliqué of shimmering white stones.

At least White Rock House lived up to its name.

Beyond the house, the graduated tree line fell off steeply in all directions. The house had been built like a medieval castle—in a strategic position to protect it from attacking Huns. It was definitely the most secluded, least accessible place she'd ever been. And despite the brilliant white rocks and a sparkling light blazing forth from every window, Meg couldn't help but think the house looked lonely on that point, cut off from the rest of the world.

"Takes a certain kind of person to build that house way the hell out here, right?" T.J. said.

"You really have to stop verbalizing what's in my head," Meg said with a half smile. "It's getting creepy."

"Oh, yeah?" T.J. beamed, as if being told he was a potential creeper was the greatest compliment Meg could have paid him.

"It's kind of cool, the communion with the elements," Ben said. He deposited Minnie's bags on the grass, then reached his hand back and helped Minnie up the last of the steps. "Don't you think?"

"Yeah," Minnie said, making a concerted effort not to pant as she finished the climb. "Elements. Totally." Her pale face was pink with the physical effort of climbing the stairs and she looked as if she might go into cardiac arrest at any moment.

T.J. nudged Meg in the ribs and she had to stare at the ground to keep from laughing.

A gust of wind ripped through the clearing and every tree on the island seemed to spring to life.

"We should get inside," T.J. said. "Looks like it's about to start raging again."

T.J. led the way across the water-logged front lawn to the wrap-around patio. He marched up to the gleaming white door and threw it open. "We're back!"

They stood in a foyer that extended from the main part of the house, almost as if it had been added as an afterthought. Before them, a hallway opened up to a massive staircase. The ceiling slanted upward to a point under one of the house's many gables, and the walls were bare and white except for a row of coat pegs holding a couple of neon-yellow rain slickers on one wall, and a low entry table against the other.

"Dude!" another familiar voice called from the hallway, followed by the sound of heavy footsteps. "Did Jessica and the girls get—"

Gunner Shields appeared in the doorway. He had one of Meg's favorite Most Unfortunate Name Combinations of all time, and it made her giggle inside every time she thought of it.

Despite the fact that it was February in Seattle, Gunner sported a deep tan, and his sun-streaked locks flopped down over each ear. He wore his usual uniform: North Shore T-shirt, baggy jeans, flip-flops. For Gunner, every day was "surf's up."

Even under his faux tan, Meg noticed the color rise in his face when he saw Minnie. "Hey," he mumbled.

Minnie leaned heavily on Ben's arm and smiled. "Hello, Gun Show. I didn't know *you'd* be here this weekend."

Gunner looked furtively over his shoulder. "Yeah, um . . . well . . . ," he stammered.

"No Jessica," T.J. piped in, saving his friend from embarrassment. "Guess we'll have to wait 'til morning."

"Dude," Gunner said with a nod at Ben. "Sucks for you."

Ben glanced at Minnie. "I'll survive."

Minnie giggled and tightened her grip on Ben's arm. Oh boy. Going after the hostess's boyfriend was probably not the best idea Minnie'd had that day.

"Babe." A short Asian girl slipped up behind Gunner. She was a punkish pixie in a black T-shirt and striped arm warmers, with a fat streak of magenta hair sweeping over her eyes. "I need your help in the kitchen."

Meg saw Minnie stiffen as Gunner and Magenta Hair disappeared around the corner. T.J. must have seen it too. "This way." He started up the stairs. "Let me show you to your room and then you can meet everybody else."

Meg was relieved as she followed T.J. up a narrow staircase. So Gunner had a new girlfriend. Good. She'd always liked his sort of good-natured doofiness. And he had worshipped Minnie, which always gave Meg a twinge of guilt since she knew her friend didn't really care about him. She was glad he'd moved on.

Without thinking, her eyes drifted to T.J. Why couldn't she move on too? That flirty closeness they'd experienced as they were climbing up to the house . . . it was the first moment of real happiness Meg had felt since the Homecoming disaster. But she had to get over him. Had to. He was a player—as Minnie brought up repeatedly—they were going to college a thousand miles apart, and her best friend was in love with him. Three strikes. She had to move on.

T.J. caught her staring at him and smiled. "I think you'll like your room."

How was she supposed to get over him when he kept smiling at her like that?

"You're playing host now?" Minnie said. Meg thought she caught an edge to her voice.

"Nah," Ben said. "When we got here, the front door was unlocked and there was a note on the table that said 'Make yourselves at home.' So we did."

T.J. nodded. "There's Wi-Fi and satellite, even an Xbox. Oh, and the fridge is fully stocked. Food, juice, beer."

"There's beer?" Minnie said.

Meg shook her head. Just what she needed. Drunk Minnie was a hot mess. She tended to a get a little . . . mean, and the booze inevitably lead to laughter, falling down, making out, screaming jags, fistfights, and tears, usually—but not always—in that order.

"Calm down, Frank-the-Tank," Meg said. "Let's at least put our stuff away before you start shot-gunning brewskis."

Minnie ignored her. "Where are we going?"

"T.J. saved this room for you guys." Ben pointed up the stairs to the top of the tower. "He thought you'd like it."

Meg stole a glance at T.J. as they rounded the staircase. It was hard to tell with his dark skin, but was his face ever so slightly pink?

The staircase narrowed and hugged all four walls as it wound its way upward around the square tower. There were bare windows that let in enough light to illuminate the entire tower, including the stairs as they disappeared through the ceiling. Meg followed T.J. up and emerged into a garret. It was a small room, plainly furnished with two twin beds, an easy chair, a dresser, and a full-length mirror. But the real selling point for Meg was the enormous row of windows on each of its four walls. She could see the lights of Roche Harbor across the bay, dim and muted through the low fog, and through another window, the dancing glow of the Taylors' house. Meg couldn't wait until morning; the views would be stunning.

"We have to sleep up here?" Minnie said, looking around. "There isn't even a bathroom."

"It's down on the second floor," T.J. said. "I'm sure we could move you if you hate it. We'll probably have to refigure the sleeping arrangements when Jessica and the others come tomorrow anyway."

"Nope, we're good," Meg said.

"But—" Minnie started.

Meg didn't let her finish. "We're good." It was the kind of room she'd always dreamed of staying in as a child, like a turret in a castle. She could picture herself up there, tucked away from the rest of the party, writing on her laptop or in her journal. It was perfect, and she wasn't going to let Minnie mess it up.

Minnie plopped down on the bed nearest the stairs. "Fine."

"Come down when you're ready," T.J. said as he disappeared down the stairs behind Ben. "We're making dinner."

FIVE

"BEN'S CUTE," MEG SAID AS SHE UNZIPPED HER backpack.

Minnie shrugged. "Yeah. He's okay."

"Just okay?"

"That's what I said."

So much for Minnie's good mood. "I dunno, seems like you were kind of into him. And it was really sweet the way he helped you across the beach and up to the house."

"I guess."

Meg frowned. Minnie was being intentionally pissy; Meg knew damn well that she had already set her sights on Ben. "Tall. Blue eyes. Hair as blond as yours. What's not to like?"

"Tons." Minnie opened the wardrobe and examined the closet space.

"Like?"

"He dyes his hair, for starters—his eyebrows are black."

"Oh." Leave it to Minnie to notice something like that. Meg was clueless. "I just thought you guys were cute together."

Minnie spun around. "What, are you trying to pawn me off on someone before you abandon me in September?"

Meg was struck momentarily speechless. She totally didn't see that one coming.

"Well, aren't you?" Minnie asked.

"What are you talking about?"

"You're trying to make me someone else's problem before you leave me."

"I'm not leaving you! I'm going to college." These arguments were starting to make them sound like a married couple on the verge of divorce.

"You could do that here."

"The creative writing program at U-Dub didn't accept me," Meg lied. "You know that."

Minnie opened her mouth to say something, then apparently thought better of it. She snapped her jaw shut and turned abruptly away.

Meg returned to unpacking. Did Minnie actually know that the closest college Meg applied to was over a thousand miles away? Impossible. The only person who knew for sure where Meg had applied was her mom, who wrote the application checks. And if there was one person on the planet who wanted to make sure Meg went to school far away from her clingy best friend, it was Meg's mom.

"You and T.J. seem pretty buddy-buddy," Minnie said out of the blue.

So that's what was bothering her. Meg had been dreading

this, ever since T.J. walked her up to the house from the dock. She'd hoped that the attention Minnie was getting from Ben would distract her from what she wasn't getting from T.J.

No such luck.

"Minnie, don't start."

"What?" Minnie pulled a strapless dress out of her wheelie bag and laid it out on her bed. "I was just voicing an observation."

Meg grabbed some T-shirts and a pair of jeans from her backpack and shoved them in a drawer, leaving her journal and laptop at the bottom of the bag. "I'm not interested in T.J."

"Could have fooled me." Minnie's voice had a singsong quality, but Meg wasn't buying it. Minnie was hurt by T.J.'s snub and was lashing out. "Seemed like you guys were flirting pretty hardcore."

They hadn't had this conversation since Homecoming, both of them preferring to let the whole incident lie untouched, unresolved. Until now.

"We're just friends, Mins," Meg said.

"Friends don't ask friends to the Homecoming dance."

"No one asked me to the dance," Meg said. She'd lied about that night so many times now, she could do it easily. "I was home sick with the flu that night." Yeah, the heartbreak flu. She'd stayed home all night pretending to be sick while she wrote pages and pages of emo, angst-filled crap in her diary.

"Promise?"

Meg forced a smile. Yet another promise she couldn't keep. "Minnie, I promise. I'm not interested in T.J. Fletcher. Pinky swear."

Meg held her pinky out to Minnie, who stared at it for half a second as if deciding whether or not she wanted to let her bitchiness go. Then with characteristic impulsiveness, Minnie threw her arms around Meg's neck and kissed her on the cheek.

"I'm sorry," she said, then sighed. "I guess I just freaked a little when I saw him."

"I know."

"Between that and you leaving me . . ."

Meg shook her head. "Mins, I'm not leaving *you*."

"But you're leaving."

That was it, plain and simple. Meg was leaving. In seven months she'd be starting a new life in LA, and as much as she tried to pretend in front of Minnie that that wasn't what was happening, they both knew it was true.

"It's not like I'm going to Europe or something," Meg said.

"You might as well be." Minnie stuck out her lower lip in her patented pout. It was a move that made boys sweat. "You're going to find a new best friend and forget all about me."

"A, that's not going to happen. B, *that's not going to happen*."

"Promise?"

"Yes, Minnie."

"And you're not into Teej?"

"Didn't we just pinky swear?"

Minnie hugged her for a second then broke away. "Because, if you *were* interested . . ."

"Minnie!"

"If you *were*," she continued with a smirk, "I'd have to warn you—that boy has the biggest—"

"Mins!" Meg plugged her ears with both index fingers. She did not want to hear a firsthand account of T.J.'s boy parts, especially not from Minnie. It was bad enough to know that Minnie and T.J. had drunkenly hooked up at a party, worse hearing a replay of it. "I'm not listening. I'm not listening. I'm not listening."

Minnie flopped on her bed in a paroxysm of laughter. "I just meant—" she gasped. "For your first time you might want—"

"I'm not listening!"

Minnie rolled onto her back and laughed even harder, and despite herself, Meg joined in. She fell backward on her own bed and the two friends giggled like kids until the tension and fatigue of the day had completely drained out of them. It was moments like this one that reminded Meg of why she loved Minnie so much. Their lives had grown in different directions, but deep down they were still two goofy twelve-year-olds who laughed at the same stupid jokes, protected each other, and were totally, utterly inseparable.

As they calmed down, Minnie reached out to Meg. "I'm sorry."

Meg squeezed her friend's hand. "I know."

"Friends still?"

"Always."

"Good." Minnie rolled off the bed and smoothed her skirt. "Let's go downstairs. I'm freaking starved."

SIX

LAUGHTER DRIFTED UP THE STAIRWELL AS Minnie and Meg wound their way down to the ground floor. They followed the hallway to the back of the house and found themselves in a spacious family room, amply furnished with overstuffed couches and easy chairs. The walls were lined with bookcases, and an enormous fifty-inch plasma television mounted above a wood-burning fireplace was lit up with the latest zombie-massacre-alien-invasion-first-person-shooter-apocalypse video game.

Two guys sat on opposite sofas, controllers in hand, eyes fixed on the game. One looked like your average skinny shredder who spent mom and dad's money most weekends up at Whistler—tight thermal shirt, baggy jeans, and long, stringy hair he kept tossing out of his eyes with a violent flip of his head. The other was a big Samoan dude. Really big. Like linebacker in the NFL big.

As they entered the room, the skinny guy caught sight of them out of the corner of his eye. He did a double take, then paused the game.

"Ladies," he said. "Welcome to Paradise."

If Paradise was two dudes playing video games in the middle of nowhere, Meg was going to take a big old Pasadena on that.

Minnie placed a slender hand on her hip. "Does Paradise come with a beer keg?"

"Bottles," the skinny guy said, standing up. He reached a hand up under his Hollister T-shirt and scratched his belly as his eyes traveled from Minnie to Meg. "Can I get you one?"

"She doesn't drink," Minnie said.

"Too bad." He continued to stare at Meg, then a sly smile stole across his face. "Does she talk?"

Meg narrowed her eyes. As much as she hated being on the spot in front of strangers, she didn't like the way this guy was looking at her. "When I need to."

"Oooo," he said, wiggling his fingers. "A sassy brunette. Papa likes."

Ew.

NFL linebacker kicked the sofa on which his friend had been sitting. "Dude. Finish the damn game."

"Fine, fine," he said, resuming his seat. He continued to smile at Meg. "More later."

Minnie grabbed Meg's hand. "Come on."

She led Meg through the L-shaped room to where the rest of the guests were gathered in the enormous stainless-steel kitchen that ran along the north side of the house.

Gunner and Magenta Hair were dancing to an electro-metal track blaring from a set of iPod speakers on the counter. Their bodies were pressed tightly together, and Magenta Hair had one hand leisurely draped around Gunner's neck while the other gripped a bottle of Stella. Ben leaned against the far wall, also with beer in hand, and was laughing with a tall, angular Asian girl whose limbs seemed too long for her body. A Stepford Wives-y-looking brunette with a sensible bob and sensible pink J. Crew cardigan buttoned up to her neck stood on tiptoe, examining the contents of the kitchen cupboards.

T.J. sat on a barstool at the island in the middle of the room. He jumped to his feet as soon as they entered. "Hi!"

Five heads all turned in their direction, with the exception of Gunner, who stared intently at a spot on the refrigerator.

"You get settled in okay?" Ben asked. He walked across to the iPod dock and dialed down the volume. Meg noticed his eyes never even rested on her, just went straight to Minnie.

"Yep," Minnie said, matching his smile. "The room is gorge."

Meg hid a grin.

T.J. touched her elbow. "You need a drink?"

"Nope," Meg started. "I'm—"

"I'd *love* one." Minnie made a beeline for the fridge and yanked it open so fiercely the bottles of condiments on the door rattled against one another. She took a cursory glance at the interior and crinkled her nose. "Where's the beer?"

Here we go. "Minnie, why don't you wait 'til we get some food first?"

"No, thanks, Mom," Minnie said with a sly smile. "I can handle it."

"I'll grab you one." Ben dashed out the kitchen door to an enclosed patio. Meg heard the slight suction of a fridge door opening, then Ben reappeared, practically falling over himself to hand Minnie her beer. As he popped the cap for her, Minnie dropped her eyes and batted her mascaraed eyelashes in a display of false demureness that would have made a southern debutante proud. Then she grabbed the beer from his outstretched hand and chugged it like a frat boy. Classy.

The girl with the sensible bob opened the fridge and rearranged the bottles Minnie had knocked askew, then bent down and opened a drawer. "Did anyone see any cucumbers in here?"

Magenta Hair snorted. "What do you need cucumbers for? We've got a house full of dudes."

Minnie and Ben burst out laughing, but Sensible Bob continued to search through the fridge. "They're for the salad," she said, clearly not getting the joke.

"Of course they are," Minnie said. She reached out her finger and poked Ben in the stomach.

Magenta Hair leaned into Gunner. "So *that's* your ex?" she said in a poorly disguised whisper.

Minnie paused midsip. "Yeah, I'm in the room."

Meg flinched. Minnie hadn't even finished one beer and she was already primed for a fight.

"Um . . ." Gunner sounded stumped, like the simple question of whether or not Minnie was his ex-girlfriend confounded him. "Um, yeah. But it's totally over."

"Totally," Minnie confirmed. She reached out and traced her

fingers down Ben's lanky arm as if to emphasize the point. "He's all yours, if that's what you're into."

Magenta Hair straightened up. "What the f—"

"I'm Meg." She dashed forward, intercepting Magenta Hair before she crossed the room and pummeled Minnie's face with her bare hands. "Minnie and I are at Kamiak with Gunner. Um . . ." Meg glanced at Gunner, who was turning bright red. "As you probably already knew."

Magenta Hair eyed Meg's hand for a few seconds, then tentatively stuck out her own. "Kumiko. I'm at Roosevelt in Seattle." She pointed to Sensible Bob. "That's Viv."

Sensible Bob closed a cupboard with a bang. "Vivian," she said sharply.

"Right," Kumiko said with a smirk. "Sorry."

Vivian ignored her. "I'm a junior at Mariner."

"Mariner?" Minnie said. "That's were they found that body in the locker room."

Vivian winced. "Yeah."

"Have they identified the body yet?" Meg asked. The idea of someone's family not knowing that their kid was dead really bothered her.

"Not yet," the tall Asian girl said. "When we left on the ferry, no one had been reported missing. We should probably check the news later for an update."

T.J. placed his hand on the small of Meg's back. "That's Lori," he said quietly.

"Scary shit," Kumiko said.

Vivian placed a stack of nesting bowls on the counter. "I know. I hope they won't suspend classes on Tuesday."

Really? She was worried about missing class after someone was murdered on her school campus?

"I'm sure we'll have class on Tuesday," Ben said. He rubbed Minnie's back.

Vivian spun around. "You go to Mariner?"

"Yep."

"Really?"

"Really," Lori said. "Haven't you seen him around?"

Vivian's eyes grew wide. "Wait, you go to Mariner too?"

Ben laughed. "Yeah, where have you been? Lori was the soloist in the spring choir concert last year." He smiled at her. "You were awesome, by the way."

Lori's face lit up. "Thanks."

"Really." Vivian seemed totally unconvinced that two people could go to her school and she didn't know them.

Kumiko leaned on the counter. "Do you think they're lying about where they go to school?"

"Did I say that?"

"Kinda," Meg blurted out. T.J. laughed.

"Well," Lori said softly. "We're not on debate team, so you might not have noticed us."

Vivian waved her hand dismissively toward the living room. "I know those two guys and *they're* not on the debate team."

The skinny guy came charging through the kitchen. "Which two guys?" He didn't pause but made a beeline for the beer cooler on the patio. His large friend sauntered into the kitchen without a word.

"That's Nathan," T.J. said, then nodded toward the NFL line-backer. "And this is Kenny."

Nathan reappeared, two beer bottles gripped in each hand, and smiled broadly at Meg. "What's up, babe?"

Double ew.

Meg felt T.J. stiffen. "This is Meg."

Nathan moved his beer-laden hand up and down, mimicking a handshake. "We've met." Then he elbowed T.J. in the arm. "I'm digging the chicks-to-dudes ratio here."

Chicks? Really? Meg bit her tongue. *Don't call him a douche bag. Don't call him a douche bag.*

"Do you think it'll get even better when Jessica shows up with half the cheerleading squad?" Nathan continued.

"Meg goes to Kamiak with me," T.J. said, ignoring the question. Was it Meg's imagination or did he emphasize the last two words?

Nathan backed up a few steps. "I dig it." Meg wasn't sure if he meant her or chicks in general, but shockingly, Nathan didn't elaborate. "Dudes," he said, tossing a beer to Kenny. "What is this, a library? This is supposed to be a fucking party. Let's rock this!"

He bounded over to the speakers and turned them up as he chugged down half his beer. Then he grabbed Vivian around the waist and started to freak her like a dog in heat.

"Stop it!" Vivian shrieked. She looked mortified, but at the same time, she wasn't trying very hard to get Nathan off of her.

"Come on, sexy mama," he said in a fake pimp voice. "Don't you want to rip those pearls off and get wild?"

Meg couldn't help but laugh at the idea of the douchey Nathan and the prim Vivian as a couple. It was so ridiculous she couldn't have put it in one of her stories for fear of it seeming too unbelievable. Gunner and Kumiko joined in the dancing, as Kenny made his way silently across the kitchen toward Lori. He whispered something in her ear, and she blushed from chin to hairline.

Meanwhile, Minnie and Ben had disappeared completely out onto the patio. Uh-oh.

"You okay?" T.J. asked.

Meg craned her head to see if she could get a glimpse of what Minnie was up to. "Yeah, totally."

"Having fun?"

"Sure," she lied. "You know, people watching."

T.J. flashed his dimply smile. "Writer."

Vivian finally managed to extricate herself from Nathan. "Jerk," she said. "How did I end up at a party with you?" But Meg noticed her eyes were laughing.

"Same as the rest of us," Lori said. "You don't turn down an invite from Jessica Lawrence."

Nathan leaned against the island, panting, and cracked another beer. "You loved it."

Vivian ignored him. She yanked the fridge door open and eyed Meg. "You know how to cook?"

Meg bit her lip. It was a well-known fact in the Pritchard household that Meg should never be allowed in the kitchen. Her involvement in family dinners usually ended in botulism or a fire extinguisher. "Not really."

Vivian grabbed two bags of lettuce out of the fridge and tossed them on the counter. "Okay. You can do the salad."

Gee, thanks.

SEVEN

AS SOON AS VIVIAN BEGAN ORGANIZING A DINNER production line in the kitchen, Nathan and Kenny made a break for the living room. Kumiko and Lori weren't so lucky, and got assigned garlic bread duty. T.J. stirred the pasta sauce, and when he wasn't preoccupied with "helping" Kumiko spread garlic butter on a baguette, Gunner occasionally remembered to check in on a pot of not-yet-boiling water.

Minnie and Ben continued to be M.I.A. Crap. If word got back to Jessica that Minnie was hooking up with her boyfriend it was going to be a train wreck.

"They're just making out," T.J. said. "Don't worry." Could he tell Meg was tweaking over it?

"Isn't he with Jessica?"

"I think it's pretty casual."

"Oh." Meg didn't understand the concept of casual relationships. She envied girls who could date a bunch of guys and be totally unattached to any of them. They always seemed confident and blissfully happy, unlike her, pining away for a boy she couldn't have. A boy who stood right next to her at the stove, languidly stirring a pot of jar pasta sauce. Somehow it was the sexiest thing Meg had ever seen, like she'd been transported to a chick flick where hot, brooding men just wanted to read Tennyson out loud and make epic meals in an Italian villa. . . .

Stop it. She needed to get a grip. Meg opened the fridge to look for salad ingredients and secretly hoped the chilled air would snap her out of her hormone-induced haze. She grabbed some tomatoes and returned to the salad.

"So did you ever decide on a school?" T.J. asked while Meg attacked a tomato with a serrated knife. "You had like three writing programs after you, right?"

Meg smiled as she reached for a cucumber. He remembered that?

"Well?" T.J. said. His dimples danced on his cheeks. "Don't leave me hanging."

"I'm going to UCLA."

Vivian appeared at Meg's shoulder as if by magic. "Hm," she said, scrutinizing the salad assembly. "Don't cut the cucumbers so big. Choking hazard."

"I'll try." What were they, six?

"And be sure not to add the croutons until dinner's ready because they'll get soggy." Then Vivian moved on to the pasta sauce. "Don't add any salt. The sodium content in that jar is already off the charts."

"Yes, ma'am," T.J. said with a salute.

Vivian narrowed her eyes, then marched off to spread her

control freakiness to another facet of dinner.

Meg wanted to shove a cucumber where the sun didn't shine.

T.J. lowered the burner and put a lid on the pot. "Oh, she's going to be fun."

"If by 'fun' you mean 'exhausting,'" Meg said without thinking.

T.J. smiled. "See, why can't you say things like that in front of people?"

Meg felt the blush rising up almost immediately. She hated it when T.J. called her out on her inability to verbalize what was in her head. "Not everything needs to be said." It was one of her mom's favorite sayings.

Oh crap. She was quoting her mom.

"Some of your comebacks are gold."

"Thanks."

He dumped a giant box of spaghetti into Gunner's abandoned pot of now boiling water. "And you shouldn't be afraid to say them out loud."

"What are you, my therapist?"

His smiled deepened. "See? Gold."

"You're killing me. Seriously."

T.J. stirred the pasta sauce. "We'll practically be neighbors, you know."

The transition was so sudden, Meg had no idea what he was talking about. "Huh?"

"You didn't hear?"

Obviously not. "I don't think—"

T.J. scrunched up his brow. "I thought Mins would have told you."

"Oh. No."

"USC. Full scholarship. I'll probably be red-shirted freshman year, but they've promised me a shot at starting."

"I thought you were going to U-Dub?"

T.J. shrugged. "I changed my mind."

Wow. So they were going to be neighbors. Both in Los Angeles. Meg's stomach fluttered.

T.J. placed a hand on her shoulder. "I thought maybe, since we'll be like a few miles from each other . . ."

Without meaning to, she leaned closer to him. "Yeah?"

T.J. looked her directly in the eye. "Since we'll be near each other, I thought maybe we could—"

"If the sauce is done," Vivian called from the dining room, "can you set the table?"

T.J. pulled his hand away from Meg's shoulder. "I've been summoned. We'll talk later."

Meg threw her chopped vegetables into the bowl as T.J. disappeared into the dining room. That was close. Her resolve to resist T.J. had wavered at the first major challenge, which was not good. She should thank Vivian for the interruption.

On the other hand, Meg bristled at the idea that she'd just been KO'd by that bossy type A know-it-all. *Really?* Had that really just happened?

Out of spite, she put the croutons *and* the salad dressing in the bowl at the same time and secretly hoped they got completely soggy.

The first thing Meg noticed when Minnie and Ben entered the dining room was that Minnie wasn't wearing any lip gloss. The second thing she noticed were the remnants of Minnie's sparkly pink MAC Lipglass smeared around Ben's mouth, cheeks, and neck.

Meg didn't really want to know where else pink glitter had been deposited on Ben's anatomy.

They came in separately, like that was supposed to allay suspicions that they'd been sucking face on the patio for a half hour. Minnie practically pranced through the room, past the hand-in-hand Gunner and Kumiko, and took a seat next to Meg.

Minnie didn't look at her, just smiled to herself as she ran her fingers through her tangled blonde hair. But the second T.J. entered the room carrying the giant bowl of salad, she waved him over.

"T.J.," she said, slightly out of breath. "Put the salad here. I'm *starving.*"

T.J. shrugged. "Okay."

"I can't believe what an appetite I worked up," she continued, heaping lettuce and chopped veggies onto her plate.

T.J. shot Meg a look that said *Am I really supposed to ask?*, then turned on his heel and disappeared into the kitchen without another word.

Meg bit her lip. She'd seen Minnie play this game before,

trying to make T.J. jealous by flaunting another guy in front of him. Last time, she'd dated Gunner for four whole months before she gave up and dumped the poor boy. Now it seemed Ben was a convenient target, though by the way she looked at him as Ben took the seat next to her, Meg suspected Minnie might actually kind of like him.

Which was good, except that he was dating their hostess. For the first time that day, Meg was glad Jessica had been delayed in Mukilteo.

A haze of white noise blanketed the dining room as people chattered to their neighbors. Kenny and Nathan discussing their video game, Minnie and Ben making fun of the old-fashioned wallpaper, Gunner and Kumiko whispering back and forth. For the most part, Meg just sat and watched, drifting from one conversation to the next, catching bits and pieces as they jumped out at her.

"Teej and the Gun Show?" Vivian laughed as T.J. carried an armful of beer bottles to the table. "They really call you that?"

"That's like a reality show, dude." Nathan laughed through a mouthful of pasta. Little specks of red sauce sputtered out of his mouth and hit the white tablecloth.

"Like a *bad* reality show," Minnie corrected.

"Oh, like M and M is so much better?" Kumiko said.

Minnie narrowed her eyes. "It's not like I picked it."

"True," T.J. said, with a glance in Meg's direction. "But it's still pretty adorable."

Minnie beamed. "I know, right?"

"So you're Tara's cousin?" Lori asked.

Kumiko nodded.

Lori helped herself to salad. "She's friends with Jessica, right?"

"Best friends," T.J. said. "You know her?"

Lori passed the salad to Kenny. "We sang in All-County Choir together last year."

"Awesome," Nathan said. "Tara's fine."

Kumiko paused midbite. "Gross."

"What?" Nathan laughed nervously, looking from guy to guy for approbation. "She is."

Kumiko nodded at T.J. "Teej dated her last year."

Nathan's eyes nearly popped out of his head. "For reals?"

"For reals," T.J. said coolly. "But not for very long."

"Dude." Nathan leaned forward. "Do you mind if I . . . you know. Try and hit that?"

Kumiko dropped her spaghetti-laden fork to her plate. "Really?"

T.J. laughed. "Yeah, dude. Knock yourself out."

At the other end of the table, Ben pointed at Kenny. "Oh my God, I'm failing too. You have Mr. de Gama, right?"

"Fourth period," Kenny said.

Ben reached his arm across the table for a fist bump. "I'm in his fifth period. Totally with you."

"I *hate* that dude," Nathan chimed in. "He totally tried to fail me last year."

Ben cocked his head. "Tried to?"

"Yeah, dude, check this out." Nathan scooted his chair closer to the table. "Douche-Gama told me I had to ace the midterm or he was going to flunk me cuz I'd be so far behind I wouldn't be able to pull my grade up by the end of the semester. I was like, 'Dude, come on.' But the a-hole had no mercy. So my man Kenny and I, we got me a little help."

"Oh, yeah?" Ben said.

"Oh, yeah. You know that weird chick that used to go to Mariner? Long dark hair, bug eyes, kinda quiet."

Ben wrinkled his nose. "I think so. She was kind of a loner, right? Always sat by herself in the corner of the cafeteria?"

Lori and Vivian exchanged a glance.

Nathan slapped the table. "That's her! Right, so, weird chick had this thing for me. Used to follow me around, wait by my car and shit. Kenny pointed out that she was totally acing his class."

"And she tutored you?" Ben asked.

"Better." Nathan smiled. "I got her to give me all the answers for the midterm. She had it before lunch and I had it after lunch so . . ."

Vivian's eyes practically popped out of her head. "You cheated?"

Nathan shrugged. "Creative test taking."

"Nice scam," Ben said shaking his head. "But how did you convince her to help you?"

"That's the best part!" Nathan helped himself to seconds. "All I had to do was pretend I was dating her for a couple of weeks. It was so easy."

"Dude," T.J. said. "That's fucked up."

Nathan shrugged. "Whatever. I'm sure she got over it."

Meg couldn't help but project herself into that poor girl's place—a popular guy like Nathan with whom she was totally in love suddenly started paying attention to her. She must have been so happy, so excited, only to realize he was just using her.

Meg's eyes involuntarily flew to T.J. Popular guys like that didn't exactly fall in love with shy nobodies like herself. Yet another reason she needed to get over him.

"I think that's awful," Vivian said.

Lori nodded in agreement. "Yeah, that girl had enough problems."

"Oh, come on!" Nathan said. "She got a little something-something out of it. Right, Kenny?"

Kenny's face flushed scarlet and he looked sheepishly at Lori. "Uh, I guess," he muttered.

Nathan laughed, then launched a piece of garlic bread across the table at his friend. "Whatever, dude."

Kenny snatched it off the table and pitched it back to Nathan, who followed with some of his salad. Before Meg knew it, the two guys were lobbing handfuls of lettuce across the table.

Kumiko and Gunner joined in, and Minnie and Ben were laughing uncontrollably while Lori tried to shield herself from the onslaught behind Kenny's bulk.

"Stop it!" Vivian shrieked, jumping to her feet. "You're making a mess. What if Jessica comes and sees—"

Vivian paused. She was staring at something across the table. Meg followed her gaze. She was staring at Ben.

It took a moment before Meg realized what was happening. He

sat frozen with his fork halfway between his plate and his mouth. It looked like he was thinking intently about something, then immediately his face deepened to dark red and his lips began to swell.

"Oh my God," Minnie said. "What's wrong?"

"Are you choking?" T.J. asked.

Ben shook his head, shoved his chair back violently from the table and began to fumble for something in his pocket. His face was purple, and in a matter of seconds it had swollen so tight his eyes were barely more than slits. He made a strangled gasping sound, then flopped face-first onto the table.

"Holy shit!" Gunner said under his breath.

Minnie backed away from Ben. "Somebody help him!"

Vivian dashed around the table. "We should get him on the ground so I can administer CPR."

Meg shook her head. "Nope." She took Minnie's chair and pulled Ben's swollen hand away from his jeans. There was something in his pocket he'd been trying to reach.

"What do you mean?" Vivian's voice practically squeaked. "I'm CPR *and* AED certified. And I'm a candy striper on the weekends."

Did she never stop? Without a second thought, Meg shoved her hand into Ben's pocket. Her fingers felt a thin, penlike object. Thank God.

"What's that?" Vivian demanded. "What are you doing?"

"EpiPen." Meg whipped off the cap and with as much force as she could muster, jabbed the needle end of the pen through Ben's jeans into the fleshy part of his thigh and held it there. No one spoke, and Meg hardly dared breathe. For a few seconds, nothing happened. Then Ben opened his mouth and took a huge gasp of air. The swelling in his face and limbs began to recede.

"Thank you," he gasped, slumping back into his chair.

"How did you know?" T.J. said. "How did you know what to do?"

Meg slowly released her grip on the used EpiPen and let it fall from her fingers, then shoved her hands into her pockets. They were shaking uncontrollably. Everyone was looking at her, expecting some sort of answer. She tried to steady her voice, but the words got tangled up. "I, um . . . my mom . . ."

"Her mom's allergic to bee stings," Minnie said. "She always carries one of those things with her."

Meg smiled at her. She was surprised Minnie remembered that.

"He got stung by a bee?" Gunner asked. "Inside the house?"

Ben sat up and shook his head. Except for a slight flush and puffy eyes, he looked practically normal again. "Nuts. I'm allergic to tree nuts. There must be some in the salad."

Vivian wheeled on Meg. "I told you to only put tomatoes and cucumbers in the salad."

Really, Iron Chef? Meg's heart was still racing and she needed several deep breaths before she could respond to Vivian with something other than a scream. "That's all I put in," Meg said slowly. "Lettuce, tomatoes, cucumber, croutons, and those feta cheese crumbles."

"And almonds," Lori said simply as she peered into the salad bowl.

"Almonds?" Meg asked.

Lori pushed the bowl forward. "Look."

Ten heads bent over the salad bowl and Meg clearly saw them. Several thin, slivered almond pieces sprinkled into the salad.

EIGHT

"THAT'S SO WEIRD," MEG SAID. "I DIDN'T PUT ANY nuts in. I swear."

Vivian planted her hands on her hips. "You must have."

Once again Meg felt nine pairs of eyes boring into her. She wished the floor would just open up and swallow her whole. Her mouth was suddenly parched, her throat tight. She knew she hadn't added the nuts to the salad. Absolutely positively not. She wanted to defend herself, but she couldn't even think of what to say.

"Hey!" Minnie said sharply. "If Meg says she didn't do it, she didn't do it."

Meg could have hugged her. It was comforting to know Minnie had her back.

Vivian clicked her tongue. "Well, someone must have."

Mumbles of "I didn't" and "Not me" rippled around the table.

Meg sat down in the nearest chair. She knew she hadn't added almonds—which meant one of the others must have. But why would anyone do something as mundane as add nuts to a salad and then not cop to it? It had to be a mistake. Someone accidentally added them, then after Ben's attack was too embarrassed to fess up.

Meg felt a hand brush against her back. "No one's blaming you," T.J. said.

"Oh, my God, no," Ben said. He grabbed Meg by the shoulders. "You totally saved my life. I don't know what would've happened if you hadn't been here."

Ben stepped away and Minnie practically tackled Meg with a ferocious embrace. "Thank you, thank you, thank you," she said, planting a kiss on Meg's cheek between each repetition.

Meg smiled. That was the Minnie she knew and loved. It was good to see her again. "You're welcome."

Silence descended over the dining room table as everyone wandered back to their seats. A few people picked at the food on their plates, but it seemed no one had any appetite left.

Ben was the first to break the silence. "It's no big deal, guys. Seriously. Happens all the time."

"Sorry," T.J. said. "It was just kind of a shock, you know?"

Ben piled his utensils on his plate and stood up. "Forget it. Let's go watch TV or something, huh? You guys are bumming me out."

He bussed his plate into the kitchen, and Minnie quickly followed, leaving her mostly untouched dinner on the table. One by one they gathered up plates and serving trays, and hauled everything to the sink. Nathan and Kenny didn't hang around to get roped into clean-up duty. Lori followed close behind Kenny, and

Vivian, after a few instructions on how the dishwasher should be loaded, joined the group in the living room. But Meg lingered.

While Gunner and Kumiko rinsed plates and loaded them in the dishwasher in the exact opposite way Vivian had recommended, Meg checked the cupboards for signs of the slivered almonds. When she came up empty, she pulled out the trashcan and used a long wooden spoon to pick through the table scrapings, looking for any sign of the almonds.

"I already checked," T.J. said. "No empty bag of almonds."

"Oh." Meg stood up and tossed the spoon into the sink.

"Weird," Gunner said. King of the Obvious.

Kumiko added detergent to the dishwasher and closed it up. "Don't worry about it. Ben's fine. Just put it out of your mind."

"Exactly," T.J. said. "You need to relax. That's what this weekend's for, right?" He disappeared onto the patio and returned with four beers. He handed two to Gunner, then popped the other two with an opener on his key ring. "Seriously, have one. I know you don't really drink but it'll help you relax."

Meg took the bottle gratefully. T.J. was right. She just needed to relax and have some fun. Stop worrying about who put almonds in the salad. This weekend was supposed to be fun.

Beers in hand, T.J., Gunner, Kumiko, and Meg joined the rest of the party in the living room. Meg expected to see a movie on the huge flat-screen television, but instead it was blank and blue, bathing the living room in a dullish cerulean light. Nathan and Kenny stood at a bookcase. They yanked DVD cases off the shelf and tossed them to Ben and Minnie on the sofa.

Minnie pried open *The Hangover.* "Empty," she said before flinging it in a large pile on the floor.

"Empty," Ben said, and added *Trading Places.*

"Empty?" Meg asked.

"Empty," Ben and Minnie said in unison.

Kenny didn't even turn around. "All of them."

"It doesn't make sense." Vivian examined the discarded cases as if she didn't entirely trust anyone else's opinion. "Why would someone put empty DVD cases on the shelf?"

T.J. picked up the remote and flipped through input devices. The result was always the same: blue screen of death.

"The satellite's out," Kenny said.

A gust of wind blasted the backside of the house as if in agreement. It wasn't the least bit cold inside, but Meg shivered.

"Must be the storm." Ben jumped to his feet and headed to the kitchen. "I'm getting more beers. I think we're gonna need them."

"We can always play board games," Lori said. "I saw some stacked in the—"

"Here's one!" Minnie squealed. She held up a shiny DVD like she'd just found Willy Wonka's last golden ticket.

"What is it?" Vivian asked.

Nathan plucked the disc out of her hand. "It's homemade." He held it up to his face and read the label: "Don't Watch Me."

"I don't know that movie," Gunner said.

Minnie snorted. "It's a burned disc, Gun Show. Not a real movie."

"Oh."

Ben handed beers around. "It's probably lame vacation footage or something."

"Or porn," Nathan volunteered.

Lori wrinkled her nose. "Why would someone label porn *Don't Watch Me*?"

Nathan shrugged. "Why not?"

Vivian sat in one of the winged chairs and crossed her legs. "I don't like this."

"You know what?" Minnie said with a dramatic pause. "This is how horror movies start."

"We've already had one near-death experience," Kumiko said.

Ben laughed. "Just an accident. Nothing sinister."

"Dude!" Nathan pointed at T.J. "You'd better watch out."

T.J. arched an eyebrow. "Why?"

"Well, if this is a horror movie, you're the first one to go. The black dude's always the first one to die."

Words flew out of Meg's mouth before she even knew what she was saying. "Really? You really needed to go there?"

"What?" Nathan looked around the room. Everyone avoided his eyes. "It's true."

Focus shifted back to Meg. She felt her throat start to tighten up, the usual shyness creeping over her. "I, uh . . ."

"Come on," Nathan said. "Say it."

Meg saw the bully come out in Nathan. And there was nothing she hated more than a bully. It pissed her off that he was trying to intimidate her, and suddenly, Meg was able to say exactly what she meant.

"Racist much? Are you going to ask if Kumiko can help you with your math homework next?"

Kumiko laughed. "Good one."

Meg smiled, surprised by her own words. She usually wasn't this confrontational. Must be the booze.

"Whatever." Nathan snatched the disc out of Kenny's hands. "Are we watching this or not?"

"Why not?" Ben handed Minnie a beer and sat down next to her. Meg saw him drape a long arm around Minnie's back. "Better than board games."

"Dude," Gunner said, his eyes wide. "Don't do it."

Minnie laughed, light and airy, as she leaned into Ben's arm. "Oh come on, it's just a video." She pointed at Nathan. "Hurry up!"

Nathan put the disc in the machine and hit Play.

The number "10" appeared on the screen. It was animated as if it had been written by hand, and then a red slash crossed right through it. "9" and "8" were drawn and slashed through in the same manner, then three images of a beach at night cycled through in rapid succession, all different locations, it seemed, but all with a prominent starry sky and waves breaking across an expanse of sand.

The numbers started again: "7," "6," "5," all with the same red slash marks crossing them out as if they were being counted down. Then more images. This time it was a collage of students in class—taking a test, arguing in some sort of mock trial, doing science experiments, running around a track, glee club.

"4," "3," "2," "1."

The screen went black and a low soundtrack kicked in. Just a few solo piano chords at first, then a soprano voice began to sing.

"Sure on this shining night . . ."

Words faded onto the screen.

When you hurt someone . . .

. . . with intent . . . with cruelty . . .

The screen went black for a moment as the song continued, then more words faded into view.

To steal someone's soul.

To break someone's heart.

The screen flashed, then filled with a quick montage of totally random images—a lightbulb turning on, a judge's gavel striking a sound block, a bonfire.

To lie, cheat, or steal.

To destroy a reputation.

More random images. Math equations scrolling across the screen. People dancing. A girl and a boy making out.

Your actions are a crime.

Now it was capital punishment. An electric chair. A firing squad. A gallows.

Even if the law does not recognize it.

Flames filled the screen.

Your betrayal, your backstabbing, your character assassination.

The music stopped.

Steps must be taken to protect the innocent.

Those steps begin right here, right now.

Suddenly the screen exploded with light and sound. The images flashed at a manic pace, moving backward as if the movie had been switched into rewind. The music was no longer a languid song but a dissonant cluster of screaming chords. The noise crescendoed as the video reached the countdown again, flying rapidly in reverse from one to ten. There was a massive explosion, along with matching sound effects, then a single line of text faded into view.

Vengeance is mine.

The screen went black.

NINE

STATIC FIZZLED ON THE SCREEN WHILE EVERY-one sat frozen in their seats, unable to move.

Kumiko was the first to break the spell. She jumped up and turned off the television with a shaky hand. "What the hell was that?"

Gunner scratched his knee. "Maybe Jessica's messing with us?"

"Backstabbing? Character assassination?" Vivian's voice seemed to have gone up an octave. "What does that even mean?"

"I can honestly say that was the weirdest thing I've ever seen," Ben said.

"Math problems?" Nathan said with a tense laugh. "And a noose? I mean, it's just a joke, right?"

"Sick joke," T.J. said. He was still staring at the dark television screen, his jaw muscles clenched tight.

"It couldn't mean anything," Vivian said.

From the corner of the room, someone sobbed. Everyone turned. Lori sat on the window bench, frantically rubbing the side of her face. Her eyes were red and swollen, and heavy tears streaked down her cheeks.

"Lori, are you okay?" Kenny asked. He heaved himself off the sofa with more agility than Meg thought possible and was across the room to her in an instant.

He placed his hand on her shoulder, and Lori started as if she'd been woken out of a deep sleep. There was a look on her face that Meg could only describe as panic. Without warning, she balled up her fists and pounded them against the wooden bench. *"Who did this?"*

Everyone froze. Stunned.

Nathan glanced at the blank television screen. "Huh?"

"One of you did it. To scare us." Lori looked around aimlessly. "I need . . . I need . . ." She spotted the beer Ben had placed next to her and polished it off.

"I'm sure it's nothing," Vivian said. She sounded less than sure. "Calm down, okay?"

"Calm down?" Lori grabbed Vivian by the shoulders. "Someone's trying to scare us. Someone's out to get us."

Meg's eyes grew wide. Did she mean everyone or just her and Vivian?

Vivian shook herself free. "That's ridiculous."

"Is it?" Lori wobbled a bit and steadied herself against the wall. "You think this is a coincidence? I know what that means. I know what you did."

"Excuse me?"

"What you did to that girl last year. Everyone knew about it."

Vivian flinched. "I don't know what you're talking about."

"Really? Please. You'd stab your own mother in the back to win that competition."

Gunner leaned into Kumiko. "What's with the freak-out?"

T.J. shook himself, then stood up slowly. "I think we all need to calm down," he said. "It's been a long day and we're probably all tired. Maybe we should call it a night?"

"I'm getting out of here. First thing in the morning." Lori stumbled down the hallway. "I'm not staying here with you liars."

Meg listened to Lori's staggering footsteps as she ascended the stairs. She'd only seen Lori drink one beer, so she couldn't be drunk. Was she *that* upset?

As soon as Lori was gone, Vivian dashed down the hall after her without saying a word. Meg was pretty sure she was crying.

"Damn," Minnie said. "What is wrong with everyone?"

"I'm sharing a room with Lori," Kumiko said. She sounded genuinely concerned. "I'll make sure she's all right."

"Okay," T.J. said. "Good."

No one spoke as they filed out of the living room. No one looked anyone else in the eye. There was zero interest in discussing what they'd just seen.

They trudged up the stairs, single file, like school children marching off for detention. At the second floor, everyone disappeared into their own rooms. The door to Vivian's room was already closed. At the other end of the hall, Kumiko approached her bedroom door, knocked softly, then entered.

The oppressive silence lingered as Meg and Minnie ascended

the stairs to the garret. They didn't speak while they got into their pajamas, they didn't speak while they climbed into bed, they didn't speak as Meg turned off the light.

Meg stared at the roof, listening to the sharp tapping of the rain as it was catapulted into the windows by a ferocious wind. She'd been so excited to stay in that room but now everything felt odd. Off in a way she couldn't explain.

Meg shook her head. Jessica would be arriving in the morning with more guests. The storm would probably blow over during the night and tomorrow things would be different. She was being silly; she just needed some sleep.

"We should see about getting out of here tomorrow," Minnie said softly. The nearest guest room was down on the second floor, yet she still whispered.

"Really?" Meg asked. "But I thought you were having a good time?"

"Yeah . . ." Minnie's voice trailed off, then she fell silent. Meg could hear her turning over in bed. "Meg?"

"Yeah."

"Will I be okay? When you're in LA?"

"Mins, you'll be fine."

A rustle of sheets and bedding. "Sometimes, I don't think I can, you know? Be fine without you. I'm not sure I can do it."

"We'll talk about it later, okay?" Meg said. "When we're home." She didn't want to have that conversation at all, let alone in the pitch-black garret at White Rock House with T.J. sleeping in a room downstairs. It made her feel even more like a traitor to her friendship with Minnie: First she was running away to college, then she was rekindling her feelings for T.J.

"Promise?" Minnie said. Another promise no one expected her to keep.

"Promise."

A roar of wind rattled every window in the garret and the rain lashed at the glass so fiercely it sounded as if someone had thrown a handful of pebbles at the side of the house. The light filtering through the white gauze curtains was muted and dull, and Meg's first thought as she squinted her eyes open was that the storm must have raged all night without letting up. Judging by the wind and the rain, they were in for another dark, damp day on Henry Island.

She shivered and pulled the quilt up around her ears. Damn, the house was freezing. Had someone turned off the heat? She rolled on her side to check the time on the alarm clock, but the digital face was completely blank. No wonder it was so cold. The storm must have knocked out the power during the night. No power, no heat, no satellite. Minnie was right—they needed to catch the first boat out of there.

Meg listened for other noises in the house, but there was only the sound of Minnie's rhythmic breathing. She lay there for a moment, eyes squeezed shut against the encroaching daylight, and wondered if she should get up and tell someone about the power outage. Eh, what could they do? No point in leaving a warm bed. She snuggled under her covers, hoping she'd drift back off to sleep.

Except she had to pee. Small bladder and too much beer. She swung her legs over the bed and tested her toes on the frigid floor, silently cursing her decision not to pack slippers. With the giant comforter wrapped around her, Meg tiptoed across the garret and down the stairs.

There was a slight breeze in the open stairwell of the tower that sent a chill racing down Meg's neck. She hitched the comforter up over her head—sympathizing suddenly with Eskimos, mummies, and women in burkas—and quickened her pace.

Pat, pat, pat. The sound of her bare feet was distant and fuzzy as it permeated the layers of thick down wrapped around her head. Her toes were so cold she could barely feel the smooth wood of the stairs, and the comforter cocoon was like having blinders on: She could only see a small oval right in front of her. She moved as quickly as her bulky wrap would allow, praying she didn't trip and send herself careening down the stairs or worse, over the railing. That fall would certainly end in a broken neck.

Why was she always thinking of the most morbid scenarios? Sheesh. Just go down to the bathroom then back to her warm, comfy bed.

Pat, pat, pat.

Creeeeeak.

Meg paused. Was that the stairs creaking? It sounded like it came from somewhere above her. Maybe the old house was straining against the storm? She rounded a corner and heard it again.

Creeeeeeak. A shadow on the white wall of the tower caught her eye. There was something odd about it, something familiar, and yet there shouldn't be a shadow there at all. The windows in the tower didn't have any curtains, nothing to cast a shadow. Meg stared at it for a second and noticed the shadow was moving, swaying slowly from left to right.

Creeeeeak.

Meg froze, her eyes locked on the shadow. The heavy form, oblong and amorphous except for the dangling appendages. . . .

Legs. Holy crap, they were legs.

Meg turned her head and came eye-to-eye with a face hanging in the stairwell. The noose around the neck. The purplish-blue hue to the skin.

Meg opened her mouth and screamed.

TEN

LORI'S BODY ROCKED SLOWLY BACK AND FORTH.

Meg wanted to look away. But her eyes were locked on those of the dead girl in front of her. She let the comforter fall to the ground and even though the air was frigid, Meg was burning up. She began to sway, mimicking the motion of Lori's dangling body, so much so that she had to reach out and grip the banister to steady herself for fear of tumbling over the rail.

Meg couldn't even blink; Lori's sightless brown eyes held her gaze. There was something in them: Fear? Confusion? In her final moments had Lori felt both? Had she regretted the choice to take her own life only after she had thrown herself over the banister? Meg shuddered. The idea of suicide, of being so full of despair that you didn't want to live anymore, horrified her.

"Holy shit!"

"Oh my God!"

A sob. A whimper.

It probably only took twenty seconds for the others to emerge from their rooms, but it felt more like twenty minutes to Meg. She was vaguely aware of the gasps and cries around her. Meg could feel the growing presence of people even though she couldn't see them. She couldn't see anything other than the eyes staring lifelessly at her.

It wasn't until Meg felt a hand on her shoulder that she could move again, blink again.

"Are you okay?" T.J. said. His arm slipped down to her waist and she let her body sag into it. She found his eyes—eyes that could feel and sense and see. She began to tremble.

"Yeah."

"Liar." He picked up the comforter and hauled it over her shoulders.

"What happened?" Kumiko's voice was high and pinched. "What the fuck happened?"

Vivian stood with her back to the body, refusing to look at it. "You were her roommate. Did she say anything?" Any trace of her emotional outburst from the night before had vanished, and the old, harsh Vivian was back.

Kumiko shook her head. "She was already in bed when I got up here last night. I thought she'd passed out."

"You didn't hear her get out of bed?"

"I . . ." Kumiko glanced at Gunner. "I didn't sleep there."

Vivian clicked her tongue. "Well, that's just perfect."

"Hey," Kumiko barked, getting up in Vivian's face. "I'm not her mom. How was I supposed to know she was that far over the edge?"

"We need to call the police," T.J. said.

"There's a phone in my room." Vivian spun around and disappeared into the master bedroom.

"Where did she get the rope?" Ben said. He stuck his head into the stairwell and gazed up to the roof beams of the tower. "And how did she get it strung up there?"

"Why are you guys yelling? I was trying to sl—"

Meg registered Minnie's voice and looked up in time to see her friend descend the stairs from the garret. Minnie stopped dead in her tracks on the second-to-last step, one hand brushing her light blonde hair away from her face while the other clutched Meg's hooded sweatshirt around her chest. Meg could see the realization of the scene dawn on her, as Minnie's eyes traveled from the body up the rope to the wooden beams of the tower, and back down.

Ben pushed past Meg and T.J. and sprinted up the stairs toward Minnie. She opened her mouth to scream, but no sound came out as her body crumpled into unconsciousness. Ben caught her just in time.

"She's okay," he said, lowering Minnie's body to the stairs. "Just fainted."

Meg wanted to go to her. But she couldn't move, wouldn't move. Not with T.J.'s arm around her.

"Dude," T.J. said, motioning to Gunner. "See if there's a note or something?"

It took Gunner a moment to process, then in typical wordless Gunner fashion, he disappeared into Lori's room. His hand brushed against Kumiko's arm as he passed her. She paused for half a second, then followed him inside.

"You're still trembling," T.J. whispered, his mouth just inches from her own. "Can I do anything?"

Meg caught her breath. T.J. was so close to her, as if he wanted to protect her. It was a new sensation for Meg, who spent most of her time trying to protect her best friend from the things in the world that might trigger her crippling anxiety and bipolar disorder. And now here was T.J. looking out for *her* for once.

"Fine," she said, not sure if she was trying to convince him or herself. "I'm fine."

"The phone doesn't work," Vivian said. She sounded slightly out of breath.

Nathan folded his arms and leaned against the wall. "That's not good."

"Wha . . . what happened?" Minnie said. Her voice sounded weak.

Ben propped her up. "You fainted."

"I did?" Minnie sat up and looked past the body, finding Meg on the landing below. "Why?"

Meg opened her mouth to respond but she literally had no words. Thankfully, Minnie would have plenty, and Meg cringed as she watched Minnie's eyes find the dangling body and the horror of it came rushing over her once again.

"Oh my God, oh my God, oh my God." Minnie's voice crescendoed with each repetition. She pointed a shaky hand down at Lori. "She's dead. It's a dead body. Oh my God. What do we do? How do we . . . I mean . . ."

Meg could hear the panic in her voice and prayed Minnie had actually packed her medications. If she didn't, this would not end well.

"Don't look," Ben said, trying to guide Minnie away from the railing. But it was too late.

"Get it out! Get it away from me!" Minnie screamed. She looked right at Meg, as if she could make it all go away.

"She's not an *it*!" Kenny roared. Meg turned and saw him standing in the doorway of his room, tree trunk–sized arms folded across his chest, brows low over his eyes. He'd been quiet the whole time, but suddenly he just exploded. His face was a deep shade of red, and he was shaking from head to toe.

"Of course not," T.J. said calmly. "She didn't mean it. She's just freaked."

Freaked was an understatement. Meg recognized a panic attack when she saw one. She snapped into caretaker mode, attempting to stem the tide. "Minnie, it's going to be okay. You're going to be okay."

"No, it's not," Minnie sobbed. "It's not, it's not."

"What's wrong with her?" T.J. whispered in Meg's ear.

"Panic attack," Meg said out of the corner of her mouth. "She needs her meds." Then she started up the stairs. "Come on. I'll get your Klonopin."

"It's okay, I'll take her," Ben said, taking Minnie's hand. He looked at her and smiled. "Do you know where it is?"

Minnie nodded slightly and they disappeared up the stairs to the garret.

Meg turned back to T.J. and caught a look of confusion on his face. "Does that happen a lot?" he asked softly.

Meg bit her lip. She'd kept Minnie's secret for so long she didn't quite know what to say. "Um . . ."

She was saved by Kumiko, who slowly emerged from the bedroom, Gunner close behind. She gripped a lined piece of paper in her hands and as she spoke, it was clear that she was trying in vain to control the tremor in her voice. "We found it. We found her suicide note."

"Dude, really?" Nathan said.

Kumiko held the page up, shielding her face. It was written on strange paper with groups of parallel lines running across it. It took Meg a moment to recognize what it was—sheet music.

"C-can't deal," Kumiko read aloud. Her hand shook. "I should just end it all now. This voice will never sing again."

Silence. Meg stared at the blue and gold runner that carpeted the second floor hallway. It wasn't a particularly interesting rug, but she couldn't bring herself to look at anyone. Maybe if she stood there long enough trying to forget what had happened, it would just go away? Maybe she'd wake up and discover this was all a horrible beer-induced dream?

Creeeeeeeak.

Meg's eyes involuntarily flitted toward the body. She couldn't help it.

"I don't believe it." Kenny's voice was strong and defiant, and clearly calmer than he'd been a minute ago. But his eyes and face were drawn, his jaw hard and defiant.

"Kenny," T.J. started. "I'm so sor—"

"I don't believe it," Kenny repeated. He stared straight at Lori's body, unblinking, unflinching. "She didn't kill herself."

"Dude," Nathan said, putting a hand on his friend's arm. "Dude, I think it's pretty clear—"

"She. Didn't. Kill. Herself," Kenny repeated. Then he turned on his heel, pushed past Nathan into their room, and slammed the door behind him.

"Kenny!" Nathan followed Kenny into the room. "Dude, I didn't mean . . ."

His voice trailed off as he shut the door behind him. Poor Kenny. Meg remembered him whispering into Lori's ear before dinner, and the blush that spread across Lori's face. She had been watching two people fall for each other, and now Lori was dead and Kenny was in shock. It seemed so . . . pointless.

Creeeeeeak.

That sound was starting to make Meg nauseous.

"Okay," T.J. said. He gave Meg's shoulder a squeeze and walked to the center of the balcony, his back to Lori's body. "We need to find a phone that works and call the police."

"On it." Gunner grabbed Kumiko's hand and half dragged her down the stairs.

"There's one in the study," Vivian called after them. She paused a moment, then ran lightly into her room and emerged pulling on an oversized sweater over her pajamas. "Better go with them," she said to no one in particular. "Just in case."

T.J. and Meg stood alone on the second-floor landing. Everyone else seemed to have a purpose—Ben was taking care of Minnie, Nathan was trying to calm Kenny down, and Kumiko, Gunner, and Vivian were calling the police. Meg felt like she should be doing something. Helping. Not just standing there like an idiot yearning for the strong arms of T. J. Fletcher to wrap themselves around her again.

Lori's suicide note fluttered off the table where Kumiko had left it, drifting to the ground like it was light and airy, not a thing of sadness and pain. Meg had a sudden urge to see it and snatched it off the floor. The words of Lori's suicide note were written on the back side of a page of music in all caps, but the handwriting didn't look shaky or erratic. It was as if Lori had found calmness in her decision to take her own life. Meg flipped it over and looked at the musical notation. It was a song with piano accompaniment and lyrics.

"Weird," she said.

"What?" T.J. peered over her shoulder at the sheet of music.

She read the lyrics out loud. "'Sure on this shining night, I weep for wonder.'"

"Pretty."

"'Sure on this shining night,'" Meg repeated. Those lyrics rang a bell. "Wasn't this the song playing on the video last night?"

T.J. cocked his head and stared at her. "You're right. How did you catch that?"

"I . . . I don't know." *Because I watch everyone all the time? Because I'm more comfortable observing than doing?* Yeah, that's not creepy.

"Writer." T.J. smiled, exposing his deep-set dimples.

"No wonder she freaked out." Meg remembered Lori's face after the video ended. She looked scared, panicked almost. And the way she accused someone of making that video on purpose. It must have been a song she was rehearsing. Her reaction made perfect sense.

Meg stared at the sheet music. There was something odd about it, the music Lori chose for her suicide note. It didn't sound like a sad song, a song of depression or longing or anything like that. Totally the opposite. "Weep for wonder" was more like crying from happiness and joy. Why would she choose that? Meg shook her head. It could have just been coincidence, the only paper in arm's reach. Still, according to the endless lineup of crime-scene investigator dramas that filled up her TiVo, suicide notes were usually deliberate. So why would Lori choose that song? How could that lead to her body hanging in a stairwell . . . ?

Meg squeezed her eyes shut, hoping the flurry of rods and cones would bleach the image of Lori's face from her memory. No such luck.

"We need to take her down," she said.

"I was thinking the same thing." T.J. climbed halfway up the tower stairs and peered at the beams that supported the roof. "I'll get the guys. I think we can lower her."

"Good."

T.J. smiled grimly. "I'm sorry you were the one to find her, Meg."

Meg laughed, short and terse. "Better me than Minnie."

"Are you always this protective of her?"

Meg bit her lip. She usually hid her enabling-codependent relationship with Minnie better than she had in the last twenty-four hours, and she was embarrassed that T.J. had witnessed as much of it as he did. "I have to be."

T.J. descended the stairs to her. "Why? Why is that your responsibility? Do you really think she'd do the same for you?"

Meg couldn't look him in the eye. He'd hit a little too close to home. "I—"

"Oh my God. *Oh my God!*" It was Vivian from downstairs.

Without a word, T.J. and Meg sprinted down the flight of stairs and found Vivian standing in the entryway, staring fixedly at the wall. All the color had drained out of her face. "Look."

Meg slowly turned her head. On the crisp white wall next to the coat pegs was a huge slash mark in dripping red paint.

ELEVEN

"WHAT THE HELL IS THAT?"

"Is this some sort of joke?"

"Do you think Lori did it?"

"Shitty joke."

Everyone spoke at once. Meg, however, heard every comment, clearly, distinctly. The world was moving in slow-motion around her. And though that world seemed to have descended into chaos, Meg felt oddly calm.

She took a step closer to the red slash mark. It had clearly been done with a brush; she could see texture in the thick red paint as it had dripped down the wall. It reminded her of the countdown in the video the night before, the numbers slashed through with animated red lines. Except now, it really did look like . . .

"Blood?" Nathan asked. "Do you think it's blood?" He stood right behind Meg, peering over her shoulder at the mark on the wall as if he was using her as a shield. So macho.

"Doubtful," she said, fighting the urge to ask him if he had, in fact, been raised by monkeys.

"How did it get there?" Kenny stood midway down the last flight of stairs, reluctant to get any closer to the mark on the wall.

Meg didn't blame him.

T.J. stepped right up to it. "Looks like Rust-Oleum. Topside paint for boats."

Nathan was unconvinced. "Still looks like blood to me."

"Well, it's not," Vivian snapped. She turned to Gunner, who stood in the doorway of the study. "Did you call the police? What did they say? Are they sending a helicopter? How long? What are we supposed to do until then?"

Girl was getting twitchy, and Meg wondered if Minnie was going to have to share her Klonopin.

Gunner shook his head slowly. "Phones are out."

"What?" Vivian said. Her voice cracked. The girl was wound tighter than a two-dollar watch.

"The phones," Kumiko said slowly like she was speaking to a slightly stupid child, "are out."

"Idiots." Vivian pushed past Gunner into the study. "I'm sure they're not out. They can't be out."

Meg rolled her eyes. Cue anxiety-driven meltdown in three . . . two . . .

"Must be the storm," T.J. said with total calmness.

Kumiko ran a hand through her magenta-streaked hair. "Did anyone notice if they got a cell signal here?"

"I tried last night," Meg said. "No coverage."

"The closest tower's in Roche Harbor," T.J. said. "Too far."

Vivian shuffled out of the study, deflated. "The phone's out."

Kumiko whirled on her. "Really? So the fact that we checked the receiver, checked the phone cord, checked the batteries, checked the receiver again . . . That wasn't enough for you?"

Vivian shrugged. "I like to confirm the facts myself."

"Awesome." Kumiko walked right up to Vivian. "Then why don't you confirm the fact of me kicking your ass."

"Hey, hey," Gunner said, pulling Kumiko back.

Vivian darted up the stairs. "Keep her away from me or I'll press charges."

"Oh, yeah?" Kumiko said, straining against Gunner's arm. "Kind of hard when we have *no way to call the police.*"

The concept sunk in. Holy crap. What were they going to do? No phones, no cells, no internet . . . A memory stirred. Something she remembered seeing in the living room. A coiled yellow cord tucked into the footboard of a bookcase.

"Internet!" she blurted out.

"Huh?" T.J. said with a tilt of his head. "I didn't see a computer."

Meg didn't wait to explain. She sprinted up the stairs to the garret where her laptop lay stashed in her backpack. She kept her head down, eyes glued to the worn, wooden steps as she rounded the landing of the second floor and wound her way up the tower.

"Minnie," she called as she emerged into the garret. "I need my—"

Meg froze. The room looked like a bomb had gone off. Every drawer of the dresser had been pulled out and their contents—primarily Minnie's weekend wardrobe—were strewn across the room. Underwear hung from the lampshade. A pair of shorts was caught on the mirror. Tanks and jeans, dresses and skirts carpeted the floor.

Both beds had been literally torn apart. Sheets lay at the foot of the bed, mattresses dislodged, pillows ripped from their cases and tossed aside.

Minnie's suitcases were overturned, clothes and cosmetics scattered across the room, as if someone had shaken out the contents of her bags. Even Meg's backpack hadn't escaped the slaughter. Her cosmetics case and journal had been unceremoniously dumped on the armchair and her precious laptop had fallen onto the floor, propped up against the dresser.

It took Meg a moment to digest the scene, a moment longer to find Minnie. She was huddled in the corner, Ben crouched by her side. Her face was red and wet with tears.

"What's wrong?" Meg asked. She'd seen Minnie in various stages of disarray, depression, and out-and-out despondency, but this? This was a first.

"Someone stole my pills," Minnie said. Despite the signs of crying, her voice had a dispassionate matter-of-factness about it that unnerved Meg.

"*Stole* your pills?" Meg pulled one of her hooded sweatshirts off the back of the easy chair and pulled it on over her pajamas. "Come on, no one would steal your pills."

Minnie's hazel eyes flashed. "Then how do you explain the fact that they're missing, huh? Some sort of magic trick?"

Meg glanced at Ben, who stayed quiet and rubbed Minnie's back. Great, no help there.

"Maybe you forgot to pack them," Meg said.

"I didn't. I double-checked."

"Maybe you misplaced them?" Meg knew the words were stupid as soon as she heard them come out of her mouth.

"Are you kidding?" Minnie sneered. She held her hands out, gesturing to the overturned room. "Don't you think we looked?"

"Meg?" T.J.'s voice floated up through the staircase. "What are you doing?"

Crap. "Look, come downstairs. Maybe someone else has a prescription."

Minnie shook her head. "No way."

"She won't go down 'til the . . ." Ben paused. "'Til Lori's gone."

"Oh, right." Meg shuddered at the idea of removing Lori's body from the stairwell. "The boys are going to take her down in . . . in a bit." She wasn't sure which was worse: leaving Lori there or taking her down.

"Are the police coming?" Minnie asked.

Double crap. Should she tell her that the phones had been knocked out by the storm? Minnie's eyes darted back and forth between Meg and Ben, clearly searching for some word of comfort. Yeah, this probably wasn't the time to bring up the phone situation. That might push Minnie over the edge.

Instead of answering, Meg squeezed her friend's hand and gave her what she hoped was a confident, reassuring grin. Then she picked up her laptop and her journal, shoving the latter into the pocket of her sweatshirt. She didn't want it lying around.

"Why are you taking your laptop?" Minnie asked. Her voice cracked. "What's going on?"

"I need to go back downstairs," Meg said.

"Why?" Minnie prodded.

Ben's eyes flitted from the laptop to Meg's face. She saw a moment of confusion, then he seemed to understand what was going on, and gave her a short nod.

"Will you stay with her?" she asked.

"Totally."

"Good. Thanks. I'll be back in a bit." Then before Minnie could ask any more questions, Meg disappeared down the stairs.

"It won't work."

Kumiko sighed. "Why not?"

"The power's out," Vivian continued, always the voice of hope and joy. "Do you think that's exclusive of the router?"

"Unless we're hardwired," Meg said as she plugged the network cable into the back of her MacBook. "If it's satellite internet the dish might have its own solar power supply."

"And if the cable comes directly from the dish, it might still be working." T.J. squeezed her shoulder. "Brilliant."

"Man," Kumiko said, with a glance at Vivian. "I'm *so glad* Meg's here."

"Whatever," Vivian said.

Meg could feel the press of bodies behind her as everyone clamored for a view of the screen. Her laptop rested on the shallow shelf of a bookcase, propped up against her knee. The network cable had been plugged in and Meg held her breath as she hit the power button, praying the battery had enough juice.

Come on, dammit. It would be her luck that this was the one time her laptop was completely drained, but just as she was about to give up hope the green light came on, indicating life of some kind. Thank God.

She felt a collective sigh of relief, including someone's breath against her cheek. Not just someone. T.J. So close that she could have turned her face and their lips would have touched. . . .

Stop it. Of all the inappropriate times to think about kissing T.J., this had to be the worst.

She forced her attention back to the computer screen. There was an agonizing moment as the rainbow pinwheel of doom blipped on, then the home screen loaded.

"Awesome!" T.J. said.

"Hurry up!" Vivian demanded. She was barely hanging on to the last threads of her cool. "Open the browser."

Meg bit her lip as she clicked on the browser icon. If this didn't work, what the hell were they going do?

"Oh my God!" Kumiko said. "Look!"

A browser window opened to Meg's homepage tabs. It worked! Her idea worked!

"Let me do it," Vivian said, pushing forward. "I'll log into my email and—"

Kumiko shouldered her back. "It's Meg's computer."

Right. Her computer. Meg quickly tabbed on the window for her email service. It was there, it was working. Most recent email was from early that morning—her mom, with the subject "Hope you're having fun!" Meg bit her lip as she hit "compose email." For some reason, seeing that email from her mom made her want to cry.

"Who should we email?" Gunner said. "The police?"

"Um," Meg said, looking around. "I don't have an email address for the police department."

"Email your parents first," T.J. suggested. "Then we can find an emergency contact online."

Meg nodded and typed both of her parents' names into the address box, then skipped right to the body of the email.

"At Jessica Lawrence's house on Henry Island. Long story. Been an accident. Phone's out. Need help."

Her parents were going to go apeshit when they found out she'd lied to them, but at that moment, it was more important to get the police out to the island. She'd deal with her inevitable punishment later.

With a shaky hand, she hit Send.

"Come on," T.J. said under his breath. Meg felt everyone lean closer to the laptop as if they were willing the email out into cyberspace, desperate to see the delivery confirmation screen.

"Shit."

The word came from seven mouths all at once. The screen, which had been actively connected to the internet a split second before, now had gone blank. *No internet connection established.*

So much for that.

TWELVE

"WHAT HAPPENED?" VIVIAN SNAPPED. "IT WAS just working."

"Hit refresh," Kumiko suggested.

Meg was a step ahead of her, but each refresh only brought the same result: *No internet connection established.*

"We must have lost the signal," Meg said. "I'm so sorry."

"It's not your fault," T.J. said. "We wouldn't have even thought of it if it weren't for you."

"Dude, let me try," Nathan said. Meg stepped aside and Nathan immediately started opening up network windows and connection diagnostic tools that she didn't even know existed. "Sometimes maintaining a connection is tricky. If it's working, I'll figure it out."

Meg wasn't exactly hopeful, but she appreciated Nathan's enthusiasm nonetheless.

"I told you it wouldn't work," Vivian said. She sat down in the window seat and crossed her legs.

"You really are a know-it-all, aren't you?" Kumiko said.

Vivian thrust out her chin. "Well, somebody has to be the voice of reason."

"You think you're the only one here with a brain?" Kumiko was fired up. "At least Meg had a good idea and was trying to be helpful. You just put on your bossy pants and think that makes you superior. Get over yourself."

Vivian slowly stood up and held her head high. "At least I'm not slutting my way through the weekend."

"What's that supposed to mean?"

"Did she just call you a slut?" Gunner said.

"It means," Vivian said, planting her hands on her hips, "if you two weren't sneaking around—"

"Nobody's sneaking," Gunner said slowly. "T.J. offered to sleep on the sofa."

Meg cocked her head. T.J. slept in the living room last night? She could have sworn he was the first one on the stairs after she discovered Lori's body.

"I'm just saying," Vivian continued, "that if you'd slept in your own room last night maybe Lori wouldn't be dead."

"That is *it*!" Kumiko lunged at Vivian, but T.J. stepped between them.

"Okay, all right," he said. "Fighting won't get us anywhere. We need to figure out what we're going to do." He turned to Nathan. "Anything?"

"Nope," Nathan said. He closed the lid to Meg's laptop, stood up, and pulled on the network cable. It snaked out from behind the bookcase in the corner of the room by the bay window.

"Looks like it goes through the wall." Without another word, he ran out of the living room into the kitchen.

"What the hell?" Vivian said.

The door to the patio slammed and from the bay window Meg saw Nathan stick his head out the side door that led to the backyard. He paused, then dashed out into the rain.

Six bodies crammed onto the window seat as they gazed out the window. Rain lashed at the pane, turning the view outside into a blurry, impressionist mess. It was kind of like looking through a kaleidoscope as Meg watched Nathan's disjointed form pick something up off the muddy ground.

"What's that?" Vivian squeaked, pushing herself right up to the window pane. "What's he got?"

Meg saw a flash of yellow in Nathan's hand and held her breath. The yellow network cable.

Nathan paused for a moment. Meg watched as he looked up toward the roof, then spun around and jogged back into the house.

Without a word, everyone sprinted into the kitchen.

"Well?" Vivian demanded. "What happened?"

T.J. tossed Nathan a towel, and he immediately started drying his face and hands. "Nothing. No go."

"Really?" Kenny asked.

"Sorry, dude. Looks like something sheered the cable in half. A branch or some debris. It's totally jacked."

"Can't we plug the laptop directly into the satellite?" Vivian asked.

Nathan shook droplets of water from his hair. "Are you going to climb up on the roof and do it?"

Vivian pursed her lips. "Do I *look* like I'd climb up there?"

"Didn't think so. I'd say we're screwed."

They were, kind of. No phone, no internet. And the closest town was across the channel. Meg thought of the houses in Roche Harbor that she could see from the garret window, lights twinkling in the distance.

Lights in the distance. Duh, how could she have forgotten? "The Taylors' house!" she blurted out.

Vivian glared at her. "Who?"

"The house across from us," Meg said. "Maybe they have a phone."

"Of course!" Kumiko said. "They had a raging party last night."

"The weather's crap," Nathan said, wringing water out of his thermal T-shirt. "Do you think we'd make it across?"

"Gunner and I can try," T.J. said.

"On it." Gunner bolted back through the living room toward the foyer, T.J. at his heels.

Meg followed with everyone else close behind. T.J. and Gunner pulled raincoats off the pegs on the wall while Meg cracked open the front door. The rain blew horizontally across the front yard in sheets so thick they obscured the view of the Taylors' house. The structure seemed to come and go between gusts of wind, as if it were fading in and out from another dimension.

"Are you sure it's safe?" she asked. She pictured a giant wave washing T.J. and Gunner out to sea and her stomach knotted up.

T.J. pulled the hood of the coat low over his head. "We've got the footbridge. We'll keep one hand on it at all times. Should be fine."

Nathan stood behind Meg and opened the door wide. "Dude," he said, pointing down at the isthmus below the house. "I don't think so."

Meg's eyes jumped to the roiling sea. A savage wave crashed over the tiny strip of land, temporarily submerging it. Then the water was sucked back out, and the isthmus emerged from its cover. Meg caught her breath.

"The bridge is gone."

"Shit," T.J. said. He pushed out onto the porch for a better view.

"That is not good," Kumiko said.

T.J. turned and walked back into the house, stripping off the yellow rain slicker. "Completely gone," he said. "The storm must have destroyed it."

Vivian stuck her head out the front door. "You can get across without it, right? The waves aren't that bad."

"Are you insane?" Kumiko pulled her back inside. "Without the bridge even a small wave would suck you under."

"But we can't just sit here."

"Then you try it." Kumiko folded her arms across her chest. "Be my guest. I'll watch you. From up here."

"Kumiko's right," Kenny said calmly. "There's no way we'd make it."

Vivian's eyes practically popped out of her head. "You mean we're stuck here?"

T.J. nodded. "At least 'til the storm lets up."

Meg gazed into the downpour. A lull in the wind and rain exposed the outline of the Taylors' house across the isthmus. It seemed so close, so comforting, and yet they couldn't get there. She slowly closed the door and leaned her forehead against it. None of her ideas had worked. They were trapped.

"What do we do now?" Kumiko asked. She had Gunner's hand gripped in her own.

"We should take her down," Kenny said quietly. It wasn't a question, and though his voice was soft—barely above a whisper—Meg got the distinct impression that Kenny was trying to contain his pain. She didn't want to see him unleash.

Apparently, Vivian wasn't worried about pissing Kenny off. "Take her down? Are you insane? That's a crime scene. The police will need to investigate."

"Last time I checked, suicide wasn't a crime," Kumiko said.

Kenny was resolute. "We can't just leave her there."

"Why not?" Vivian asked.

"It's disrespectful."

"It would be disrespectful to move her. What if we destroy evidence?"

"Calm down, CSI," Kumiko said.

Meg thought of Minnie huddled on the floor in the garret. While she appreciated Vivian's point—God help her—without any way to contact the police and without any idea of when Jessica might arrive, it seemed too horrible to leave Lori's body hanging there. What if they were stuck on the island until Monday?

"I agree with Kenny," she said. "We should take her down."

T.J. nodded. "Me too. Anyone else opposed?"

Nathan, Gunner, and Kumiko shook their heads.

"Fine," Vivian said. Her face flushed red with anger. "But I'm not taking any responsibility for this. If the police ask me, I'll tell them it was your idea and I tried to stop you. You'll all get in trouble. Not me." And with that, Vivian stormed off down the hall.

"If she stomps off every time she doesn't get her way," Kumiko said, smiling after her, "can I have permission to disagree with every single thing she says?"

"That shouldn't be hard," Meg said.

"Now what?" Gunner asked.

T.J. looked at Meg. "Do you really think we should take her down?" Even though he'd effectively taken leadership of the group, he still seemed intent on her input. Meg wasn't sure why, but she kind of liked that. And while she had a split second of panic when she realized that everyone was waiting for her answer, she was excited by the idea that T.J. cared what she thought.

Meg swallowed. "Okay." They couldn't just leave Lori hanging there. It wasn't right. "Let's do it."

THIRTEEN

IT TOOK JUST ABOUT EVERYONE'S HELP TO LOWER Lori's body down to the ground floor of White Rock House. The rope had been flung up over the top rafters of the tower, with one end tied securely to the banister at the bottom of the garret stairs. It was a knot worthy of a sailor, and Meg was surprised Lori had been able to both secure the knot and loop the rope over the rafters in what must have been a distraught state of mind.

The guys gradually lowered Lori's body while Meg and Kumiko waited at the bottom of the stairs. Meg had found some old sheets in a linen closet that they could wrap the body in. She and Kumiko spread one out on the floor while the body crept downward.

The horror of Lori's suicide was nothing compared to seeing her body descending from above. It jerked and wiggled like a marionette as the guys strained against her weight. Inch by inch, the dark figure grew larger as it approached, the tangled hair hanging lank around her face. The beams at the top of the tower creaked and groaned as the body twisted slowly, rotating first to the left, then unwinding more rapidly before twisting back again.

Meg's stomach lurched as Lori's dangling feet passed over her head. She stepped back and dropped her gaze, unwilling to see the lifeless eyes again. She waited until she heard the sound of the body touching down before she dared look up.

The guys at the top of the tower must have felt the change in weight and eased up on the rope, letting it slip through their hands. All at once Lori's body crumpled to the floor, lifeless and rigid. Meg and Kumiko scampered out of the way as the rope cascaded down from above.

"Sorry," Ben called from the top of the tower. "Everyone okay?"

"Yeah," Kumiko said. "We're good."

Everyone except the dead girl, Meg thought as she brought a second sheet over to cover Lori up.

Her body lay facedown—left arm caught beneath her, right arm twisted unnaturally at the shoulder. She looked like a doll that had been taken apart and put back together with all the parts reversed. The noose still encircled her neck and the rope had draped itself over her body in a series of loops and turns as it fell.

Meg unfurled the sheet and draped it over Lori's body, then together, she and Kumiko folded the top and sides over to form a kind of mummified bundle.

Ben, Gunner, and T.J. gathered at the bottom of the stairs, with Nathan trailing behind. "Should we say a prayer or something?" he asked. "Seems like we should."

"Know any?" Kumiko asked.

"Heh," Nathan laughed. "No."

"We're here to say good-bye to Lori Nguyen," Kenny said from the top of the first flight of stairs. He had taken possession of Lori's mourning. "Never again will we see her smile. Never again will we hear her voice. I wish—" Kenny caught his breath, smothering a sob. He paused and wiped his eyes with the back of his hand. "I wish we'd gotten to know each other better. We could have been . . ."

His voice trailed off. Meg saw Nathan shift his feet uncomfortably as he glanced up at his friend, but he didn't say a word.

"Well, whoever did this, whoever caused this . . ." Kenny said after a pause. "They're going to pay."

Meg winced. It was the second time in less than a day someone had mentioned revenge. Meg realized that Kenny was upset, but couldn't he just accept that Lori had killed herself instead of looking for someone else to blame?

Vivian poked her head out of the study. "We should move her in here. Then we don't have to look at her."

"Is she really that clueless?" Meg said under her breath.

"Apparently," T.J. said.

Kenny took Lori's head, Gunner and T.J. held her legs, and Nathan propped up the middle as Vivian guided them into the study. She kept up a constant stream of directions. "Don't knock over the lamp. Be careful of her head. You're too close to the desk. No, the other side." Meg was amazed at her energy. It was sort of pointless and negative, as if just being in charge was the most important thing in the world, and yet she appeared to have an endless supply of it.

"Is it gone yet?"

Everyone turned. Minnie stood on the second-to-last step. While everyone else was still in their pajamas with coats and sweatshirts thrown over them against the cold, Minnie was fully dressed in jeans and platform flip-flops with a long-sleeved cashmere sweater. She seemed to have recovered her poise after the frantic search of the garret, but Meg couldn't help but cringe at her friend's total lack of empathy in the current situation. Kumiko and Gunner exchanged a look that bordered on disgust, and Meg could practically feel Kenny's glare burning a hole through Minnie's skull.

"Her name," he said, in that same soft tone that gave Meg a creeping feeling up the back of her neck, "was Lori."

"Oh," Minnie said. She seemed vaguely aware of her misstep. At least that was something. "Sorry."

"Right," T.J. said, changing the subject. "Let's go sit down. We need to figure out what we're going to do next."

Meg picked at a piece of bread with some room-temperature butter smeared on top, ripping off little pieces, which she forced herself to eat. Most of the people gathered around the dining room table weren't faring much better, though the tragic events of the day hadn't dampened Minnie's appetite.

"What I don't understand," Ben started, "is why now?"

T.J. glanced at Meg. "Something, um, must have triggered it."

"Maybe," Vivian said with a shake of her head. "But why come to a house party if you were depressed and planning to kill yourself?"

"Too bad it wasn't you," Kumiko muttered to Meg's left.

"Huh?" Vivian asked.

"Nothing."

Nathan shrugged. "Seems as good a place as any. I mean, if that's your thing."

If that's your thing. Like suicide was a thing. A quirk. A personality flaw.

"We need to figure out what we're going to do now," Ben said, then took a bite of his doughnut. Like Minnie, Lori's death hadn't affected his appetite. Wow, they *were* the perfect couple.

"Maybe there's a generator in the house," Nathan suggested.

"We already searched for one, Gunner and me," T.J. said. "Nothing."

Nathan slouched in his chair. "Damn."

"We should wait for Jessica to get here," Vivian said. "Then we can have the ferry call the police."

A massive gust of wind rocked the house, sending a shudder from the foundation to the roof.

"I think," T.J. said after a pause. "I think we need to face the fact that Jessica might not be coming."

"What?" Minnie said through a mouthful of bagel. "What do you mean, not coming?" She dropped the half-eaten food to her plate. "She has to come. She has to. Meg, she has to come. You promised."

Meg was having a hard enough time keeping her own fear in

check. The idea of calming Minnie felt like trying to scale Mt. Everest barefoot.

Thankfully, Ben stepped in. "It's going to be okay," he said, and rested a hand on top of Minnie's.

"There's the boathouse," Gunner said. That was all. He didn't elaborate.

"Gee, thanks for that," Vivian said.

Kumiko immediately came to his defense. "Oh, yeah, Miss Brilliant? If there's a boathouse there might be a boat. And a boat probably has a radio."

"A radio?" Meg sat bolt upright.

"Yeah," T.J. said. "All vessels have a Marine VHF radio."

"Do you know how to use one?"

T.J. nodded. "My uncle owns a fishing boat. I used to work for him during the summer."

Meg glanced at Minnie. Her mood seemed to have recovered since Lori's body was interred in the study, but how long would it last? Without her antidepressants or her antianxiety meds, it was only a matter of time before a serious meltdown occurred. Like Chernobyl serious.

She had to avoid that. At all costs.

T.J. seemed just as eager to check out the radio. "Let's go, then."

"All of us?" Minnie asked, glancing at the raging storm outside.

"Nah." T.J. winked at Meg. "I'll just take Meg."

"Oh." Minnie stared straight ahead of her, not looking at either of them.

Ugh. Even with Ben around, Minnie was still territorial over T.J. Just one more reminder of why Meg had to get over him.

T.J. definitely wasn't reading her mind this time, though. "Come on, Meg," he said. "Throw on your raingear and let's go."

FOURTEEN

MEG RAN UP THE STAIRS TO THE GARRET AND sifted through the mess for her boots and raincoat. Her heart pounded in her chest, but it wasn't from the mad dash up the stairs. She was in decent enough shape to handle that. She was excited, plain and simple.

T.J. wanted her help.

Stop it.

Meg sat down on the side of her bed and pulled on her rain boots. The hardened look on Minnie's face flashed before her. She had to control her feelings for T.J. Had to. Minnie would never forgive her if she found out, and besides, she was going to Los Angeles, starting fresh.

Except T.J. would be in LA too.

What is wrong with you? It was like her brain was trying to sabotage her. She'd made a decision on Homecoming night. She and T.J. would never happen. She needed to stick with that. Besides, once he got to USC, he'd be an even bigger rock star than he was in Mukilteo. He'd have hot LA girls swarming all over him.

Celebrities, probably. Didn't USC football players always date celebutantes? It was part of their contract or something—full scholarship, plus a Kardashian as a girlfriend. He wouldn't even remember Meg. She'd be a speed bump on his road to fame.

She just had to get through this weekend. Find a radio, get off the island. *Move on.*

Meg got to her feet and searched around for her coat. She found it on top of the dresser where Minnie had launched it during her madcap search of the room. Meg pulled it down and started to put it on when something caught her eye.

Sitting on the dresser was a framed photo of a girl.

Meg didn't recognize the photo at first. It seemed so incongruous, so out of place in that room. The pale skin, the look of sadness on her face, the stringy hair that hung in front of her face like a tattered curtain. Black hair. Black and foreboding.

It dawned on Meg slowly, like a fog clearing from her mind. She knew this girl.

It was Claire Hicks.

Holy shit. Claire Hicks? What was a photo of Claire Hicks doing in her room?

Questions flooded her mind.

Had the photo been there when they arrived? Meg tried to remember. She'd come up the stairs the first time and been so dazzled by the garret room, maybe she hadn't noticed. No, that was stupid. A thick black frame around a photo of Claire Hicks? She'd have remembered that.

Okay, but if it wasn't there last night, *how did it get there?*

Obviously it didn't appear out of thin air. Someone had to have put the photo on the dresser. *Who?* Ben and Minnie had been up there for an hour or so, but in the chaos of the morning, anyone could have been in the garret. It would have been pretty easy.

Which led to the most important question: *Why?*

There was the mundane answer, of course. It had fallen behind the dresser and someone, maybe Minnie or Ben, found it there and put it back. Logically, it made the most sense. But even if that were true, Meg returned to her initial reaction: *Why was there a photo of Claire Hicks in her room?*

Meg stared at the photo. Claire. She looked so much like the creepy dead girl in *The Ring* that Meg was more than a little afraid that Claire was going to crawl out of the picture frame into the room.

Which made it even more disturbing that her family had used that photo for her obituary.

Why, why, why was it in her room? Claire wasn't related to the Lawrences in any way. If anything, Jessica Lawrence and her circle had avoided Claire like the plague. They weren't openly hostile, and honestly, it wasn't like Claire needed any help ostracizing herself at school. She had transferred to Kamiak at the beginning of fall semester, and within weeks of her arrival, rumors were flying. Accidents seemed to happen to people who were mean to her.

Bobby Taylor had a car crash two days after purposefully tripping Claire in the hall. Afterward he swore up and down that his brakes had failed.

Tiffany Halliday cut herself on a jagged piece of metal hanging from her locker a week after someone circulated a Photoshopped picture of Claire around Facebook. She got this weird infection from it and spent two weeks in the hospital getting transfusions. Meg remembered the blood drive and the scary days when no one was sure if Tiffany would make it. She did, thankfully, and the police declared the whole thing an accident.

After that, everyone pretty much left Claire alone. Even the teachers. And Claire seemed to like it that way, which is why even though she was a freaking mess, it was a complete surprise when she was found hanging from the ceiling fan in her bedroom the day after Homecoming.

Now another suicide by hanging. And there was Claire's photo looking out at it all in this big creepy house in the middle of nowhere. Was it supposed to mean something? Maybe Lori had put the photo in their room while they were sleeping? Was she somehow connected to Claire?

Meg shook herself. She was letting her imagination take over. Stupid. She needed to stay calm, go with T.J. to check out the boathouse, and hopefully find an easy way off Henry Island. It was going to be fine.

With more force than she intended, Meg flattened the frame against the dresser. She was about to leave when she noticed some writing on the back of the picture frame. With one finger, she spun the frame around so she could read the words.

They were written in red ink: *I will repay.*

What in the hell did that mean? Someone's idea of a practical joke, no doubt, but things were officially getting a little bit too weird. She backed her way out of the room until she felt the lip of the first stair, then turned and ran down as quickly as her boots would allow.

T.J. was waiting for Meg at the bottom of the stairs. "What took you so long?"

"S-sorry," Meg stammered. Her mind raced. Lori's death. The photo of Claire. The mysterious red slash and the freaky DVD. Were they all just coincidences or were they somehow related? And if so, how?

T.J. stepped in front of her. "Are you okay? You look . . ."

"What?"

"I don't know. Kind of shaken."

Meg raised an eyebrow. "You think?"

"I meant," T.J. said with a sigh, "you know, something other than Lori."

Meg opened her mouth. She wanted to tell T.J. about the photo of Claire, but she stopped. He'd changed out of his pajamas and into jeans and a thick cable-knit sweater under his raincoat. Meg even caught a trace of aftershave. Meanwhile, she'd tucked her flannel pajama bottoms into her rain boots and thrown a coat over her sweatshirt. She hadn't even run a brush through her hair or put it up in its normal ponytail. She must have looked like some dorky tween just up from a slumber party . . . who was about to go down to the boathouse with a hot boy. Alone.

Wow. She was such an idiot.

Nope, she wasn't going to say anything. More than likely, her imagination was just running rampant again. The last thing she needed to do was make herself seem like any more of a silly little girl envisioning monsters in the closet. Yeah, that would send him running.

"You're lost in your head again," he said. "What's wrong?"

"Nothing," she lied.

"Good. Come on."

They turned toward the foyer, but T.J. immediately paused. It was like he didn't want to pass by that slash on the wall. Meg didn't blame him, and she secretly rejoiced when instead of using the front door, T.J. headed down the hall, through the living room. They passed Kumiko and Gunner spooning on the couch, and Nathan flipping through a magazine on the window seat, but no one said a word. In the kitchen, Vivian leaned against the counter sipping a room-temperature Diet Coke.

"You're going down to the boathouse," she said simply.

"Yep." T.J. opened the door to the back patio. "With any luck, we'll find a radio."

"Right," she said with an arched brow. "The radio. I'm sure that's all you're doing down at the boathouse."

"It is," T.J. said flatly. "Come on, Meg."

Vivian followed them to the patio door. "Are you *sure* you know how to use one?"

She just could not stop micromanaging, could she?

T.J. ushered Meg through the door onto the patio. "Yep."

Vivian took a few steps toward them. "Maybe I should come with you just in—"

"Nope," he said with a smile, then closed the door in her face. "Damn, that girl is a pain in the ass," he said under his breath.

"Understatement of the century."

T.J. opened the door that led to the backyard, exposing the full force of the storm. Sheets of rain obscured the view of the trees beyond the yard, and the temperature was at least twenty degrees colder than it even was in the heatless house.

"Stick with me, okay?" T.J. said. "The path down to the boathouse is kind of treacherous."

Treacherous? Great. "I'll try."

"Ready?" T.J. buttoned his coat up to his chin, whipped his beanie out of his pocket, and pulled it down to his ears.

Meg lifted her hood over her head. "Ready."

T.J. dashed down the steps into the rain. With a deep breath, Meg followed.

FIFTEEN

THE GROUNDS AROUND WHITE ROCK HOUSE WERE a muddy mess that sucked at Meg's boots as she trekked across the yard. It felt as if she were slogging through ankle-deep sand, and it took twice as much strength as usual to put one foot in front of the other. The wind was even more brutal than it had been the night before, gusting across the island, trying to uproot every tree and topple every structure in its path. Towering Douglas firs cowered before the tempest, and though Meg should have been able to hear the shuddering branches and the waves crashing against the rocks below, the only sound in her ears was the relentless, howling wind.

Meg struggled to keep up with T.J. He was at least six inches taller than she was, and his star-football-player legs had no trouble driving through the muck of the yard. He reached the tree line a full thirty seconds before she did and hardly seemed to notice when she plodded up behind him.

He stared off to the right and Meg followed his eye. Cutting through the forest was a series of wooden walkways leading down the side of the hill. They were the same kind as the footbridge that had been washed off the isthmus. The beams were rough and water-damaged, their once-brown wood now grayed and pitted with age. T.J. stepped on the first deck and tested his weight against its solidity. The walkway bounced a little, but it appeared sturdy and sound.

"Should be okay," T.J. shouted through a wall of rain. He grabbed her hand and led her down through the trees.

The walkways were slanted and uneven—some took ten steps to traverse, others took three—and even the rubber grip on the bottom of Meg's boots had a difficult time retaining traction on the waterlogged planks. Meg tried not to let her eyes stray over the side of the hill, where a steep drop-off ended on the jagged rocks below.

Maybe this trip to the boathouse wasn't such a good idea. Rickety wooden land bridge? Check. Storm of the century? Check. Certain death at the hand of the rocks on the beach? Check and mate. Just like Nathan's painfully racist joke last night: This was how horror movies started.

Up ahead, the walkways turned abruptly. The path was slanted at a precarious angle, and Meg watched T.J. hydroplane a few inches before he caught his balance. "Careful," he shouted. "It's a bit—"

Too late. As soon as Meg's rain boots hit the slanted planks, they lost their grip on the wood. Meg slid down the walkway, totally out of control, and pitched forward toward the rail. She saw a flash of the hillside barreling toward her and pictured her body careening headfirst down the cliff. She reached her hands out to brace herself against the railing, and prayed the rickety wood would stop her. No such luck. The wooden railing gave way and Meg squeezed her eyes shut. This was it.

But instead of falling, Meg felt a strong arm around her waist. With a grunt, T.J. hauled her body away from the edge and spun around, pulling them both back to safety. They slid against the large tree that supported the walkway on the inside of the hill, and Meg leaned her body into his as they stood there panting.

"You okay?" he asked. His arms were still around her waist.

"Yeah," Meg said. Her heart pounded in her chest, though whether it was from the near-death experience or from feeling T.J.'s body pressed against her own she wasn't entirely sure.

"That was close." He gazed over her shoulder toward the bend in the path. "Someone should really fix that."

Meg didn't even want to think about what would have happened if T.J. hadn't been there.

With his arm still around her, T.J. eased her down to the next platform that wound back around the hillside. Slowly, carefully, they continued on toward the boathouse, until T.J. suddenly paused.

"Shit," he said.

Meg looked up at him. "What?"

"There were some flashlights by the patio door," he said. "I forgot to grab them." He looked down toward the boathouse, then back up to the house past the dangerous bend in the path as if weighing his options. "Shit," he said again. "We'll need them. Stay here?"

Stay on a hillside by herself in the middle of nowhere? After almost plummeting to her death? Um, no. She started to protest, but T.J. didn't give her the opportunity. Faster than Meg could react, he reached down and gave her a quick kiss on the lips, then whirled around and headed back up the hill.

Meg felt dizzy. Had he just kissed her? Had T. J. Fletcher just *kissed her*?

Several thoughts filled Meg's head simultaneously.

Number one—she was quite possibly going to pass out from joy.

Number two—had he meant to kiss her? Had it been a mistake? No, that was silly. How could it possibly have been a mistake unless he was trying to lick something off her face?

Number three—was there any way Minnie might have seen them?

The last was the most disturbing. Meg blinked through the onslaught of rain and craned her head to try and get a view of the house. She could just make out the line of windows along the enclosed patio, and even then it was just a glimpse of glittering white through the trees. No, she was safe. Unless Minnie had followed them to the boathouse. Meg stepped up to the higher walkway and tried to follow the path back to the house, but the angle of the hillside and the thickening trees made it impossible to see more than a hundred feet behind her.

Good. If she couldn't see the house, Minnie couldn't see her.

Meg leaned back against a tree for support. The rain was falling in sheets, so fast and so heavy that she couldn't differentiate the individual drops anymore. Every few seconds the wind would shift, giving Meg a face full of rain. The storm was fierce, unrelenting, and Meg could barely keep her eyes open in the face of its violence.

She squinted down at the rocks below. The waves crashed against the rocky island so viciously she could feel their impact, though oddly, she couldn't hear them. She couldn't hear any individual sounds, actually. The wind and the rain created a kind of white noise backdrop that drowned everything else out. Meg opened her mouth and yelled into the storm, then laughed to herself. She could barely hear her own voice.

Meg quickly realized it wasn't funny. No one could hear her scream. That was the truth. As she stood, lashed by rain and straining against the wind to even stand upright, the whole island took on a more sinister feel.

Meg shivered. How long had T.J. been gone? Surely long enough to run back up to the house and get back to her. Still, she didn't want him to rush. One misstep on those slippery wooden walkways and he'd go crashing headfirst onto the rocks below. Why would anyone build such a dangerous path? It was almost as if—

A hand grabbed Meg's shoulder. She screamed, her heart leaping to her throat, and spun around to find T.J.

"You okay?" he yelled through the rain. He had two orange-handled flashlights sticking out of each of his coat pockets. He wasn't smiling.

Meg nodded.

"Your teeth are chattering," he said.

"They are?" Meg took mental stock of herself. She was

drenched from head to foot and yes, her teeth were indeed chattering. She was so lost in T.J.'s kiss and the weird ambiance of the island that she hadn't even noticed.

"Come on," T.J. said.

Meg blindly stumbled behind him. Just above the rocky shore, the walkway stopped at a set of steep wooden stairs. The railing was wobbly, but T.J. took the steps one at a time, slow and careful. Then together they pushed open the rickety door of the Lawrences' boathouse.

SIXTEEN

DRIPPING WET AND CHILLED TO THE BONE, T.J. and Meg trudged inside. There were cracks in the roof allowing beams of dull, muted light to filter in, illuminating a million particles of dust kicked up as they shuffled across the wooden floor. Rain dripped steadily from two dozen spots in the roof, but at least the wooden walls blocked the wind. Meg sneezed as T.J. latched the solid, cross-beamed door behind him.

T.J. whipped the cap off his head. "You okay?" he asked, wringing the water out of it.

Meg fought the urge to shiver. Her flannel pajama bottoms were soaked and clung to her thighs in a way that could not possibly be flattering. Beneath the waterproof layer of her teal-green raincoat, her skin was goose-pimpled with the cold, and she silently cursed her airheadedness in forgetting to put on a bra.

"Yeah." Meg pulled the hood off her head and shook out her hair. "Totally fine."

"Good." He shoved his beanie into his coat pocket and handed

Meg a flashlight. She switched it on and scanned the interior of the boathouse.

They stood on a wooden platform that stretched the length of the floating building. A large blue tarp covered a pile on the far wall. Meg traced its outline with the beam of her flashlight and saw where a corner of the tarp had been folded, exposing a stack of gasoline cans beneath.

"At least there's plenty of gas," she said.

T.J.'s beam joined hers on the pile. "So we can start a bonfire?"

"No." Meg snorted. "If we have to drive a boat out of here, at least we'll have fuel."

T.J. stepped in front of her and smiled. "Oh, yeah? And are you going to pilot the boat?"

His dimples—the left one slightly deeper than the right—taunted her. So many times she'd dreamed about running her fingers over them, feeling the soft indentations with her fingertips, then tracing the strong, square line of his chin. She'd even journaled about it, much to her own personal embarrassment. Nothing like reading over your own diary entry and realizing how pathetic it sounded.

T.J. took a step toward her and Meg caught her breath. Was he going to kiss her again? Oh my God. She hadn't French kissed a guy since she'd cut her tongue on Tim Eberstein's new braces when he kissed her after band practice in junior high. She'd bled like crazy, drooling a mixture of blood and saliva down the front of her white T-shirt. Tim had shrieked like a girl and run away, and Meg had to go to the nurse's office and spin a ridiculous story about a wicked paper cut caused by licking envelopes for the spring concert invitations.

It was a less than romantic experience.

Meg shook herself out of the memory. *T.J. doesn't have braces, what are you freaking about . . . ?*

It was then Meg realized that although T.J. was standing mere inches from her, his eyes were fixed on something over her right shoulder. She turned and saw that he was staring at a boat.

Well, not a boat. It was huge, forty feet long at least, with a long, pointed bow and a raised pilothouse towering above them. The boat was painted white—like the house—with its name painted in bright red letters up near the bow: *Nemesis.*

"It's beautiful." T.J. sighed.

Really? A boat? An inanimate object was more enticing than she was? This was so exactly her life.

"Man," T.J. said, sidestepping Meg. "My uncle had one of these when I was a kid. I haven't seen one in years."

"Creepy name for a boat."

"Not just a boat," he said. "A Grand Alaskan Trawler. They're perfect for small island travel, personal fishing. Real workhorse." He unlatched the side boarding gate and climbed on board.

"Oh." She had absolutely no idea what he was talking about.

"This is probably like early seventies." He knocked on the side of the boat with his knuckles. "Wooden hull. Portuguese bridge. A total collector's item. I can't believe it's just sitting out here in the middle of nowhere."

Meg sighed. "Awesome?" She knew next to nothing about

boats. Her Upper East Side, New York–transplanted parents hadn't exactly taken to life on the Seattle coast, and the only boats Meg had ever been on were ferries.

"Totally." T.J. turned to her and smiled again, his dimples wreaking havoc with her nerves. Then he held his hand out to her. "Come on. I'll show you the pilothouse."

Meg stepped aboard and followed T.J. up a short, narrow flight of stairs to the raised pilothouse. The boat showed signs that it had been well taken care of once upon a time, but in the last few years had been totally neglected. The mahogany-lined wheelhouse appeared to be decked out with more modern technologies than would have been available when it was constructed. Modern navigation screens felt anachronistic with the old-fashioned spoked pilot's wheel and wooden railings that lined the stairs leading belowdecks. And while there were no obvious signs of decay or damage, a thick layer of dust had settled on every surface.

"Damn," T.J. said, tracing a line in the dust-caked captain's chair and wiping the remnants on his jeans. "Shame this baby's just sitting up here. Somebody put a lot of work into her, but beneath the upgrades, this girl is a classic. They don't make them like this anymore."

Wow. So T.J. was a boat geek. Who knew? Somehow this knowledge made him slightly less intimidating. "I didn't realize you knew so much about boats," Meg said with a half smile.

"Heh," T.J. said, shuffling his feet. "I don't share it much."

"I can see why. It's pretty nerdy."

T.J. pried his eyes away from the ship's gadgets and gizmos

and stared at her. The smile dropped from his face and his brows crinkled up like he was trying to figure out if she was making fun of him or not.

"I was just kidding," Meg said, feeling her face flush red. Why was she such a spaz? "I mean, I'm totally way nerdier than you. I'm a writer, for chrissakes. We're like the ultimate nerds. And you don't even want to see my baseball card collection. . . ."

Meg's voice trailed off. Ah, yes. Cue her verbal diarrhea. *So not sexy, Meg.*

"I don't think you're a nerd," T.J. said. His voice was soft yet firm, as if he were making a very serious clarification. "Not even a little."

"Oh." So he didn't think she was a nerd. Was that good? Was that bad? Holy crap, why was she so unsure of herself?

T.J. took a step toward her. This time his eyes were fixed fully on her face. "Meg . . . ," he started, then paused.

"What?" Her voice was breathless, probably caused by the fact that her heart was racing so fast she thought she might pass out.

"Are you okay?"

Why did he keep asking her that? "Yeah."

T.J. placed a hand against her arm. "You're trembling."

Meg hadn't even noticed but as soon as T.J. mentioned it, her teeth began to chatter again. She was either going hypothermic or the adrenaline rush of being alone with T.J. was spiraling out of control. Probably both.

"Just cold," she said through chattering teeth.

"I'm sorry," he said. He let his hand linger on her arm and she could feel his grip tighten slightly through the fabric of her coat. "I didn't mean to drag you out here in the cold. I just . . . I wanted to talk to you."

Meg's stomach had by this time permanently relocated to her throat. She'd dreamed a hundred times about T.J. proclaiming his undying love for her, but even now, as they were alone together in the boathouse, she couldn't quite bring herself to believe it was true. He had his pick of girls to choose from. Everyone wanted to go out with T.J. Fletcher. Why on earth would he choose her?

"I know we didn't talk much after . . . well, after Homecoming," he started. She felt his fingers graze the back of her hand. "I mean, I was pretty pissed off and I guess I avoided you after that."

Homecoming night. She'd been so excited when he asked her to the dance, though it all came crumbling down when Minnie confronted her.

"But I've missed you," T.J. started again. He brought his face close to hers. "Since Gunner and Minnie broke up, I never see you."

At the mention of Minnie's name, Meg's entire body stiffened. Minnie. Oh crap, what would she say if she saw the two of them on the boat together? Minnie would never forgive her if she knew about this conversation. It would crush her. It would ruin their friendship.

T.J. leaned into Meg's body. "And I guess what I'm trying to say, is that I—"

"We need to look for the radio," she blurted out. She couldn't hear anymore. What had she been thinking? She couldn't date someone her best friend was in love with. That was the ultimate betrayal.

T.J. jerked his head back like Meg had just slapped him. "Huh?"

"The radio." She pulled away from him and started rifling through the gadgets on the control panel of the wheelhouse. "And then get back to the house."

"Oh." T.J. stood still for a moment, then walked over to the captain's chair. "Right."

Meg turned her back to him. She wanted to cry. Why couldn't she at least wait to hear what he had to say? Why did she have to go and make a mess out of everything?

"That's weird," T.J. said.

Meg wiped a stray tear off her cheek. "What?"

"The radio's gone."

"What?" The tension between them was gone in an instant. Meg peered up to where T.J. pointed above the window.

"Gone. It's been removed."

SEVENTEEN

"SOMEONE TOOK THE RADIO OUT OF THE BOAT?" Meg stared at a gaping hole in the boat's console. "Why would anyone do that?"

T.J. shook his head. "No idea. But judging by the prints in the dust here"—he pointed at smudge marks on either side of the radio's former location—"I'd guess it was removed fairly recently."

"Is that normal?" Meg asked. She was grasping at straws, attempting to quell the uneasiness in her gut that threatened a full-scale panic. "Like for maintenance or something?"

"Nope."

"Oh."

They stood in silence. The idea that yet another hope for communication with the mainland had been purposefully removed was still sinking in, and while the reality of their situation weighed on her, Meg's mind raced with possible solutions.

"What about the boat? Can we drive it to Roche Harbor?"

"No keys."

"Oh." Duh. Somehow she'd expected a more dynamic answer.

"Can you hotwire it?"

T.J. tilted his head to look at her. "Do I look like I know how to hotwire a boat?"

"You don't *look* like you'd know how to drive one, but apparently you do."

"Good point."

Now it was Meg's turn to tilt her head. "So do you?"

"Do I what?"

What was this, twenty questions? Meg threw up her hands. "Do you know how to hotwire the boat?!?"

T.J. pursed his lips. His dimples sagged ever so slightly. "Yeah, no."

Meg's eyes roamed the wheelhouse. "Maybe they're here somewhere? The keys?" That was logical, sort of. Why not keep the keys in the boat somewhere? It wasn't exactly as if a boat-jacker was going to steal the thing way out there in the middle of nowhere.

"Honestly, Meg, I doubt it."

"We should still check."

T.J. sighed. "Fine." He climbed down a short staircase that led belowdecks. "I'll check the cabins, you look up here, okay?" He didn't sound particularly optimistic.

"Okay." Meg wasn't about to let T.J.'s pessimism daunt her. She was going to find those keys, dammit.

The wheelhouse seemed to be the most logical place to keep a set of boat keys. She combed the control panel with her flashlight, hoping the gleam of the metallic keys would catch her eye amid the gears and gizmos. No dice. Then she rummaged through a few drawers and cabinets on either side of the steering wheel. She found charts, a tool box, a can of WD-40, a dusty compass, a Seattle Mariners baseball cap with a heavily creased brim, a battery-operated fan, dusty coffee mugs, and an array of adapters, plugs, and extension cords that didn't appear to go with any specific electronics whatsoever.

Ugh.

There was a closet door on the back wall next to the stairs. Last chance. Meg crossed her fingers, held her breath, and opened the closet.

Not only were there no keys, but the space was oddly empty. No mops, no brooms, no coats, no anything. Weird. The rest of the wheelhouse compartments were stuffed with junk, but this one had been completely cleaned out.

She scanned its length from top to bottom, then paused as her flashlight beam caught something on the ground. It was a stain, a ring-shaped stain, of red paint.

"T.J.!" Meg called out. "Come here!"

The boat shifted as she heard T.J.'s footsteps pounding up the stairs. "What?" he asked as his head popped over the rail. "Did you find them?"

Meg shook her head. "Look."

T.J.'s light joined hers on the red stain on the floor of the closet. He crouched down and dabbed at it with his finger. A smudge of red paint appeared on the tip of his middle finger.

Meg gasped. "It's still wet?"

T.J. didn't answer. He held his finger to his nose and sniffed a few times, then abruptly stood up. "I think . . . ," he started. "I'm pretty sure it's the same paint that's on the wall up at the house."

Meg's heart was racing. Missing radio, missing paint . . . "Someone took them both," she said. "Recently."

It wasn't a question and T.J. didn't respond. The unspoken "why" lingered in the air between them, but Meg was afraid to ask. Afraid of the answer.

"What do we do now?" she asked instead.

T.J. glanced from the closet to the missing radio bay, then to Meg. "We go back."

It wasn't raining nearly as hard as it had been thirty minutes ago, and the wind was no longer attempting to wipe the island clean of all its inhabitants, flora and fauna alike. But Meg still felt as if she were battling the elements as she slowly climbed back up the wooden walkways toward White Rock House.

T.J. led the way as before, but he didn't hold her hand this time. Instead he was easily ten feet in front of her by the time they were halfway up the hill. He hadn't turned around once to make sure she was okay.

Not only was their chance at contacting civilization gone but she'd managed to piss off the love of her life. Again. Awesome, Meg. Well done. Why don't you just throw yourself off the side of the island right now and . . .

As she thought the words her eyes drifted off the walkway down the rocky hill. But instead of the jagged rocks and washed up driftwood she expected to find, she saw something else. A splash of neon yellow. An inflatable raft maybe? What would that be doing way out here? Meg squinted into the rain, blinking her eyes to try and get a better look. The shape, the size. Too small for a raft. It looked almost like . . .

Oh God.

"T.J.!" Meg yelled. She wasn't sure if he could hear her. She called out again, her eyes still fixed on the rocks. "T.J., come he—"

"What's wrong?" He was at her shoulder in an instant, but before Meg could even verbalize what she was staring at, he'd followed her gaze and seen it with his own eyes.

"Holy shit," T.J. said. He vaulted over the handrail and started to pick his way down the side of the hill.

Meg didn't hesitate. She shimmied under the rail and followed straight behind him. Her clunky rain boots made the climbing slow, and T.J. easily outpaced her as he half climbed, half slid down the muddy hillside. He was at the bottom a full minute before Meg made it down. When she stumbled up behind him, T.J. spun around and grabbed her.

"Don't look," he said, placing himself between her and whatever lay on the rocks.

"What?" she said. "What is it?"

T.J.'s face was pinched. Instead of answering he pulled her to him and hugged her so fiercely she could barely breathe. She could feel his hands shake as he slowly peeled himself away from her.

"There's been an accident."

"Is it Minnie?" Meg could barely control the panic in her voice.

T.J. shook his head.

She let out a breath. If Minnie had been injured trying to follow them down to the boathouse Meg would never have forgiven herself.

"Maybe you should go up to the house," T.J. said.

"Let me see. I want to see what happened." Meg sounded far braver than she felt, but somehow, in the midst of all the strange events of the last twenty-four hours, she needed to see.

T.J. didn't protest. He merely stepped aside.

Behind him, lying on her back, was Vivian. Her eyes were wide open, frozen in fear and pain. She wore a yellow raincoat buttoned up over her sweater and silk pajamas. Blood trailed slowly down her arm, dripping off her fingers into the pooling water beneath her. A jagged piece of driftwood protruded from her chest; it had impaled her from behind.

"Is she . . ." Meg's throat closed up.

"Yeah."

"Oh my God."

"Yeah."

Meg had no idea what to think. Vivian must have followed them down to the boathouse. But how did this happen?

"She must have slipped on the walkway," T.J. said, answering Meg's unasked question. "If she came down behind us in that rain . . . I mean, it was pretty dangerous."

Vivian's eyes stared blank and unseeing at the rocky hillside Meg and T.J. had just traversed. Her head lolled off the edge of the log, her arms splayed out on either side of her body. Meg pictured Vivian hurrying after them, convinced they wouldn't be able to find or operate a radio without her assistance. She was rushing and slipped on the wet walkways. She toppled head-over-heels down the hill and landed right on the jagged log, which literally stabbed her through the back. Her micromanaging was her undoing.

What were the odds? Two deaths in just a few hours? Meg shook off her fears. Lori's was obviously a suicide, Vivian's a horrific accident. Right?

The rain increased as Meg and T.J. stood beside Vivian's body. Large drops hit her open eyes and caused the eyelids to flutter slightly, as if Vivian was trying to wink at them. Meg forced herself to look away before she was sick.

"What should we do?" she asked.

"There's that tarp in the boathouse," he said. "I'll get it. We should cover the body but maybe not move her until . . ." His voice trailed off.

"Until Jessica comes?" Meg said. She couldn't hide the sarcasm in her voice. "Or until the ferry comes back tomorrow? That seems a better chance at this point."

T.J. looked down at her. His lips were pressed together so tightly they'd turned pink. "I'll get the tarp," he said, refusing to reply to her sarcasm. "You go back up to the house and tell them what happened."

Meg and T.J. scrambled up the side of the hill. The rain made the ascent in water-logged flannel pajamas and clunky rubber galoshes even more precarious, but by almost pure force of will, they managed to haul themselves back up on the nearest walkway. They sat panting for a moment—wet, muddy, mentally and physically exhausted. Meg couldn't stop looking down at Vivian's body. Just like Lori, her eyes were still open, empty and soulless. Meg couldn't get either death mask out of her mind.

Without a word, T.J. stood up and lifted Meg to her feet. He gave her a short nod, then carefully made his way back down to the boathouse. Meg watched him go for a few moments before she reluctantly turned her eyes to White Rock House, just visible through the trees. She was going to have to tell a house full of already weirded-out people that there'd been another accident. Minnie . . . oh God, Minnie was going to completely freak. And without her meds.

Meg was just approaching the sharp turn in the walkway when she stopped dead. At exactly the point where she'd lost her footing and almost fallen down the hill, the railing was gone, broken clean away.

A lump rose in Meg's throat. This must be the spot where Vivian had slipped, just as Meg had an hour earlier. And if T.J. hadn't been there to catch her, it could easily have been her own body down there on the beach impaled on a log.

Meg didn't want to think about it. She turned away and hurried up to the house, desperate to be inside. The storm picked up strength as Meg emerged from the trees. Never before had wind and rain felt so ominous, like it was mimicking the cold misery Meg felt inside. Vivian and Lori were dead. There was no radio in the boat. They were quickly running out of options.

To make matters worse, the back door to the patio was locked. Dammit. Vivian must have locked it when she left the house. God, this day just kept getting better and better. With her mood sinking faster than the *Titanic*, she made her way to the front of the house.

Meg took a deep breath. She could do this. There were eight of them at White Rock House. Strength in numbers. They'd just hunker down and get through the night. Monday morning the ferry would be back and this whole nightmarish weekend would be just a memory.

Okay. She had to be strong. Meg turned the handle and marched into the house.

But all her bravado, all her false courage and confidence died the second she stepped into the foyer.

On the wall, next to the first, was a freshly painted red slash.

EIGHTEEN

MEG WASN'T SURE HOW LONG SHE STOOD IN THE foyer dripping muddy puddles on the floor. She hardly remembered why she was there. All she could focus on were the parallel slash marks on the wall. Two slashes. Two dead bodies. There was no way in hell it was a coincidence.

But what did it mean? Someone was messing with them, obviously. Trying to scare them. Freaking sick sense of humor. Probably just a practical joke that happened to come at the same time as Vivian's accident. Or . . .

Meg's stomach dropped. Or someone else knew that Vivian was dead.

"You okay?"

Meg snapped back to the present and found Nathan standing in the hall with a half-eaten turkey sandwich in his hand.

"Did you guys find a radio? Where's T.J.? Do you want some of this sandwich? It's pretty go—" Nathan stopped midword as his eyes found what Meg had already discovered.

"What is that?" he roared. His sandwich fell to the ground as he stormed across the foyer to the slash marks. "What the fuck did you do?"

"Me?" she said. What the hell was he talking about?

He swung around and got up in Meg's face. "There was only one mark before, now there are two. Do you think this is funny or something? Trying to make them look like that stupid video we watched?"

Meg pulled away from him. "I didn't do it."

"Dudes!" Nathan crossed into the hallway and yelled again. "Everybody downstairs. Now!"

Kumiko and Gunner came first, then Kenny, all from the living room. Ben and Minnie leisurely strolled down the stairs.

"Why is everyone screaming?" Minnie said through a yawn.

"It's her," Nathan said, pointing a finger at Meg. "She did it."

"Did what?" Kumiko asked.

Nathan nodded toward the wall and everyone filed into the foyer.

"I didn't do anything," Meg said. She felt six pairs of eyes on her and she wished desperately that T.J. had come with her. "I came into the house and saw it just before Nathan found me."

"It didn't just get there on its own," Kenny said, backing up his friend.

Kumiko wasn't so easily convinced. "Then where's the paint? If she'd just painted the wall, she'd still have a brush and a can or something."

"She could have stashed them after she used them," Nathan said. He wasn't giving up his case.

"Then why would she come back to the scene of the crime, moron?" Ben asked. "Just to throw you off?"

"Well . . . um . . ." Poor Nathan. He clearly hadn't thought things through.

"Besides," Ben continued. He walked behind Meg and gestured to the trail of dirt and water she'd left as she came into the house. "She's dripping wet and covered in mud. Clearly her footsteps stop right where she's standing. She never went anywhere near the wall."

Meg could have hugged him.

"I guess," Nathan grumbled. He sounded less than convinced.

"Wait," Kenny said, looking around. "Where's Vivian?"

"And T.J.?" Minnie added.

Crap. As scared as Meg had been to tell everyone about Vivian before, the second slash mark made it even worse.

"There's . . . ," she started. She looked from face to face. How would they take this? Would they blame her? "There's been an accident."

T.J. had managed to get Vivian's body pretty well covered by the time Meg led the rest of the group down the side of the hill. He'd anchored the tarp with heavy rocks from the shore and tucked the sides down beneath the log onto which she'd fallen. Nathan and Kenny insisted on seeing the body for themselves, and Meg wasn't sure if it was because they didn't believe she was dead or didn't believe she'd died as the result of an accident. Either way, the two of them traipsed down the muddy hill and

T.J. carefully pulled the tarp away. From where Meg stood on the walkway, she couldn't see the body, but the shocked, drawn looks on the boys' faces reminded her only too well of what they found underneath.

Meg was the last one to climb back up the walkways to the house. She lingered behind, not wanting to partake in the inevitable conversation happening ahead of her. The deaths, the slash marks, the fact that they were currently cut off from the rest of the world. She didn't need to hear it again. Even the relentless rain was preferable.

Once again, she paused at the spot where Vivian must have lost her footing and fallen to her death. It seemed so pointless, so preventable. Her eyes traced the broken railing. If only it hadn't been raining, or the railing hadn't been so freaking old. It must have been rotted to have given way like that. Without thinking, Meg bent over to examine it.

While the one side of the wooden railing had been splintered by the impact of Vivian's body, the other side, the spot right at the turn in the walkway, was broken cleanly most of the way through, then, just at the back, looked as if the wood had snapped. There was a vertical groove that permeated almost all the way through the beam. It was clean and man-made.

As if someone had taken a saw to it.

Oh my God.

The railing had been cut intentionally.

Meg reared back. Half of her wanted to tell someone about her discovery, but would they believe her? Nathan was still convinced she'd painted the second slash on the wall, and if this discovery meant what she thought it did . . .

"You okay?"

T.J. stood on the platform above her. She beckoned him over. "Look at this."

T.J. carefully picked his way down the precarious walkway to the broken railing. "Isn't this the same spot you almost fell?"

"Yeah." Meg pointed to the broken railing. "And check this out."

T.J. bent down and examined the splintered wood. "She must have slipped too, only there was no one here to catch her. How horrible."

"But look," Meg said, tracing the saw mark with her finger. "That's no accident."

T.J.'s fingers grazed against Meg's as he felt the vertical cut. "You think someone did this on purpose?" he said after a moment.

"Maybe?" Meg was suddenly nervous, afraid of saying exactly what she thought.

"It could still have been an accident," T.J. said, his eyes fixed on the broken railing. "Someone could have been doing repairs and just forgotten to finish this section."

"Do you think we should tell someone?"

T.J. stood up suddenly. He gazed down at the tarp that covered Vivian's body, then up to the house. Finally, his eyes rested on Meg. "Not yet," he said. "Let's wait and see what happens, okay? I think everyone's on edge. This might make it worse."

"Okay." He was right, of course. After Nathan's reaction over the last red slash, Meg was pretty sure he'd be accusing her of cutting the handrail as well. Still, it seemed weird not to say something. Maybe if they figured out a way to contact the police, she could mention it.

Meg shivered. *If.*

"Come on, let's get you inside." T.J. guided her up the walkway toward the house. "You need some dry clothes."

Meg's skin was icy cold by the time she reached the garret. She stripped off her coat, then her sweatshirt, and kicked off her boots and soaking-wet pajama bottoms. She pulled her journal out of her pocket—dry, thankfully—and tossed it on the bed while she dug through a pile of her clothes and grabbed the warmest items she could find. Jeans, a long-sleeved shirt with a sweater over it, thick socks, coat, and her fingerless gloves. She couldn't find her brush so she borrowed Minnie's and dragged it through her wet hair, pulling it up into a high ponytail.

Meg lingered in the garret. She didn't want to go downstairs. By the time she and T.J. made it back to the house, everyone had gathered in the living room to discuss what they should do next. But after her discovery on the walkway, she kind of wanted to squirrel herself away in the garret until the ferry came back the next morning. Despite T.J.'s conviction that the whole thing was a tragic accident, the details surrounding Vivian's death nagged at her. Was it *really* an accident? Or could it have been intentional?

She was overreacting. There could have been other reasons for the man-made damage to the handrail. Like T.J. said, maybe the Lawrences had been doing repairs to the walkway last time they were at the house, and that section was left unfinished. That made sense. They might not even have known the railing was damaged.

But what about the paint? That was a problem she couldn't explain away. There had been red paint in the closet of the *Nemesis*. It had been removed recently—like within the last twelve hours—and there were red paint slashes on the wall of the foyer. Two of them. Both corresponding to deaths. Someone had known that both Lori and Vivian were dead before their bodies were discovered by everyone else.

Someone knew they were going to die.

Meg leaned against a window sill and stared out into the cloudy grayness. She felt knotted up inside, a mix of fear and apprehension and disbelief. Her mind raced. Was she really suggesting that Lori and Vivian had been murdered? Or at least that someone had known about their deaths and not told anyone? It was ludicrous. Wasn't it?

And yet there were two deaths. One might have been a tragedy, but two? She couldn't believe Vivian's death was just an accident. Not with the sabotaged handrail. And the slashes. Even if Lori had painted the first slash herself as some sort of morbid "screw you" to the world, who made the second mark?

Something had been off ever since they arrived on the island. Meg had tried to ignore it—the strangeness of the guest list, Jessica's absence, and then that creepy nonsensical DVD. The DVD . . . Meg recalled the conversation Lori and Vivian had after the video ended. *Someone's out to get us. I know what you did.* Lori and Vivian had been talking about something or someone, an incident at school that no one else knew about. What if they were connected?

Meg pulled away from the window and sat down on the edge of the bare bed. She desperately wanted to talk to someone about it, but bringing all of this up in front of everyone downstairs seemed about as appealing as walking through a field of broken glass barefoot, and T.J. thought she should keep it to herself for now. Still, her mind raced. She needed to organize her thoughts.

Without thinking, she reached out a hand for her journal.

The moment she held it in her hand, Meg realized something was wrong. She always kept a thin silver pen tucked into the journal. But it was gone. No bulge between the pages. She gazed down at the black fake-leather book and though it looked exactly like her own journal, the cover was more worn, more aged in a way Meg couldn't quite put her finger on. Kind of prematurely old. It felt heavy, brittle, like a book that had been dropped in the bathtub then left to dry out in the sun for a month. The attached ribbon bookmark hung in tatters between the pages, sticking out the bottom like a splayed peacock's tail, and the whole thing smelled musty.

One thing was for sure—it definitely wasn't Meg's journal.

Two thoughts jumped into her mind. Where the hell was *her* journal, and how did this one get in her room? She glanced around the disaster that was the garret—her journal must be somewhere in the mess. And this one was probably in the room, left there by a former resident or guest, and Minnie had uncovered it in her mad search for her meds.

Meg wanted to put the book back in a drawer. As a fellow journaler, she felt a pang of guilt about reading someone else's private thoughts and hidden secrets. She imagined the horror she would feel if someone found and read her own journal. The mere idea sent chills down her spine. So on that level, she wanted to shove the old diary back into the drawer where it had sat for who knows how long gathering dust and hoarding its secrets. She wanted to leave it alone. She wanted to walk away.

She didn't.

I'll just read the first page, Meg said to herself. *To find out who the owner is. No harm in that.*

Meg furtively glanced around the garret to make sure she was still alone, then sat on the floor beneath a window where there was enough muted light to see words on a page. It was like a forbidden book. Meg desperately wanted to open it.

It must be older than it looked. So old, the owner had probably forgotten it even existed. The author had left it here, after all. It couldn't have been that important to him. Perhaps he was dead and gone by now. That meant it was okay to read, right? Kind of like posthumously publishing someone's letters. Really, there was no harm in just peeking at the first page and seeing who it belonged to. No harm at all.

Meg took a breath and opened the diary.

Is this book yours? No? THEN STOP READING IT. NOW.

The words were centered on the title page, written in red ink. It should have been ominous. It should have kept Meg from turning the next page.

Not so much.

Seriously. I'll find you and hurt you.

Meg laughed out loud. Not that the words were funny, or the intention, but she had this flashback to an old picture book she used to love as a kid, where Grover from *Sesame Street* is trying to keep the reader from turning pages because there's supposed to be a monster at the end of the book. Of course, as a child she had a fiendish delight in continuing to turn the pages, despite Grover's preventative measures such as ropes, two-by-fours, and brick walls. Apparently things hadn't changed much in ten years.

The third page had a single line of text.

And their doom comes swiftly.

The words seemed familiar to Meg but she couldn't quite put her finger on it. A line of poetry maybe? Shakespeare? Crap, she should know it. Whatever it was, the author of the journal seemed passionate about it. The word "doom" was underlined like three times, and it looked as if the author had gotten increasingly excited with each repetition: by the last underline, the pen dug into the paper so fiercely it actually marred the next two pages in the diary.

Okay. Crazy much?

"What are you doing?"

Meg started at the voice, whipped her head up from the journal, and cracked her skull against the wall. Her vision blurred for a split second, then as it cleared, she saw Minnie's head and shoulders poking up from the floor, her lower half hidden on the stairs.

"Nothing," Meg said. She slapped the journal closed, feeling very much like she'd been caught doing something naughty.

"Oh." Minnie didn't look like she bought it. "You need to come downstairs. We're trying to figure out what to do."

"Okay." Meg stood up, furtively dropping the journal into her coat pocket as she pulled it on. There was nothing she wanted to do less than go down and face whatever conversation was going on, but Minnie was right. She needed to be there. She needed to be present.

The mysterious journal could wait.

NINETEEN

A MODEST BLAZE CRACKLED IN THE FIREPLACE, which made the living room the warmest spot in the house. Some of the chairs and the large sofa had been dragged in front of the fire, and everyone sat around talking. Meg entered quietly and stood near the window, half hoping no one would notice her.

"And no one saw anything?" T.J. said. He leaned against a bookcase with his hands shoved deep into his pockets.

Minnie curled up on a sofa next to Ben. "*We,*" she said emphatically, "were together up in the tower. Didn't see anything."

"You were the ones outside, dude," Nathan said. Meg didn't like his accusatory tone.

"Down at the boathouse," T.J. said. "You can't see the path from down there."

"What was there to see?" Kumiko said. "Vivian slipped and fell. It was an accident."

"Whatever," Nathan said. "I'm tired of just sitting here talking about it."

"What do you suggest we do?" T.J. asked.

Nathan bounced his leg furiously. "I think we should try to get across instead of waiting around for another 'accident.'"

Nathan's inflection on the word *accident* made Meg flinch. Did he suspect there was more going on too?

"What do you want to do?" Kumiko said. "Swim for it?"

"The storm's let up some," Kenny said. "We could make it across."

Ben shook his head. "Did you see the waves crashing over that strip of beach? It washed the bridge away. No way we'd make it."

"We don't all have to go," Kenny said. "In fact, we shouldn't."

T.J. stood up straight. "What's that supposed to mean?"

"Dude," Nathan said. "Are you mental?"

"No, I'm just the black guy. Which means I should be grateful I'm still alive at this point, remember?"

"It was a joke," Nathan said. His leg continued to bounce up and down.

Gunner edged forward in his chair. "Not funny."

Nathan did the same. "Not my fault you and your boyfriend don't have a sense of humor."

"So now it's gay jokes?" T.J. said. He clenched his fists. "Racist *and* homophobic?" He nodded at Kenny. "Why are you friends with this guy?"

Kenny pushed himself off the sofa. "Only matters that I am."

Kumiko threw herself between them. "Oh my God, what is wrong with you guys?"

Nathan wasn't about to back down. "Those marks on the wall? They didn't appear by magic."

The room fell silent. It was what they'd all been thinking, but

Nathan was the first to say it out loud. There was no one else in the house. One of them had made the marks on the wall.

"Look!" Kenny kicked the leg of the sofa so fiercely Meg jumped. "One of us is an asshole. And I'm not going to sit around and wait to see what happens next."

It was as if Kenny's whole demeanor had changed since Lori's suicide. That first night he'd seemed like a soft, gentle giant who barely said a word and just smiled a lot. Now he was a ticking time bomb.

"Exactly," Nathan said, resuming his seat. "So excuse us if we don't want everyone"—he looked pointedly at Meg—"along for the ride."

Meg opened her mouth to protest, but T.J. beat her to it. "She's the one who discovered the paint was missing from the boat. Why would she point that out if she was responsible?"

"Maybe she's trying to throw us off."

"She didn't do it," T.J. said through clenched teeth.

"Yeah?" Nathan said. His leg bounce was so manic Meg could actually feel it through the floorboards. "And we're what, supposed to take her word for it?"

T.J. squared his shoulders. "Hers *and* mine."

Meg glanced at Minnie, hoping her best friend would jump in and add her endorsement of Meg's innocence. Instead, Minnie stared at the coffee table.

"Excuse me if that's not good enough." Nathan got to his feet again. "Kenny and I are heading to the other house," Nathan said. "Alone."

"Whatever," T.J. said. "Good luck."

Nathan and Kenny stormed out of the living room without another word.

"That was ridiculously dramatic," Kumiko said.

"Shouldn't we try and stop them?" Meg asked. "They'll never make it."

Ben stood and stretched his long arms over his head. "I'm sure they'll be fine. The sooner we get hold of the police, the better." He placed a hand on Minnie's shoulder. "Why don't you get some rest? It's been a long day."

Minnie jolted in her chair as if Ben had just woken her from a nap. She got to her feet without so much as a nod or a smile and followed him out of the room.

Meg was worried. It was so not like Minnie to be this calm, this stoic. Her usual MO was what Meg had witnessed that morning—total freak-out followed by slightly dramatic narcissism. So this reaction was . . . odd.

"Minnie, wait up," Meg said, hurrying after them. She caught up to her at the bottom of the stairs. "Hey, are you okay?"

Minnie glanced at her briefly. "Why wouldn't I be?"

"Um . . ." Was Meg the only one who remembered the epic meltdown just two hours earlier when Minnie literally ripped their room apart looking for her meds? Ben was a few steps ahead of them, the only one within earshot. "You know. Without your anxiety medication? I'm worried everything that's happened today has been—"

"I'm fine."

"Oh."

That was a first. In six years of friendship Meg had always been the only person Minnie confided in. And as bad as Minnie's mood swings had gotten over the last year or two, Meg was used to that role. The shoulder to cry on. The one who fixed everything. Made it all better. That was the pattern. Maybe it wasn't the healthiest of relationships, but it was the norm, and something about it made Meg comfortable. Now this? Had to be the lack of meds. Had to be.

They reached the second-floor landing and Ben peeled off to his room. Minnie started up into the tower, then turned abruptly.

"I'm going to take a nap," she said matter-of-factly. "I need some time alone." And with that she ran up the stairs two at a time, disappearing into the garret room before Meg could ask another question.

"Okay," Meg said to no one in particular.

Meg stood on the stairs for a full minute. Alone time was Minnie's nemesis. Her kryptonite. Her Achilles' heel. In the face of a depressive episode, Minnie would call Meg at any hour of the day or night, keeping her on the phone for hours because she was so terrified of flying solo. And now in the midst of this nightmare, she wanted to be alone? Of all the freaky stuff that had happened in the last twenty-four hours, that topped the list.

Slowly, Meg turned around and wandered back downstairs. Was it her? Was she the social leper in the house? Nathan and Kenny clearly thought she was behind the slashes on the wall.

T.J. had disappeared. Minnie didn't want to be in the same room with her. . . . Well, crap.

At the bottom of the stairs, Meg paused. Where was she going? The study had a dead body in it. The foyer had the ominous red slashes that she didn't want to be caught within twenty feet of. Part of her wanted to go upstairs and find T.J., or Kumiko and Gunner, just for the sake of having some company.

She needed something to do, something to occupy her time. Meg's hand crept into the pocket of her coat and fingered the worn cover of the diary. Or she could find someplace quiet and find out exactly what was in that journal.

The pull was too great. Living room it was.

The room was icy and dark. The fire had died down and even when Meg stoked it, only a shuddering of orange sparks fluttered up the chimney. There wasn't any more firewood in the log rack, so Meg was left with the dullish glow of dying embers that barely penetrated the gloom of the house. Definitely not enough light to read by. So despite the chill, Meg sat in the window seat, where at least she had some dullish sunlight by which to read.

With a slight shiver—caused by the cold or nervous anticipation, Meg wasn't sure—she opened the diary.

> They'll know when I'm gone what a mess they made of things. Maybe they'll be sorry? I don't know. But at least they'll know they caused this. It was their fault and someday they will pay.
>
> All of them.

Whiskey. Tango. Foxtrot. What in the hell was that? The

entry was written in black ink, uneven and smudged in places where the paper was slightly warped, as if drops of water had been sprinkled over the page. Tears maybe? Meg thought of all the tears she'd shed while writing some of her own journal entries and could almost picture the author doing the same.

It was hard to tell from the language whether this was a recent entry or something written years even decades ago. And still no hint as to the author's identity.

Once again, Meg felt like she should close the diary, leave it on the window seat, and walk away. She shouldn't be doing this. And yet she felt compelled, despite the author's warnings, to continue. She was totally hooked.

Still, it was wrong, and Meg knew it. These were someone's private thoughts, and when you read people's private thoughts . . . well, things could go horribly wrong. Meg thought of what Minnie or T.J. or even Jessica Lawrence would think of her if they read what was in her journal. Just like most of Meg's life, there were some things better left unsaid.

Which is why she kept a journal.

And yet Meg's journal was, in some ways, the most concrete thing in her life. It was totally real and authentic, the only place where she could always be herself, always say exactly what she wanted to, when she wanted to. She was never tongue-tied, never shy, never unsure of herself.

She should have put the journal down.

Instead, she turned the page.

TWENTY

I'M SO EXCITED!

Today was the first day at the new school and I think it's going to be awesome. I can feel it.

Mom's in a good mood. The move went well. She loves the new house and it's closer for Bob to get to work so we can all have dinner together like a real family. I hope she stays this way.

Dr. Levine says the move will be good for me, too. New house, new school, new friends. I think he's right. I feel lighter already. And hopeful.

I'm starting over. Reinventing myself. No one knows what I was before I came here. Everything is going to be different.

Meg caught her breath. She could have been reading her own journal. She vividly remembered being the new girl in school when her parents moved the family from New York to the Seattle suburbs before the start of seventh grade. The excitement and the apprehension. Just like this author. *I'm starting over. Reinventing myself.* How many times had she written almost that exact same thing? It was one of the reasons she was going to college out of state.

> I met a few people, but not too many. There's a really cute guy in my Spanish class. I can't believe I'm even thinking about boys already! Dr. Levine says I should focus on making friends first. Just friends. But I couldn't help it. He cracked a lot of jokes in class, and when I laughed at one, he smiled at me. Not mocking, but an actual smile. He noticed me in a good way.

Holy crap. Were she and the author living parallel lives? Meg remembered the first day she had an actual conversation with T.J., something more than just a passing "What's up?" at a party or in the corridor at school. They'd been paired up for a project on *The Grapes of Wrath* and met at a coffee house after football practice to come up with a plan.

At the time, they were practically strangers. What Meg knew about T.J.: (a) he's a player, and (b) my best friend's in love with him. What T.J. knew about Meg: (a) she gets good grades, and (b) her best friend may or may not have a crush on me. It was a stiff and awkward meeting.

Then T.J. made a stupid joke, and Meg followed it up with one of her comebacks. T.J. had paused and looked at her. Really looked at her, maybe for the first time. Then he smiled, that perfect, dimply smile.

And Meg melted.

Not that she'd admit it to herself. Day after day, she'd write in her diary about how they were "just friends," more to convince herself than anything. She knew she was falling for him, and she felt like a horrible friend for doing so. Minnie had been in love with T.J. for so long, and Meg was the only one whom she'd told. Even if something happened between Meg and T.J., how would she ever tell Minnie? It would be the ultimate betrayal.

And yet Meg had continued to go out of her way to see him. They spent way more time together working on the project than was necessary. But Meg couldn't help herself. T.J. was more than just a jock—he was smart, quick-witted, playful. There was substance to him, something deeper and more real than the other guys he hung out with. Meg saw that there was more to him than just the star wide receiver—and she desperately wanted him to realize how perfect they were for each other.

Until he did.

> Choir was the best part of the day. We all had to audition and the director seemed really impressed with me. I don't think any of the other sopranos sang as well as I did, except maybe one girl. She's really sweet, though. She helped me find a folder and had me sit next to her. It felt so good to find a friend, you know? But I'm going to feel bad when I beat her out for the solo at the next concert.
>
> Hee. Can you believe I just wrote that? See, I'm different already! Tom said I would be. I feel like I can do anything!!!!!

Meg grinned. She couldn't help but feel a connection to this girl, whoever she was. There was such hope, such joy in her voice.

Meg could almost picture her sitting in bed, a huge smile on her face, writing these words.

There was also a pang of guilt. She really shouldn't be reading this. Clearly, this was not a journal written twenty or a hundred years ago. It must be relatively recent. Meg felt hypocritical. If anyone found *her* journal—which didn't even have the aggressive warning at the beginning—she'd be mortified if they read even a page. But here she was, barreling on. She needed to know what happened with the boy in Spanish class. It reminded her so much of how she and T.J. met. . . . She needed to know if this had a happy ending.

Meg turned to the next entry.

I can't believe it's been a week since I wrote last. Well, yes I can because it's been completely crazy!!! I joined . . . wait for it . . . the debate team!

I know. I told you it was crazy. But Dr. Levine said it might be good for me to do group activities, kind of force me to meet more people.

I'm willing to try, you know? So I signed up for choir and then on Friday, the girl who sits next to me in history was telling everyone about how the debate team is traveling all over the area and how she knows people at like every school in the state and I thought, "That's exactly what Dr. Levine was talking about."

So I did it. I joined. The first meeting is after school tomorrow!

The people here are pretty nice, though there is this

one blond guy in P.E. that kind of makes me nervous. He was joking with his friends on the track yesterday and I think he was pointing at me. But I'm just going to ignore it, like Tom told me. I'm sure it's nothing.

Also, we got the audition song for the spring concert solo yesterday. It's SO beautiful. I can almost feel the music in my bones when I sing it. My friend loves it too, and she's also going to audition for the solo. We were talking at lunch today (see? I already have lunch buddies!!!!) and she was saying that our choir director really likes it when his soloists kind of do their own thing. Riff on the music a little. He thinks it shows their musicality. So I'm going to practice and see where the music takes me, and hopefully impress him.

The auditions are in two weeks. I know I can get this solo and then when The Boy hears me sing it, he'll totally fall in love with me.

Meg's heart sank. She was doing it for a boy? That just couldn't end well.

The Boy notices me sometimes, but not as much as I'd like. I watch him in class a lot, hoping he'll see me and smile. He's SO gorgeous when he smiles. I couldn't even begin to describe it. But I know if he'd just see me—actually see me . . .

So I want to get this choir solo.

I have to.

Meg cringed. The girl was pinning her hopes on getting that

choir solo, and in Meg's experience, whenever you wanted something that desperately—say, for the guy you're in love with to ask you to the Homecoming dance—that's when things go horribly, horribly wrong. It felt like she was watching a train wreck in slow motion. She wanted to turn away, but she couldn't.

The next entry wasn't surprising.

> How could he give the solo to HER?
>
> The list of soloists was posted on the choir room door after school today. He gave it to my friend. She sang exactly what was on the page. Word for word. It was stiff and boring and she wasn't showing that she understood the music AT ALL. And I actually interpreted the music. Like the composer and I were working together to create something new and amazing.
>
> And now everything's ruined! The Boy will never notice me. What am I going to do?
>
> Tom thinks I should go talk to the director at rehearsal tomorrow, ask him what I did wrong so maybe I can improve for the next audition, but I feel like it's over.
>
> I should just end it all now.

TWENTY ONE

I SHOULD JUST END IT ALL NOW.

Wasn't that what Lori wrote in her suicide note? Like, word-for-word?

Meg dropped the journal. Suddenly it felt dangerous. Off. Just like everything else in that house.

Maybe it was just a coincidence. "Ending it" must be a common sentiment in suicide notes, and though the author of the journal didn't sound like she was on the brink, there was clearly something slightly troubled about her. So yeah, it could just be a coincidence. Right?

Meg shook her head. Too many coincidences this weekend. How did that journal end up in her room? Another coincidence? Like the song from the DVD being the same as the sheet music from Lori's suicide note? And the damaged handrail?

No. Meg didn't believe it. And T.J. thought there was more to it than just a series of accidents too or else he wouldn't have asked her to keep quiet about the railing. He was worried everyone would suspect there was something weird going on and they'd panic. She wanted to show him the journal immediately, but she had no idea where he'd disappeared to. Damn.

She needed him to see what she was seeing. Somewhere in the deep recesses of her brain, a little light had gone on. These occurrences were all related. They had to be. And she needed to know why.

Meg picked up the journal and turned to the next entry.

> It's happening again.
>
> They told me things would be different this time. That I could start over. Tom promised me things would be different.

Meg's mouth went dry. Promises you could never keep. Once again, the journal sounded all too familiar.

> I know I haven't written in a month but, ugh, it's been awful. I had to drop out of choir. I went to talk to the director, just like Tom said. He told me that I had a really beautiful voice, but he expects his soloists to sing what's on the page. And my interpretation of the song was too freestyle.
>
> I felt like someone had kicked me in the stomach. My "friend." She was the one who told me to improvise, to take it off the page. She lied to me on purpose so I wouldn't get the solo. I thought she was my friend. Yeah, some friend.
>
> I tried to explain that it was all a misunderstanding, but instead of hearing me out the director got angry. Really angry. In front of the whole choir. He said that if I had a

problem with his decision I was free to resign.

Everyone stared at me. I wanted to fall through the floor. And how could I stay in choir after that? Now I don't get to sing at all and The Boy will never love me. All because of her.

I went to confront her at lunch but she wouldn't even look at me. Wouldn't acknowledge me standing there. Just ignored me. I couldn't help it at that point. I started crying right there in the cafeteria. That jerk from P.E. was sitting at the table behind me and he started fake crying, "Wah, wah, wah. Poor baby." When I looked at him he yelled, "BURN!" Then he and all his friends laughed. It was a nightmare.

But I'm going to try and put it behind me. I still have debate team, so I'm going to focus on that.

Maybe then The Boy will notice me.

First the choir, then debate team. She seemed so manic in her need to be wanted and included. It was something Meg understood too well.

Back in seventh grade, when Meg was the new girl in town, she was always saying the wrong thing at the wrong time. No one understood her jokes. The kids in her New York City school always did, but in Mukilteo, she was suddenly a freak. She didn't dress the right way, walk the right way. She had met Minnie in P.E. and had sort of tagged along with Jessica Lawrence's group of friends through her. One day Jessica had drawn a line in the sand: Meg was lame, Minnie had to choose between them or her.

In a move that to this day still shocked Meg, Minnie chose her.

Meg squeezed her eyes closed, pressing those painful memories to the back of her mind. It was a debt she could never repay. Minnie had been her only friend at a time when she desperately needed one, and that was why she'd pushed T.J. away.

The whole thing made her sick. Los Angeles. She was going to Los Angeles to start fresh. At least she had that, unlike the poor author of this diary who was trapped in a school with no friends and no allies.

Meg turned the page.

He does love me! I can't believe it.

I was eating lunch today and The Boy's best friend came up to me. He asked what I was doing after school because The Boy was wondering if I wanted to get coffee.

OMG! I started shaking, I was so excited and nervous.

The Boy knows who I am. He noticed me!

We met for coffee and he's SO sweet and SO cute. He said he noticed me in Spanish class but that he was kind of shy. And we talked about school and class and he admitted that he's having a hard time in algebra so I offered to tutor him. He seemed so surprised and happy! So now we're going to meet after school every day. . . .

happy sigh I knew he loved me. I knew it. I can make him happy. I can make him better. All those girls always hanging off him—they don't really know him. But I do. They don't mean anything to him. We have a connection no one else can understand.

Meg blushed. She recalled a diary entry she made over the summer about a night that Meg wished she could forget. Minnie threw herself at T.J. at a house party, and as the night went on and everyone got drunker and drunker, Minnie's approach seemed to be working. The next thing Meg knew, people were whispering about how T.J. and Minnie had gone upstairs together.

She remembered the panic she felt, knowing the guy she was in love with was upstairs nailing her best friend. Meg never thought T.J. would actually hook up with Minnie. She thought she knew him better than that.

Apparently not.

She never asked Minnie what happened, and Minnie never completely shared. Just hinted. But Meg always remembered the pain she felt that night as she poured her soul out into her journal. She needed to protect herself from it, so she'd never feel it again. And maybe that was why she pushed T.J. away over and over. . . .

Meg had been angry that T.J. was so close to her but didn't see her in that way. Just like the author of this journal, though for her, at least, things seemed to be working out with The Boy.

> I don't know what happened.
>
> It was fine. Everything was fine. I was tutoring The Boy almost every day. I was trying really hard on debate team. I was starting to feel good again after the choir thing. Confident. Then all of a suddenly it all came crashing down.
>
> The president of the debate team came to me on

Monday, the day before our biggest meet of the semester, and told me they'd all taken a vote and they thought I should leave the team.

LEAVE THE TEAM? I told her it wasn't fair, but she said I needed to think of the greater good because the team would be much stronger without me.

I told her I didn't want to leave, that it's the one thing I'm actually enjoying at school. Then she got nasty. Told me that if I didn't leave I'd "be sorry" and that she could make life at school pretty miserable for me.

I talked to The Boy about it when I was tutoring him after school. He told me not to worry. That I had him, so who cared about debate team? He's right. I should be happy with what I have. I was just so hurt by that backstabbing. . . . Ugh. Never mind. I'm trying to get over it.

Something else is bothering me though. The Boy asked me to do something. He said if I really loved him, I'd help him because if I didn't it would be like I was shooting him through the heart.

I want to, but . . . I don't know. I kind of don't think it's right if I

Meg turned the next page, desperate to know what The Boy wanted her to do, but there was a gap in the pages, as if several had been torn out. At the top of the next page, the sentence began midway through.

. . . is coming this weekend. He promised. He'll know

what to do. He takes care of me, and I always feel better when he's here.

Right beneath was a photo. It was in color, printed out on a low-quality inkjet printer on regular computer paper, and pasted directly onto the journal page. It was a girl with long black hair, swept away from her face by a flowered clip. She was smiling, not a boisterous, laughing smile. More like a tight grin. But it was definitely a smile of happiness and her blue eyes crinkled at the corners. She was wearing a heavy winter coat, and there was a gloved hand draped over her shoulder as if someone had been standing next to her. But the face of the other person in the photo had been snipped out along with the corner of the journal page it had been glued to.

Below the defaced photo, in small, all-caps handwriting that didn't match the other script, was a quote of some kind.

FOR THE TIME WHEN THEIR FOOT SHALL SLIDE.

Weird. And totally random. It absolutely made no sense.

Or did it? There was something familiar about everything—the stories in the journal, the apparently arbitrary quote, and the girl. Especially the girl, but Meg couldn't quite place her. And yet she knew that girl, didn't she? Or someone who looked like her? Something was so different. The smile? The eyes? The hair?

The hair. Meg's eyes grew wide. She pictured that same face with dirty, stringy hair hanging in front of it and suddenly she knew who it was. Claire Hicks.

Meg slammed the cover shut. Holy crap.

She was reading Claire Hicks's diary.

TWENTY TWO

MEG FELT SICK. SHE'D BEEN READING A DEAD classmate's diary. There had been something familiar about the journal, something Meg couldn't quite put her finger on, but she'd never imagined it belonged to someone she knew. And not just anyone, but Claire Hicks.

Claire's diary. Claire's photo in her room. Why? What was the connection?

The sun was low on the horizon, the daylight, such as it was, rapidly retreating. How long had Meg been reading the diary? Two minutes or two hours, she couldn't even tell. It was as if time had stopped. The diary had sucked her in and cut her off from the rest of the world.

Meg stared at the black pleather cover. She never should have read past the first page. She felt sacrilegious, almost as if she had betrayed Claire somehow. And it was so sad, so infinitely sad that Claire had no one. She must have been writing about the school she was at before she transferred to Kamiak. Maybe all this drama was why she came to Meg's school in the first place.

Meg's heart went out to Claire. She'd been the new girl in school once too. The new girl that no one liked. No one except Minnie. It had been so hard for her to make friends—every time she opened her mouth it was like she was offending someone. She'd learned to just keep her mouth shut.

But at least she had Minnie. Claire had no one.

Claire Hicks. Her photograph and journal both ended up in Meg's room. No coincidence. Could she somehow be related to what was happening at White Rock House?

Meg got to her feet. She had to find T.J. Now. She had to fill him in about the journal and see if he had any theories about what was going on. She took a step toward the hall, then stopped.

Meg saw something out of the corner of her eye.

Just a movement, a flash of darkness through the rain-smeared windows. Immediately Meg heard a muffled stomping as someone ran up the outside steps to the patio; then the door creaked as it opened and banged shut.

Oh my God. It had to be Nathan or Kenny coming back from the Taylors' house. They'd found someone, called the police. Finally!

Meg ran into the kitchen. She expected to see one of them tramp into from the patio, dripping wet from the storm outside. But no one was there.

"Nathan?" she called.

There was a moment of agonizing silence, then Meg heard pounding footsteps as someone ran down the side of the house.

"Kenny?" Meg dashed out onto the patio. To the right was

the door that led to the backyard. To the left, the patio stretched the length of the kitchen and dining room, then bent sharply as it followed the far side of the house. The footsteps rang out in the distance and Meg could feel their vibrations through the wooden floorboards.

"Guys?" She ran down the patio and around the corner just in time to see a door at the far end closing as someone ducked inside the house.

What the hell? Another way inside the house? Why didn't they just come into the kitchen? Meg trotted down the side patio toward the door. She passed a dark coat on the ground. It was drenched in rain and flecked with mud and looked as if it had been stripped off and discarded while someone was on the move. Beyond the coat, two rain boots. First the right, then the left, also thrown off by whoever had just passed that way.

Meg stopped abruptly.

What was going on? Someone was clearly sneaking around the house, but why? Meg thought of the red slashes on the wall and of the handrail that had clearly been tampered with. What if she was right? What if they were both intentional?

That would mean someone in the house wasn't exactly who or what they pretended to be. But who?

Meg never got a chance to answer her own question as a muffled scream pierced the silence of the afternoon.

Meg took off down the patio. The screams continued, coming from inside the house. She pulled the door open, unsure where it would lead or what she would find.

The study. The patio wrapped all the way around the house and opened onto the study off the main staircase. Meg barely registered the large bundle that was Lori's body, still wrapped in its cocoon behind the desk, as she rocketed through the room. The screams were coming from the foyer. She stumbled through the door into the hall and found Minnie, standing in the middle of the foyer, pointing a finger at the wall.

A third slash.

Meg grabbed Minnie by the shoulders and spun her away from the wall. "What happened?"

"I-I couldn't sleep," Minnie said. Her eyes were red and puffy. "So I came downstairs and . . . I don't know. I wanted to look outside and maybe see if the guys were back and then I saw . . . I saw . . ."

"Did you see anyone?" Meg asked. "Did someone come through here?"

Minnie looked at her, confused. "No, no one's here." She looked over Meg's shoulder toward the study. "Where did you—"

"But someone must have come down the hall," Meg said. She looked around the foyer. There was no place to hide. No closet doors, no crawl spaces or cupboards. Nothing.

"Oh man," Gunner said. He and Kumiko stood in the hallway.

"If it means what the first two meant," Kumiko said. "Then . . ."

T.J. ran down the stairs. "Who's missing?"

Meg felt Minnie catch her breath. Oh God. It was Ben.

"NO!" Minnie screamed. She pushed past T.J. and sprinted up the stairs.

T.J. followed close on Minnie's heels, then Kumiko and Gunner. Meg trailed behind. She didn't run with the same sense of urgency as the others. Truthfully, she was afraid of what they'd find. Another body, this time Minnie's new crush.

Meg paused on the landing outside Ben's room. Everyone else was inside, but Meg waited, terrified of what she'd see. With Minnie's already fragile state of mind, Meg wasn't sure she could handle what she'd find in that room. Part of her wanted T.J. or Gunner to deal with Minnie's imminent breakdown. She wanted to turn around and walk out of that house and never go back.

"NOOOOOO!" Minnie wailed.

Shit.

Minnie's weeping filled the room as Meg slowly walked through the door. She felt like a condemned prisoner approaching final judgment. Kumiko leaned into Gunner, her face buried in his burly arms, and T.J. stood at the end of the bed gripping the bedpost so fiercely his knuckles shone white.

"Who did this?" Minnie cried. "Who did this?"

On the far side of the bed, Minnie knelt on the floor, cradling Ben's head in her lap. He lay facedown and all Meg could see of him was his mussed blond hair. His left arm was stretched out toward his backpack on the floor near the window as if he'd been trying to reach it.

Minnie rocked back and forth. "It's not fair. It's not fair."

Meg knelt down beside Minnie and put an arm around her shoulder. Minnie flinched.

"This wasn't an accident," Minnie said. It sounded like an accusation.

Despite the panic rising inside her, Meg fought to remain calm. "I didn't say it was."

"Someone did this. Someone did this on purpose."

T.J. cleared his throat. "What happened? I mean . . ."

"He's dead," Minnie screeched. Her eyes flashed. "Murdered."

Meg shivered as the word filled the room. "Minnie, maybe it was . . . I don't know."

"A mistake? An accident?" Minnie jerked away from her. "Three deaths in a row? Can you really explain that away?"

No. No, she couldn't. But she also couldn't admit that fact to Minnie, who was already on the brink of a total meltdown. Minnie sank her head to her chest, nuzzling her forehead against Ben's blond hair. Meg could feel her sobs.

"Meg," T.J. said, his voice barely above a whisper. He beckoned her to the other side of the bed. "Come look at this."

T.J. crouched beside the nightstand. Next to him, a plastic water bottle had been tipped over, spilling its contents on the hardwood floor. T.J. bent to the ground and examined the liquid.

"Do you see what I'm seeing?" he asked.

She got down on her knees to get a closer look at the pooling liquid. The light from the window was dim but there appeared to be small bits of something solid floating in it. Meg sniffed.

"Oh my God," she said, jerking her head back. "It smells like—"

"Pecan pie," T.J. said.

Meg sat back on her heels. Someone had deliberately put

ground pecans in Ben's water, just as someone must have deliberately added almonds to the salad. If she'd been hesitant to believe that the deaths on this island weren't necessarily accidents, that hesitation evaporated in an instant.

She'd been trying to deny it, all day. Perhaps as far back as when she arrived on the island. Something was wrong. Something was off. She should have trusted herself, listened to her gut. And now there was only one logical explanation.

Murder.

Panic welled up inside her. They'd lied to their parents about where they were going. Dear God; no one knew where they were. They could die on that island and no one would ever find them.

She looked at T.J. His brows were hunched low and pinched together above his nose, like he was in pain. He'd been trying to be a leader and keep everyone calm. That's why he wanted Meg to stay quiet about the damage to the handrail, maintaining the line that everything was just a coincidence. Had he believed it himself? Meg wasn't sure. All she knew now was that he was scared. Just like everyone else.

He stood suddenly, grabbed her by the shoulders, and lifted her to her feet. "We're going to be fine, Meg. I promise. I'm sure there's some logical explanation for all of this."

More promises. More coincidences. Not this time. They had to face the truth.

"No, there isn't." Her voice was shaky but she meant every word. She grabbed T.J.'s hand and led him out of the room. "We need to talk."

TWENTY THREE

GUNNER SAT ON THE STAIRS WITH KUMIKO IN his lap. "We didn't do it," he said immediately.

"Do it?" T.J. said.

"Kill him. K and I didn't do it."

T.J. held his hands up in front of him. "Hold up. No one said anything about—"

"It was murder," Meg said. She was surprised how calm she sounded.

T.J. looked at her sidelong. "Are you sure?"

Meg nodded. "Positive."

"See?" Kumiko said.

T.J. continued to look at her like he wasn't totally convinced. "How can you be sure?"

"How can you *not* be sure?" Kumiko said.

T.J. paused, then nodded his head, finally giving in to the fact that all three deaths on the island had been intentional.

"Exactly," Kumiko said. "There's a killer in the house. We need to get the hell out of here."

Gunner stroked her arm. "I'm sure the guys will find a phone."

Kumiko turned on him. "Really? What if one of them is the killer? What if *both* of them are the killer?"

"Hold on," T.J. said. "We can figure this out. We just need to think."

He was right. Three deaths. If they assumed that each one was murder, then they should be able to figure out who the killer was.

"Any of us could have killed Lori," Meg said. She still couldn't believe she was speaking those words.

T.J. nodded. "True."

Gunner shook his head. "K was with me."

"Right," Meg said. "I meant theoretically." She wasn't ready to go pointing fingers at people. She'd known Gunner since freshman year and found it hard to believe he might be a cold-blooded killer.

"What good does that do us?" Kumiko said. "Anyone could have killed Vivian, too."

T.J. reached out and touched Meg's arm. "Meg and I were together. We can vouch for each other."

Meg was about to tell Kumiko and Gunner about the damage to the handrail, when Kumiko threw her head back and laughed.

"What?" T.J. asked.

"You really think that's going to fly?"

Meg bristled. It was the first time in her life she'd been accused of a capital crime. Not a good feeling.

"It's the truth," T.J. said.

"Maybe," Kumiko continued. "Like you wouldn't give each other an alibi? Same with Gunner and me. Maybe we're in it together."

"Hey!" Gunner said. "Not cool."

"I'm not saying that we did it," Kumiko said. "Just making a point."

T.J. pursed his lips. "Which is?"

"Yeah," Gunner echoed. "Which is?"

"*Which is?*" Kumiko said. "Oh come on!" She tilted her head, gazing at Gunner with a look that said *Really? You don't get this?* "We can't trust anyone."

"What if it's not one of us?" Meg said.

T.J. turned to her. "What do you mean?"

"I mean there's another possibility."

"You mean you think there's someone else in the house?" T.J. asked.

Kumiko snorted. "Wouldn't that be convenient?"

"I saw someone," Meg blurted out. "Coming into the house through the back patio right before Minnie found the third mark on the wall."

"For reals?" Gunner said. "Who was it?"

Meg shook her head. "I couldn't tell. I followed them around to the side door that opens into the study and then—"

"Oh, isn't that perfect," Kumiko said.

"Hey!" Meg said. She was tired of the finger-pointing, tired of the accusations. "I saw someone."

Kumiko narrowed her eyes. "Sure you did. And then you just *happened* to be in the foyer when Minnie screamed?"

"Stop," T.J. said. "We can't turn on each other."

"I read *Lord of the Flies*," Gunner said. Meg was impressed he'd actually finished the book. "It didn't end well."

Kumiko pushed herself off Gunner's lap. "News flash, we're already like halfway through our own *Lord of the Flies*, people. We've got dead bodies piling up and I don't know about you, but I don't exactly want to be next."

"What do you suggest we do?" T.J. said. Meg could hear the edge in his voice. He was barely containing his temper. "Sit in locked rooms until someone comes looking for us?"

Meg nodded toward Ben's room. "Yeah, because that always works out so well."

"It's not funny!" Minnie screamed. She stood in the doorway to Ben's bedroom, one hand firmly planted against the frame as if to balance herself, the other gripping the door handle behind her. With a flick of her wrist she slammed the door, then stormed right up to Meg.

"None of this is funny."

"Of course not," Meg said. "No one thinks it is."

She could see Minnie's eyes darting around the stairwell—from her to T.J., Gunner to Kumiko and back, up to the top of the tower where Lori's body had been found, then back to Meg. She was losing it. Minnie's new crush was dead. Her ex-boyfriend was holding hands with his new girl. And she was convinced that her ex-crush was interested in her best friend. Chernobyl had begun.

"We have to find out who did this," Minnie said. "Which one of *you* did this."

"Hey!" Meg was getting pissed off at being included in the list of suspects. While she recognized that someone like Kumiko, who didn't know her from Charles Manson, might not trust her innocence, at the very least she expected Minnie to believe her. Right?

Minnie grimaced. "Everyone's a suspect."

Apparently not so much.

"Look," T.J. said. "There's got to be another explanation."

"Like what?" Kumiko said. She'd refused Gunner's silent pleas to get her to sit back down on his lap. She shook off his hand and leaned against the wall.

"Well . . ." T.J. glanced at Meg. He looked confused, like his mind had drawn a blank and he was hoping Meg could fill in the pieces. Minnie didn't miss it. She emitted a sound somewhere between a growl and a sigh, and turned her back on them.

"Well . . . ," Meg said. Her brain snapped into overdrive. "Well, for starters, what if Lori or Vivian killed Ben?"

She saw Minnie jerk her head back, but she didn't turn around.

"How?" Kumiko asked.

"The nuts were in his water bottle," Meg said with a shrug. "Anyone could have put them in there at any time. I mean, we all witnessed the incident at dinner last night."

"But don't you think it was the same person?" T.J. asked. "They started out with the nuts in the salad, then had to move on to his water bottle?"

"Maybe," Meg said. She wasn't exactly sure her argument was convincing, but motivation-wise both options made sense. "Could be either."

Kumiko remained unconvinced. "What about the others?"

"Um . . ." Okay, Meg. Think. "If Lori tried to kill Ben, then maybe she killed herself out of remorse?"

T.J. folded his arms across his chest. "And Vivian?"

"Could actually have been an accident," Meg lied. She saw T.J. flick his head in her direction, but he didn't correct her.

"Hm." Gunner nodded. "It makes sense."

"Barely," Kumiko said.

"Or it was Nathan or Kenny," Meg said.

"Shit." Gunner looked deflated. "They're totally not going to call the cops if one of them is a killer."

T.J. jolted. "Gunner, you're right."

"I am?" Gunner tossed his streaked hair out of his face, exposing a rather confused smile.

"Totally." T.J. looked at his watch. "They left almost three hours ago. They should have been back by now."

That made Minnie turn around. "Do you think something happened to them?" she said, her eyes wide.

T.J. checked in with Meg before replying. "You know, probably not." He forced a laugh. "They're probably just enjoying a hot meal or something and forgot about us."

Meg thought of Kenny's face when they discovered Lori's body that morning. She seriously doubted he was enjoying anything that had to do with the weekend. "There's only one way to find out."

Yikes. Had those words really come out of her mouth? Was she really suggesting a field trip across the isthmus in that weather?

"No way," Kumiko said. Always the optimist. "We'd never make it."

"We totally could," T.J. said with conviction. "The storm's let up. We could make it."

Minnie backed away from the group. "I'm staying right here. I don't trust any of you."

"Minnie!" Meg couldn't hide the hurt in her voice. "What are you talking about?"

"You're full of lies. All of you."

Meg grabbed her arm. "Minnie, think about what you're saying."

"Please." Minnie flinched away from Meg's grip. Her face was hard set. "You hide more lies than any of us."

"Wow," Kumiko said under her breath. She was back by Gunner's side and he stroked the back of her leg with his hand. "How long did you date her?"

Minnie sucked in a breath. "What did you say?"

T.J. tried to keep them focused. "We should all go. Together. Safety in numbers."

"Hell, no," Minnie said. She'd backed all the way up to the door to Ben's bedroom. "I'm not going anywhere."

"Oh, come *on*!" Meg said. The drama was getting unbearable, even by Minnie's standards.

"I said *NO*!" Minnie screamed. She spun around, marched back to Ben's bedroom, and slammed the door behind her.

Kumiko paused a moment, her eyes fixed on the door to Ben's room, her face a mask of confusion. "As much as I hate to admit it," she said slowly, "I kind of agree. I think we should stay here."

"Me too," Gunner said quickly. Meg honestly couldn't tell if he agreed with Kumiko or not. Neither could he, probably.

"You sure, dude?" T.J. said.

Gunner looked to Kumiko. She gave a slight nod. "Yeah," Gunner said. "I'm sure."

T.J. shrugged. "Guess it's just you and me, Meg."

TWENTY FOUR

MOTHER NATURE FINALLY TOOK PITY ON THEM.

The rain had diminished as Meg and T.J. started down the stone steps of White Rock House. All that remained of the raging storm was a steady, light drizzle that soaked Meg's ponytail within minutes, but it was so much better than the relentless, abusive hammering they'd received the last two times they were outside that Meg was grateful for the break.

There was no mystical parting of the clouds to allow sunshine to break through. No such luck. A thick cloud cover still blanketed the island, and mixed with the rapidly setting sun, there was barely enough light to see by.

The wind had also diminished. Instead of gales that might register on the Fujita Scale, it was more of a playful breeze that whipped damp strands of Meg's hair across her face. The waves that had pummeled the isthmus and washed away the footbridge now merely lapped at its western shore, and though the sand was waterlogged and strewn with debris, at least Meg and T.J. could get across without fear of being washed out to sea.

Shorebirds hopped along the sand, pecking at dinner, and larger seagulls circled above, reemerged from wherever they had weathered the storm. There was life to the island, which made Meg smile despite herself, and a kind of prettiness to the gray, sodden world around her. A crispness to the air as it filled Meg's lungs that she found energizing. A delight in the way the sand and stone crunched beneath her feet. She could see why people like the Taylors and Lawrences had built houses out in the relative wilderness. In the aftermath of the storm, it was peaceful in a sort of untamed way, where nature reminded you she was boss and could kick your ass any time she wanted.

Under difference circumstances Meg might have enjoyed it.

She wanted to talk to T.J., to tell him about Claire's journal and how she might somehow be related to White Rock House, but he seemed distant, locked up in his head. He hardly even looked at her as they picked their way over the enormous trunks of Douglas firs the storm had washed ashore. So she waited. Maybe they'd find Nathan and Kenny at the Taylors' house, waiting patiently for the police to arrive, and Meg could turn the diary over to the authorities and be done with it.

They kept to the high ground, just at the center of the isthmus. It was slow going, but Meg was happy to be *doing*, instead of sitting around waiting for something to happen. That was a change, but somehow the idea of staying at White Rock House with the bodies, and Minnie's oscillating moods, and Kumiko's finger-pointing . . . well, anything seemed better than that.

As T.J. helped Meg navigate a slick pile of seaweed-covered

logs, he cleared his throat. "Is she always like that?"

"Who?"

"Minnie."

Meg's mind was so far away it took her a minute to realize T.J. wasn't talking about Mother Nature. "Oh, right."

"I mean, Gunner said she could be a little . . . erratic. But she was kinda psycho back there."

Meg bristled. As true as the statement was, she didn't like her best friend referred to as a "psycho." Besides, it wasn't Minnie's fault that she was bipolar. It's not like she chose to be that way. And even though Minnie's mom tried to ignore the fact that something was wrong with her daughter, Minnie's dad had made sure she saw a therapist and got the right prescriptions. He'd even had a private talk with Meg about it, asking her to look out for Minnie and make sure she was taking her medications.

No one else knew about it. Just Meg. And she was fiercely protective of Minnie's secret.

"It's not her fault," she said firmly.

T.J. stopped and turned around. "Not her fault she treats you like crap? Like you're her sidekick or something?"

Meg winced. That hit a little too close to home.

If T.J. noticed, it didn't deter him. "Not her fault that she clearly has no respect for you? That she only thinks of herself?"

Meg sighed. "She's not always like that."

"That's not an excuse. Not for you or for her."

"You don't understand."

"I understand that she expects you to always be there for her yet can't or won't return the favor. But what I don't understand is why you put up with it."

"Look, I can't . . ." Meg's face grew hot. *I can't tell you*. It was more embarrassing than anything. Meg thought she was the only one who noticed the way Minnie had been treating her lately. Apparently not.

"You can't what?" he asked.

Meg opened her mouth to protest, then stopped. He was right, at least on some counts. It wasn't that Minnie was a bad friend, only that most days she couldn't really see past her own pain and her own needs. And that was partly Meg's fault, because she'd been enabling Minnie for so long she didn't know what other kind of friend to be.

"You deserve"—T.J. took a step toward her—"better."

Meg looked up, straight into T.J.'s eyes. All she saw was sadness.

T.J. felt sorry for her. The idea turned her stomach. It was so pathetic. *She* was so pathetic.

"You don't understand," she repeated. It was true on so many levels.

"Then explain it to me."

Meg pressed the palms of her hands against her eyes. The pressure felt good, a relief from the throbbing stress-headache that was beginning to form at her temples. She wanted to explain Minnie's illness and her struggles with medication and treatment, and how it had changed her over the past year or two. She wanted to tell T.J. how she'd gotten thrust into this position as Minnie's caretaker, how Minnie's parents relied on her to keep an eye on their daughter, and how she was running away to college to break free of the cycle.

"What?" T.J. said. His voice was sharp. "Come on. Explain to me what I don't understand."

Meg dropped her eyes. It wasn't her secret to tell. "I can't."

"Dammit!" T.J. yelled. He stepped away from her and kicked a baseball-sized rock with his foot. It skipped across the muddy path and bounced off a dead log. "Why are you always protecting her?"

Meg squared her shoulders. "That's none of your business." She didn't owe T.J. an explanation. She didn't own him anything.

"I care about you. That makes it my business."

Now it was Meg's turned to be pissed off. And for once the words weren't locked up in her head. "You care about me? Really? Then how come I haven't heard from you in months? How come you've never noticed until now how Minnie treats me? How come the only news I hear about you is how you've been dating every cheerleader from here to the Canadian border?" Meg couldn't believe the words came out so easily. Fear and fatigue were catching up with her.

T.J. turned his back on her. "I was angry."

"Yeah, I know. I'm sorry, okay? I'm sorry I canceled on you that night."

"Are you?"

"Of course!"

T.J. whirled around and stormed up to her. "Then why did you do it? Why wouldn't you go out with me?"

"Because Minnie—" Meg stopped herself.

The muscles around T.J.'s jawline bulged. "Minnie. Really? Again? What the hell does this have to do with her?"

"She's in love with you," Meg blurted out. Ugh. She wasn't making things better.

Meg expected T.J. to be shocked or surprised. Instead, he laughed.

"What's so funny?"

"The only person Minnie's in love with," T.J. said, calming down, "is herself."

Meg was so used to defending Minnie she couldn't stop herself. "Don't talk about her like that."

"She doesn't even know what love *is,* Meg. It's just a game with her. Just a way to get attention."

"And you know so much about love? You and your forty ex-girlfriends?"

All the sadness and sympathy melted away from T.J.'s face, replaced by a hardened mask of anger. She'd done it again. Dammit, what was wrong with her? Every time she said exactly what was on her mind, someone ended up pissed off.

"We'd better hurry," he said flatly. "It's getting dark."

"Yeah," Meg said. She turned away from him. "It is."

They continued in silence.

The Taylors' vacation home was built on a raised wooden deck in a clearing on the other side of the isthmus. It was as different from White Rock House as was architecturally possible. A modern home with a wall of windows facing the ocean, it had sparkled and shone the night before when Meg had passed it from the beach. Less than twenty-four hours ago there had been life in that house. A light in every window. Music blaring. The sounds of laughter and tinkling glass drifting on the wind. Now everything looked completely . . .

"Dead." T.J. paused at the bottom of the wooden stairs that led to the front door. "This place looks dead."

"Awesome choice of words."

Despite the strain between them, T.J. laughed, short and dry. "Sorry."

"Maybe they're in the back." Meg tried to sound hopeful. There had to be someone in the house, otherwise Nathan and Kenny would have returned.

T.J. forced a smile. "Let's find out." He marched up the steps and rang the bell.

Good news. Whatever the power situation was at the house, at least something worked.

Bad news, they waited what seemed like forever and the only answer they received was silence.

Ever the optimist, T.J. rang the bell again. Through the closed doors, Meg could hear the electronic ding echo through the house.

Her stomach did a backflip. Nothing. Not a voice, not a cry, not even the sound of feet moving across the floor of the house. The only sound Meg heard was the pounding of her own heart. This couldn't be good.

T.J. grabbed the door handle and pressed down on the latch.

It clicked and he pushed the door open. He waited a few moments, then called out. "Hello?"

No response.

Without looking at each other, both Meg and T.J. reached out and grasped hands. The anger and resentment she'd felt toward him a few moments earlier vanished in an instant. There was something very wrong about the house, and whatever they were about to find, they'd discover it together. With a deep breath they stepped inside.

The house was deathly quiet. And dark. Other than the ambient light of the rapidly descending sun, there wasn't a single bit of luminescence, man-made or otherwise. Not only that, but it smelled musty and damp, like an old, abandoned warehouse. Meg shivered. The house was even colder than White Rock House. It didn't feel like the kind of place that had hosted a raging party the night before. It was more like a mausoleum.

They tiptoed from the entryway into the living room and Meg realized right away why the house was so cold. Every window was open. The gauze curtains were soaked through and billowed heavily in the breeze. Beneath her feet, the carpet squished with water, and every piece of furniture within ten feet of an open window was sopping wet.

"What's going on?" she whispered. She wasn't sure why. It wasn't like there was anyone within earshot to hear her, apparently.

T.J. gripped her hand tighter and whispered too. "I don't get it. Where is everyone?"

There was a flash of light, a whirl of movement and sound. Suddenly the whole room sprang to life. Every light in the living room illuminated—overheads, standing torches, wall sconces.

Even faux flickering "candles" around the fireplace. The room danced in warm, yellow light. The ceiling fans whirled to life, spinning at breakneck speed, dangerously close to ripping free of their moorings and catapulting across the room.

The speakers kicked in at full volume with a thump of sound that almost knocked the breath out of Meg. She screamed but could barely hear herself above the noise. The volume was maxed out, the bass was cranked up, and Meg could feel the beats of the music ricocheting through her body. There seemed to be two tracks playing at the same time: one was a '40s-esque big band track with pulsating conga drums and a screaming brass section that made her ears bleed; the other was like canned party music complete with unintelligible conversation and chinking crystal. A lady giggled on the soundtrack, high and piercing. It was meant to sound cheerful, but in that lifeless room it chilled Meg to the bone.

She wanted to run, but her feet were rooted to the soggy carpet.

T.J. released her hand and covered his ears as he scanned the room. After a moment, he dashed to the entertainment unit on the far side of the living room and dialed down the volume.

Instantly both the music and the sound of ambient party chatter dissipated.

"What the *fuck* was that?" T.J. panted. He was out of breath, like he'd just run a mile.

Meg was shaking from head to toe. "I . . . I don't . . ." She couldn't even put a coherent thought together, let alone verbalize it.

T.J. looked at his watch. "It's exactly five o'clock."

"Exactly?"

"Exactly."

Meg's head cleared as she realized what was happening. The lights, the music, the party. It was all fake. All of it.

"Oh my God." She felt the warmth drain out of her body. "It's on a timer."

"That means . . ." T.J. paused and looked her straight in the eye, his face reflecting the terror building inside. "That means there's no one here."

THE ROOM SPUN. MEG BRACED HERSELF AGAINST the wall as the horrifying revelation washed over her.

The house was dead.

There'd been a sense of comfort, however distant, in the idea that there was another house party going on here, just across the isthmus from White Rock House. Kind of like long-distance chaperones in case anything really bad happened. Only apparently the whole thing was a sham. The party, the people, the sense of warmth and safety. All of it was gone in an instant. It was all an illusion.

"What about Kenny and Nathan?" Meg said. Her voice was tight, her words choked off. She was having difficulty breathing and she shook from head to toe. "Do you think—"

"Hold up," T.J. said. The calmness in his voice was instantly soothing. "First things first."

He crouched down and yanked the entertainment center away from the wall. The flat-screen TV teetered and crashed onto the floor, but neither she nor T.J. even flinched. It didn't matter.

"There's a timer with two power strips attached. Looks like every electronic device in the room is plugged into them." T.J. passed a hand over his head. "Maybe it's just some kind of alarm system?"

"What, for all the cat burglars roaming around Henry Island?" Meg said. "And with every window open and the door unlocked? Not likely."

"Okay," T.J. said. "Then it's here for a reason."

The truth was horrifying. "To throw us off. To make us feel at home."

"Which means whoever did this—"

"Killed Lori, Vivian, and Ben."

T.J. nodded. "And probably—"

"Stop." She knew what he was going to say. *And probably Nathan and Kenny*. "I don't want to hear it."

"Okay," T.J. said calmly. "But there's another option."

Meg's voice shook. "One or both of them is the killer."

"Yeah." T.J. scanned the area at the back of the living room. "The stairs are near the kitchen," he said. He took her hand lightly, as if he was afraid he would break her. "We should go together."

She didn't want to. She wanted to flee, to start running and never stop. But she knew T.J. was right: They needed to search the house and see if Nathan and Kenny were still there. They had to know.

Side by side, Meg and T.J. slowly walked through the living room. The curtains ballooned toward her and Meg cowered against T.J.'s arm. It was like they wanted to enfold her, keep her in that house forever. Everything felt tainted, and Meg didn't want to touch anything. There wasn't enough antibacterial soap in the world to wash away the feel of that house.

The living room opened into a large kitchen separated by a staircase. A phone was mounted on the wall at the bottom of the stairs. Meg held her breath as T.J. picked up the receiver and hit the CALL button. The house had electricity. Maybe, just maybe . . .

The handset's ON light glowed in all its green glory. Meg waited, not even daring to breathe, desperate to hear the monotonous drone of a dial tone.

Silence.

T.J. clicked the power button a few times, but still nothing. "It's charged, but no phone line."

"No, it has to work. It has to." She snatched the phone out of his hand and frantically hit every button on the receiver. "There's power, so the phone has to work."

"Meg." T.J. placed his hand on top of hers. "Meg, there's no dial tone."

Meg couldn't look at him. Tears welled up in her eyes, thick and blinding. All she could do was stare at the handset as T.J. slid his hand up her arm and around her shoulders. They were so close to safety. This stupid cordless phone that she so often took for granted could have been their salvation, their connection to the outside world. The phone was charged, it was on, glaring back at her indignantly, flashing the last number called. . . .

Lawrence, John and Jean 360-555-2920

Meg straightened up. "What are Jessica's parents' names?"

"Huh?"

"Her parents. What are their names?"

"Uh . . ." T.J. shook his head, trying to get a handle on what she was asking. "Her dad's John. And her mom's . . ."

"Jean?"

"Yeah, I think so." T.J. pulled his arm away. "How did you know?"

Meg shoved the phone in his hand. "Look."

T.J. stared at the handset for a moment, then scrolled through the call log entry. "I think this is the number for White Rock House," he said. "And it looks like they called it—" T.J. froze. His eyebrows pulled together in a look of utter bewilderment.

"What?"

T.J.'s eyes met hers. "It looks like they called White Rock House yesterday afternoon."

Meg's heart pounded in her chest. "That means someone's here," she screamed. "Someone must be in the house. Someone alive!"

She spun around blindly, as if expecting to find the Taylors standing there in the kitchen making dinner.

T.J. shook his head. "Meg, I don't think—"

"No!" she snapped. "Someone's here. We just have to find them." Meg's eyes drifted to the staircase. Of course! They must be upstairs sleeping or something. Without a second thought, she bolted up the stairs.

"Meg, wait!"

But she wasn't listening. She took the stairs two at a time, desperate to get to the top. She knew there'd be someone there. Someone who could help. Had to be. There had to be someone. There had to be—

Meg never even saw what she tripped over. As she raced up the stairs and onto the second-floor landing, her foot hit something big and heavy on the ground. She lost her balance and flopped face-first over the object, landing half on it, half off it, and smacked her forehead on the thin rug.

"Meg, are you okay?" T.J. was just steps behind her. "What happened?"

Meg rolled onto her side, rubbing her head. "I'm fine. Just tripped on . . ." She looked back to see what she had fallen over.

It was a body. A huge body.

Kenny.

Her face was just inches from his. So close. His eyes were closed and his face peaceful. He wasn't stiff and cold like Lori had been, evidence that he hadn't been there long. And though Meg wished she could believe he was just taking a nap there on the floor, his body was utterly still, breathless and unmoving, and several red streaks marred his forehead and cheek, cascading downward from his skull.

Meg scrambled away from the body as if it had been covered in poisonous snakes. Dead. Kenny was dead. She clawed at her clothes, trying to wipe the death off of her. It was too much. It was all too much.

"Meg!" T.J. had his arms around her in an instant, helping her off the ground.

"I can't take it," she sobbed. "I can't take it anymore."

T.J. stroked her hair. "I know, baby. I know."

Meg buried her face in his shoulder. "When I saw the phone call I thought . . . I thought . . ."

"I know," he said quietly. "But, Meg, that was the call I got. The one that was supposed to be from Mr. Lawrence."

Meg pulled her head back. "What?"

"Yeah. The caller ID marks the call at the exact time we heard from Jessica's dad. Or someone pretending to be Jessica's dad, I guess. The connection was pretty bad."

Meg wiped the tears from her cheeks. "It was the killer."

"Yeah."

They stared at Kenny's body. Neither of them bent down to check for a pulse. Neither of them made a move to touch him.

The hair on the back of his head was slick and wet. Beside the body lay a black mallet, and Meg could see a chunk of Kenny's dark, curly hair stuck to the metal head. Someone had bludgeoned him from behind. Kenny probably never even saw who hit him. Maybe that was a good thing, not seeing the approach of death. Maybe that made it easier? Or at least less painful.

A sudden noise brought Meg's disconnected consciousness back into the terrifying present. Both she and T.J. froze. There was a rustling—like the movement of fabric—coming from a half-closed door to their left.

Meg held her breath. Nathan. It had to be Nathan. He'd had the opportunity to kill Lori and Vivian, and he could easily have put the ground-up pecans in Ben's water bottle. And now Kenny.

All of them went to Mariner—Nathan was killing them off one by one.

She grabbed T.J.'s jacket. "Nathan," she mouthed, not daring to make a sound. She tried to pull him back down the stairs. "Nathan's the killer."

T.J. had something else in mind. He pressed his finger to his lips, then noiselessly lifted a large iron candelabra off an end table in the hall. He raised it above his head as he tiptoed to the door.

Meg followed right behind him. She wasn't sure why, but she felt like she needed to be there, to be his backup, in case Nathan attacked him. Together, they could stop him before he killed someone else.

T.J. glanced at her and she watched as his lips silently counted.

One . . .

Two . . .

Three.

TWENTY SIX

T.J. THREW HIS WEIGHT AGAINST THE DOOR AND they barreled through. Meg half expected to be assaulted by a wild-eyed Nathan, wielding an ax. But no one lunged at them. In fact, nothing in the room moved, with the exception of ornate silk damask curtains, which like their lighter counterparts downstairs, billowed in front of open windows.

So much for Nathan.

Though being attacked by an insane killer might have been better than what they found.

Meg's eyes drifted from the curtains to the bed in the center of what appeared to be the master bedroom. Two people lay in bed together, spooning. The man was older—early sixties perhaps, judging by the thinning wisps of gray hair combed across his head. He had his arm draped across the woman, who looked about the same age but with highlighted brown hair.

Like Kenny, they looked like they were just asleep, and Meg wished with all her heart that she could believe it was true. But their facial features sagged unnaturally, and their skin had a white-gray pallor. There was a smell in the air, putrid and nauseating. Meg pulled her sweatshirt sleeve down over her hand and held it over her nose and mouth.

Dead. Just like Kenny.

T.J. covered his nose and mouth as well as he edged his way around the bed. He used the candelabra to pull the curtains away from the window just to make sure no one was there. Then he checked the closet.

Meg turned away. She knew—she just knew—that there was no one alive in that house. She was tired of death, tired of feeling the weight of it pressing in on her. She desperately wanted to be out of the house, off the island, away from all of it.

Meg turned to leave when something caught her eye. The door to the bathroom off the master suite was wide open. It was dark inside, but Meg could see something on the mirror. It looked like writing.

Without thinking, she reached her hand into the bathroom and flipped on the light.

"What you are doing?" T.J. asked.

Meg stepped inside. "Look, there's something—"

Meg froze. Staring back at her from the mirror was Nathan.

Only instead of a crazed killer rushing at her, Nathan's face was a lifeless mask of fear and pain. His mouth hung open in a silent, unfinished scream, his body skewered to the bathroom door with an arrow through the heart.

It was too much. Meg stumbled back and covered her mouth, bile rocketing up her throat. Then she spun on her heel and ran.

Meg bent over, elbows on knees, trying to catch her breath. It was as if her lungs wouldn't cooperate. She gasped sporadically for air between frenzied sobs. Meg was so lightheaded she thought she might pass out, and the muddy ground in front of the Taylors' house came in and out of focus with each pounding thump of her heart.

She didn't hear anyone come up behind her.

"Hey."

Meg screamed. She tried to run but there was an arm around her. She panicked. There was a murderer loose. She could be next. She had to get off the island. She had to get Minnie and herself off that freaking island. Meg pumped her legs, attempting to break free of the strong grip around her waist. But she couldn't.

"It's okay," a familiar voice said. "You're safe, you're safe. It's just me."

T.J.

Meg let her body sag in his arms. "It's not fair, it's not fair," she repeated. Hot tears poured down her cheeks.

"I know, baby," T.J. said. He pulled her toward him. Before she knew it, her face was buried in his chest, his arms holding her close as she sobbed uncontrollably.

"Why is this happening? What did we do? Why us?"

T.J. took her face in his hands. He gently wiped the tears off her cheeks with his thumbs, and she watched as his eyes scanned her face from hairline to chin and back again. Then without warning, he bent his face down and kissed her.

Meg had fantasized about kissing T.J. about a zillion times. The moments would come to her randomly: waiting for the bus after school, sitting across from him in Honors English, catching sight of the smiling dimples on the far side of the cafeteria, and, most poignantly, in those moments between sleep and consciousness when she lay in bed waiting for the snooze setting on her alarm to kick in and force her into the world of the living. Those were the most delicious moments. She would imagine his lips pressed against hers, one hand at the small of her back, the other ripping the ponytail holder from her hair before lacing his fingers in her brown curls.

And as amazing as those moments were, they were nothing compared to the real thing.

It wasn't a romantic kiss. It wasn't Mr. Darcy kissing Elizabeth in the carriage after their wedding. It was a desperate kiss, frantic even. T.J. pulled her to him so tightly that she could feel every inch of him, even through their raingear. His hand moved up under her coat, grasping her as if he was afraid she would disappear.

Meg surprised herself by matching his intensity. She kissed him as if she'd been doing it all her life. Strong, fierce. She unbuttoned his coat and had a hand up under his sweater before she could even register what she was doing. His skin was hot and smooth and she wanted to feel every inch of it, right then and there, regardless of what was going on around them. Or perhaps because of it? Meg had no idea. She only thought of T.J. and how desperately she wanted him. She didn't care about anything else—not the murders, not being stranded on the island, not the strange writing on the bathroom mirror that seemed oddly familiar. . . .

"Wait." It was her voice, not his. Though considering how intertwined they were she wasn't entirely sure.

T.J.'s hand cupped her cheek as he pried his lips from hers. "Huh?"

"Wait."

"Why?"

"We need to go back inside." Meg couldn't believe what she was saying.

T.J. paused for a moment, then took her hand and started to lead her back across the isthmus toward White Rock House. "Right. You're right. We'll be safe there."

"No," she said, pulling him back. "We need to go back inside the Taylors' house."

T.J.'s eyes grew wide. "No freaking way."

"I know," she said. Meg pictured the four dead bodies inside and felt instantly sick again, but there was something she needed to see. The writing on the mirror. The way Nathan had been killed. It all seemed familiar somehow. "I need you to look at something."

"Yeah, no. I saw everything I needed to see in that house."

"Look, I know I'm asking a lot but . . ."

He pulled Meg to him and wrapped his arms around her.

He felt so strong, so safe. She wanted to stay there forever. "But what?"

Meg sighed. She could hardly believe what she was saying. "Something's wrong."

"Something's wrong? You mean more than that Kenny was bludgeoned to death, the Taylors died in their sleep, and Nathan has an arrow through his heart kind of wrong? Could there be a worse kind of 'wrong' than that?"

"I'll explain later. Right now, I need to go back in there and—"

He brushed a stray strand of hair out of her eyes. "And you don't want to go by yourself."

Meg nodded. She wasn't sure she was strong enough to march back into that house without him. "There's no one else I trust, and we need to figure out what's going on before—"

Once again he finished her thought. "Before one of us is next."

"Yeah." Meg glanced back at the Taylors' house. It still looked inviting and comforting from outside, fully lit, just as it had twenty-four hours earlier when she'd trudged across the beach. But something sinister lingered in the house now, something that appeared to be stalking them all. Could she escape it? Even if she ran to the other side of the island, would she really be able to escape whatever it was that was after them?

No, she had to go back in. She had to figure this out if they had any chance of escaping with their lives. She felt the weight of the journal in her coat pocket. That was the key to the mystery. It had to be. She was so close to figuring it out. She had to push on. And she needed T.J.'s help.

T.J. leaned his forehead against hers. She felt him inhale deeply, then slowly let all the air out of his lungs. "Okay. Let's go."

Meg felt like a sleepwalker as she entered the Taylors' house. She saw everything clearly and accurately, the toppled television, the rippling curtains, the bright lights glowing from the wall sconces. But it was as if she was completely removed from the situation, like she was watching it on a video screen. She knew what awaited her on the second floor and yet somehow that knowledge actually stemmed the tide of panic. Once she made the decision to go back inside, she was oddly calm. T.J. seemed to have the same mindset. He walked confidently by her side. Detached, almost, from the horror around them.

Maybe the killer felt that way too? After the first or second murder, maybe it got easier, so by the time he or she bludgeoned Kenny and shot Nathan with an arrow, it was a very detached, businesslike event.

Meg couldn't believe she was comparing herself and T.J. to a killer. What was going on with her?

They stepped over Kenny's body and went straight into the master bedroom. They moved quickly, not wanting to stay in the house a second longer than they had to.

The bathroom light was still on, and Meg marched straight up to the mirror, trying to keep her eyes on the writing, not Nathan's face.

She'd caught barely a glimpse of the words before she'd seen Nathan's body and fled the room. But they were familiar somehow, written in red paint, just like the slash marks at White Rock House.

For the day of their disaster is near. The phrases were coming together. From the video, from the back of Claire's photo, from the journal, and now here.

"That's weird," T.J. said. Meg saw his face reflected in the mirror. But he wasn't looking at the phrase of text; he was staring at Nathan's body.

"What?"

T.J. stepped around her and moved to the far side of Nathan's body, examining the arrow wound. Meg turned and looked at the body straight on for the first time. Shot through the heart with an arrow, Nathan hung from the bathroom door. His body slumped forward, arms hanging limp, head lolled to one side with jaw open in a horrifying soundless scream.

T.J. pulled the door away from the wall, swinging the body closer to Meg. She stumbled back against the sink. Her stomach clenched and she had to cover her mouth with her hand, fighting to maintain her composure.

"Sorry," he said.

Meg swallowed. "What are you doing?"

T.J. tugged on Nathan's shoulder, prying his body a few inches away from the door. Then he stepped away and shook his head. "Look." He pointed to Nathan's chest, from which the thin, metal arrow still protruded. It was amazing to think something so small could take a human life. "See where the arrow is? And the blood . . ." T.J. pointed to the thin circle of red on Nathan's shirt, radiating outward from where the arrow pierced his body. "It's coming from the wound, right? But then what's this?"

T.J. moved his finger down to Nathan's stomach and Meg immediately saw what he was getting at. Closer to Nathan's abdomen there was another ring of blood.

Meg's curiosity got the better of her. She stepped close to the body, her nose just a few inches from it, to examine the spot T.J. indicated. Not only was there a second circle of blood, but it looked as if there had been some damage to the fabric in his sweatshirt, almost as if . . .

Despite her revulsion at the dead body, Meg quickly unzipped Nathan's hooded Abercrombie & Fitch sweatshirt.

"What are you doing?" T.J. gasped.

Meg didn't care. She had to see if her theory was right. She tugged the sweatshirt open and there, just above Nathan's stomach in the middle of the second blood ring, was a hole in Nathan's thermal shirt. A second arrow wound.

"He was shot twice," Meg said, breathless.

"Whoa." T.J. sat back on his heels.

"The way the fabric of his shirt and sweatshirt is pulling away from his body," she said, feeling more and more confident in her discovery, "it looks like he was shot through the back first."

T.J. glanced back toward the bedroom door. "The killer was behind them. On the stairs. He brained Kenny, then followed Nathan into the bedroom and shot him in the back."

Meg nodded. "Yeah. Yeah, that makes sense."

"And look." T.J. swung the door so Meg could see it from the side. Two metal towel hooks were draped over the top of the door. Nathan's body flapped slightly as T.J. stopped the motion of the door, and Meg clearly saw what he meant. Nathan had been hung there. The hooks dug into the fabric of his sweatshirt.

"The first shot must have killed him," T.J. said. "Then he was hung here and shot again, probably with the same arrow, point-blank through the heart."

The heart. Something nagged at Meg's brain. *He said if I really loved him, I'd help him because if I didn't, it would be like I was shooting him through the heart.* "Oh my God."

"What?"

The writing. The deaths. A suicide note written on the back of sheet music. Images of a gavel like they use in debate team. Math problems scrolling across the screen. *Vengeance is mine.*

Choir. Debate team. A boy she was tutoring in algebra and his stupid friend.

Meg reached a shaky hand into her pocket and fingered the journal. Dear God, could it be? Lori, Vivian, Nathan, Kenny—could all of the victims have been in Claire's diary?

It was insanity, and yet it all made sense. Lori, Vivian, and Nathan were all connected to Claire. It couldn't be a coincidence, not with all this evidence staring her in the face. Nathan was the final proof.

She laughed, a sudden release of fear and frustration.

T.J. grabbed her by the shoulders. "Meg?"

She had the answer. She had the key to the murders. She spun around, taking in all sides of the room.

"What's wrong with you?"

"You don't understand," she said, trying to suppress hysterical laughter.

"You're right, I don't."

Meg took a deep breath. "I know what the verse means."

T.J. tilted his head. "What verse?"

She pointed to the mirror. "That line. It's part of a verse. We've been getting it in pieces so I didn't recognize it right away."

"Getting it in pieces?"

"Vengeance is mine; I will repay.

For the time when their foot shall slide.

For the day of their disaster is near.

And their doom comes swiftly."

T.J. shifted his gaze from the mirror back to Meg. "What are you talking about?"

Meg looked T.J. right in the eye. She pulled the journal from her pocket and held it up in front of his face. "I know who the killer is."

TWENTY SEVEN

T.J. WANTED MEG TO EXPLAIN THE DIARY RIGHT then and there . . . in a room, in a house full of dead bodies. Thankfully, Meg's brain had rebooted and pulled her sanity back from the brink of no return. It was funny—suddenly she was collected, her brain running a mile a minute, where half an hour ago she was ready to curl up in the fetal position, squeeze her eyes tightly shut against the realities of what was happening, and pray she'd wake up from a horrible nightmare.

That said, no freaking way in hell was she going to plop down at the kitchen table in the House of Many Dead People and start dissecting the diary of a killer while surrounded by his or her victims. Screw that.

Despite his initial frantic need to find out what Meg was talking about, T.J. acknowledged that she was right in her desire to get the hell out of the house of death as soon as was humanly possible. So with a short sojourn into the kitchen on a successful hunt for a lantern and batteries, Meg and T.J. put as much space between themselves and the Taylors' house as quickly as the weather and relative darkness would allow.

Once across the treacherous isthmus, T.J. started up the steps to White Rock House, but Meg stopped him.

"What?" he asked. He held the battery-operated lantern up to her face. She could see the light rain falling in its beam.

"We can't go back up," she said, squinting into the light. "Not yet."

T.J. sighed loudly. "Why?"

"Because," Meg said with a significant glance up toward the house. "The killer . . . could be up there." She almost said "is up there" but decided against the panic that statement might induce, particularly in herself. She was afraid of what her discovery meant, and she needed T.J.'s opinion on the matter before she jumped to conclusions.

T.J. seemed to understand. "Okay," he said calmly. "Let's go to the boathouse."

They took the shorter route along the beach and up through the trees to the boathouse. With the sun fully retreated beyond the horizon, the bone-chilling cold had returned, and while the boathouse offered a reprieve from the relentless drizzle, Meg still shivered as she and T.J. huddled around the lantern.

"Spill it," T.J. said unceremoniously.

Meg noted the edge to his voice. "I found this earlier." She reached a shaky hand into her pocket and retrieved the diary.

"Where?"

"In my room. I thought it was mine, but . . . not so much." Meg opened the first page and held the diary before the light.

"'Is this book yours?'" T.J. read aloud. "'No? THEN STOP READING IT. NOW.'" Despite his fatigue and strain, T.J. gave her a half smile. "So naturally you read on."

"Funny," she said. The fact that he could still find humor in their current situation bolstered her courage. "It gets weirder though." She flipped two pages ahead to where the line of the quote had been copied in the center of the page.

"'And their doom comes swiftly.'" He looked up at her. "The poem you read back at the house, right? How does that fit in?"

"It's a quote from the Bible that starts with 'Vengeance is mine.'"

Even in the relative darkness, she could see T.J.'s eyes widen. "The video."

"Yeah."

"Holy shit."

"I know."

"So whoever is stalking us wrote that?"

Meg bit her lip.

"What?"

It was too impossible, too bizarre to believe. There was no way in hell Claire was the killer since she'd been dead for three months. And yet, everything pointed in that direction. Ugh. Meg didn't trust herself. She needed T.J.'s unbiased opinion. "Just read it."

"Fine." T.J. lifted the book from her hand. He held it close to the light, examining both the front and back covers, then opened to the first entry. Meg sat silently at his side while he read the first few pages. Meg stopped him at the point where the pages had been ripped out, covering the photo of Claire with her hand as she took the journal away from him. She didn't want him to see it. Not yet.

"Okay" he said. "So this girl had some problems she needed to work out. How does that relate to us?"

"Don't you see?" she said. "It's like a hit list. The singer. The two-faced bitch. The heartbreaker."

"Look," he said. "I know we were talking theoretically back at the house, but Vivian's death had to be an accident. You almost went over the hill at that point yourself."

"Teej!" she said, losing her patience. "We both saw that the railing had been tampered with. That was no accident."

T.J. wasn't convinced. "It could have been."

"But it wasn't," Meg said, her mouth dry. "Listen, Lori was a singer."

"Right."

Meg stared into the darkness. "Vivian was definitely a bitch, and Lori even said she'd probably kill her own mother if it meant she'd get the best grade or win a competition. And don't you remember what Nathan said at dinner? About conning some poor girl at school into helping him pass algebra?"

"So?" T.J. clearly hadn't made the same leap.

"Don't you get it?" she said. Why was he being so obtuse? "Lori was a singer. The diary talks about a singer who beat the author out for a solo."

"Okay," T.J. said begrudgingly.

"And Lori was strangled. By a noose. It crushed her vocal cords."

"That's just a coincidence."

"Yeah? Was it a coincidence that her suicide note was written on the sheet music for her solo from the last concert?"

"Okay." T.J. nodded. "What else?"

"Then Vivian," Meg said, speaking fast, as if she was afraid she'd forget what she wanted to say halfway through. "Two-faced pain in the ass who was completely self-serving."

"Heh." T.J. smirked. "Tell me how you really feel."

Meg narrowed her eyes. "Are you finished?"

"Maybe."

"*Such* an appropriate time for sarcasm."

"You're gorgeous when you're angry."

Meg rolled her eyes. "Come on. This is important."

T.J. sat back and crossed his legs in front of him. "Fine, fine. Go on."

"The diary talks about a back-stabber who got the author kicked off the debate team. And Vivian just *happened* to be stabbed through the back?" She didn't wait for him to respond. "Then Nathan," she said. "The heartbreaker. The author said she hoped the boy who broke her heart would have the same done to him. And Nathan was shot through the heart."

T.J. shook his head. "But in the diary, the author and The Boy are perfectly happy. No mention of him being a heart-breaker at all."

That was true, Meg couldn't deny it. But if "The Boy" and Nathan were the same person, the diary would chronicle the same story Nathan told over dinner, about conning some poor girl into helping him cheat on his algebra midterm by pretending he was in love with her.

There was only one way to find out. Meg flipped to the next entry and began to read out loud.

> This can't be happening. She did this, I know she did. That backstabbing bitch must have said something to The Boy.
>
> The big test was yesterday, the one we'd been working so hard on. I did something I shouldn't have done, but I just wanted him to pass, you know? I texted him last night to see how he thought he did. He didn't respond so I called and he didn't pick up. Then today I didn't see him anywhere, but I found his best friend and told him I wanted to talk and could The Boy meet me after school at the usual place? His friend sort of nodded, but wouldn't look me in the eye. And then after school . . . The Boy never came.

Meg swallowed, trying to control the emotion in her voice. She could feel the pain coming through the page. The tone of the entry was frantic. The handwriting grew more and more erratic as it went on so that by the last line the words blurred together and the letters were almost unintelligible. It looked as if that passage had been written in a fit of pure despair.

> My heart is breaking. I feel like everything's been taken away from me!!!! I bet his friend didn't tell The Boy I was waiting for him. Idiot. Someone should just beat him over

the head. That has to be it. I know The Boy wouldn't have abandoned me.

He wouldn't do this if he knew how much it was hurting me. Does he know how I feel? Does he know what it's like to have your heart ripped out of your chest? I wish someone would tell him how much it hurts.

TWENTY EIGHT

T.J.'S HEAD SNAPPED UP AS MEG FINISHED reading. "Head beaten in? And a heart ripped out?"

"Yep."

T.J.'s jaw dropped. "You're saying that each of them was killed in a specific way?"

Finally. "That's exactly what I'm saying."

"Hm." T.J. scratched his leg through his jeans, then shook his head. "It doesn't add up. I mean, what did the killer do, convince Lori to hang herself, then just get lucky that Vivian fell on a log that stabbed her in the back?"

Was he being intentionally dim? "T.J., you're the one who just told me that it looked like Nathan had been shot once through the stomach and then someone shot him again through the heart."

"Yeah, to make sure he was dead."

"Or to follow the pattern. And Vivian's death could have been the same thing. We're not the police. We don't know how she really died. Maybe she broke her neck in the fall, then the killer staged the body after her death."

It sounded plausible, and not just because she'd watched too many episodes of *Dexter*. And as she watched T.J. mulling the situation over in his mind, she saw him wrestling with the idea that she might be right.

"All the people who went to Mariner are dead. But how do the rest of us fit in? And Ben?"

Meg held out the journal. "Maybe . . . maybe we're all in here."

T.J. looked directly at her. Whether it was stress or the crappy lighting, he seemed to have aged twenty years. Deep worry lines creased his forehead and the arcs around his lips and nose were heavy, his usually full lips pressed tightly together, disappearing into a thin line.

"You said you knew who the killer was. Back at the house."

"I think . . ." Meg bit at her lip again. She was going to sound like a crazy person if she told T.J. what she really thought. "I think the killer knew about this journal."

"And is using it for revenge or something?"

"Yeah."

"But for whom?"

Again, Meg balked at saying the name. It was all too surreal. Claire Hicks couldn't be the killer. But then who, exactly, was hunting them?

"Maybe we should read it together," she said.

"Okay," he said. "But we need to read fast. They're waiting for us."

"Right." Read fast. No pressure.

Meg opened the diary to the next entry, bent her head close

to his, and together they began to read.

First day at the new school.

Yay.

New school. It must have been Kamiak. Claire had started that fall, and Meg remembered the rumors that she'd been at like five or six different high schools already. More like two, apparently. She'd been at Mariner before she transferred to Kamiak. But before that? Still a mystery.

Three schools in two years. That's got to be some sort of Guinness Book of Freak Shows record. My mom and Bob really believe every time that it'll be different. So did I. But not now. Now I know better. There's no point in even trying anymore.

And I'm pretty sure I'm being haunted by the past. Yesterday I saw someone from sophomore year. That was two schools ago, but it feels like a lifetime. And she didn't even recognize me. Or at least she pretended not to.

Why should she? I wasn't anything to her. Just a scapegoat so she could get her precious A in physics. I bet she never expected to see me again after I transferred to Mariner.

She's not the only one haunting me. Today I saw that blond jerk from my P.E. class at Mariner. I was at the grocery store with Mom and there he was. I never understood why I was the butt of all his jokes. I remember every one of his taunts. They're imprinted on my brain forever.

"Hey, freakshow, how's the circus? BURN!"

"What's the lunch menu like in the psycho ward? BURN!"

"When you go to the zoo, are the animals scared of you? BURN!"

I want to make him choke on those words. Him and his stupid bleached-blond hair. Really? I was the freak?

Meg gasped. Choke on his words . . .

"What? T.J. asked.

"The blond guy."

"Ben?"

"Yeah."

T.J. shook his head. "I was thinking the same thing."

What are the odds I'd see them both in two days? I don't even go to school with them anymore! It's like a bad joke. What was she doing way up here from the city anyway? I wanted to march right up and smack her. I mean, it wasn't my fault we got paired as lab partners in physics. I wouldn't have chosen her, that's for sure. But we got stuck and we were supposed to work together. As a team. Not one of us making decisions and the other just agreeing to them. Which is really what she wanted.

Until it all went horribly wrong. I told her the way she routed the circuits wouldn't work, but would she listen to me? No. Apparently she was the only one who was surprised when the lightbulb didn't go on and we got a failing grade.

She went to our teacher and blamed the whole failure

on me. She got to redo her experiment. Which she passed. I still got an F.

How could they believe her? The teacher never even asked me what happened. How is that fair? Tom said it was a conspiracy but either way, it sucks.

"Damn," T.J. said, flipping to the next page. "A conspiracy in high school physics?"

"The only conspiracy is that they force us to take physics."

"Gold." T.J. smiled faintly. "Any idea who she's talking about?"

Meg shook her head. "Let's keep reading."

He's the one. I know it.

Everyone here acts like they don't see me but he's different. He smiles at me sometimes. He notices me. I think maybe he wants to talk to me but his friends wouldn't approve.

I just need to get him by himself—no friends around—and then maybe we could talk.

Meg's empathy was back. She pictured that messed-up girl with her dirty hair and her sadness and her pain. Meg found it hard to believe that any of the guys at school had shown interest in her, but it sounded like she truly believed they did. Probably the same thing that happened with Nathan. Meg wondered who the guy had been at Kamiak.

T.J. turned the page.

It's all the same. Nothing changes.

He asked someone else to Homecoming. I've been trying for days to catch him alone. Waited for him outside the boys' locker room after practice. Sat next to his car after a game. But he was always with someone.

Today I was hiding in the copy room, waiting. He always comes on Thursdays at the beginning of third period. But as usual, he had someone with him. That stupid friend of his. They didn't see me but I heard what he said. "I've got a date for Homecoming."

His friend laughed. "That stringy-haired freak that's always following you around? Dude, something's wrong with her."

"Um, no."

"Good. I'd rather shoot myself in the head than get stuck taking that chick to Homecoming."

Stringy-haired freak? That's me. That's me his friend was talking about! Sabotaging me. Now he'll never even think of me as anything more than some crazy girl that follows him around. IT'S NOT FAIR!!!!!!

Now I have to confront them. They'll probably go to one of the bonfires at the beach after the dance. I'll find them and I'll confront them.

T.J. gasped. "Oh my God."

"What?"

He gripped her hand. "You said you knew who the killer was. Back at the house."

"Yeah."

"You think it's the person who wrote this journal?"

Meg cringed. "Or someone who knew about it."

"Meg." T.J. pulled her hand close to his chest. "Meg, I know who wrote this."

She wasn't expecting that. She hadn't told T.J. about the photo. "How do you know?"

"The copy room. That was me. I go every Thursday at the beginning of third period and make weekend itineraries for Leadership. The week of Homecoming Gunner came with me. I was telling him that I asked you to the dance."

"Oh, no."

"She must have been there. I mean, I'd noticed her hanging around my car and stuff, but after what happened to Bobby and Tiffany it's generally safer just to stay the hell away from her, you know?"

"Oh God." The realization hit her. If T.J. had been the guy Claire was talking about, that meant the girl she was going to confront, the girl she was going to make pay . . . was her.

"But it's impossible," he said, running a hand over his bare head. "It couldn't possibly be her . . ."

"Because she's dead," Meg said.

T.J.'s head flicked up. "You know who it is?"

Meg nodded. She flipped the journal back a few pages to the photo. "Claire Hicks."

TWENTY NINE

T.J. SAT BOLT UPRIGHT. "IF CLAIRE'S ON THE island, we need to get back to the house to warn the others."

"Okay, let's not get crazy," Meg said, fighting back the fear. "It can't be Claire."

"Why not?"

"Come on! What, you think this is her ghost back from the grave or something?"

"Uh, no," T.J. said. "But how do we know she's really dead?"

"Obituary. Funeral. The usual."

"But that's all circumstantial. Did you *go* to the funeral? Did you *see* the body?"

Meg looked at him. "You think her death was faked."

"I'm just saying it's possible."

Meg squinted into the darkness and tried to get a read on T.J. Was he messing with her? Suggesting that Claire Hicks somehow faked her own suicide and was now getting revenge on people who wronged her in life was a bit much even for a writer to believe. But as she watched T.J. rubbing his forehead with his index finger as he stared at the discarded diary, she was convinced that he really believed Claire might be behind it all.

Meg? Not so much.

"Okay," she said. "Let's pretend for a minute that it *is* Claire."

"Okay."

"Lori, Vivian, Ben, Nathan, and Kenny knew her from Mariner. The five of them. And she was obviously in love with you, so I get why she might hate me but . . . I don't know. Why would she want revenge on you? Or Minnie and Gunner?"

T.J. rubbed his mouth but didn't say anything.

"Did she confront you like she said she was going to? Did she show up at Homecoming?"

T.J. averted his eyes. "Kinda."

"Kinda?" Homecoming night. Everyone was always dancing around it, and Meg always let it go because the thought of that night made her physically ill. But suddenly she wanted to know more than anything what happened.

There was still one entry left. Maybe it would have the answers. Meg picked up the journal and flipped to the last entry.

"What are you doing?" T.J. asked. He sounded alarmed.

"There's one more," Meg said, holding the journal down by the light. "I need to know what happened."

"Meg . . . ," T.J. started.

"Yeah?"

His eyes met hers for a moment. His face was tight, almost as if he was in pain.

"What's wrong?"

"Nothing," he said. He wiped his brow with the back of his hand. "Read it out loud."

This is the end.

And I'm ready now.

I can deal with their ridicule, their snobbery, their cliques. I can deal with being the outsider. I never wanted their friendship. I was only at the bonfire to stake my claim on T.J. Meg Pritchard needs to understand that.

I never even saw her there. She must have been hiding, because she sent her blonde pit bull to attack me. She humiliated me in front of him and he

Meg turned the page, but there was nothing else. No more words. Only a jagged fringe near the spine.

The last page of Claire's diary had been torn out.

"Dammit!" Meg said.

T.J. slumped his head against his hands. "We don't need it. I can tell you exactly what happened."

Meg's hands shook as she flipped back a page and reread the last line. *Blonde pit bull.* It could only be one person.

"That was Minnie, wasn't it?"

T.J. nodded. "She'd basically had a whole six-pack by that point. And you know how she gets when she drinks."

"Tell me about it."

"But . . ." T.J. stood suddenly. He paced back and forth in front of the wall of gas cans. "Look, it's not Minnie's fault. We were all pretty drunk, Minnie, Gunner, and me for sure. I was really pissed off, trying to forget you. And Minnie, after the first three or four beers, started hitting on me again. Right in front of Gunner."

Meg winced. She wasn't sure who she felt more sorry for, Minnie or Gunner.

"And I'd told her off. Kind of dragged her away from the crowd so no one heard, but I told her I was never going to date her and whatever the hell she thought was going on between us was all in her head."

"You told her that?"

"Yeah." T.J. stopped pacing. "Only I think that made it worse."

Meg could almost see Minnie's face as T.J. informed her that they would never, ever be a couple. A mix of disbelief and defiance.

"That's when Claire showed up. She marched right across the beach to me and everything got real quiet. She looked like a ghost or something, with her black hair flying in the wind. I don't even think she saw Minnie there with me. Just walked right up and said 'I want you to know I love you and I think you feel the same way.'"

Meg groaned. She knew what was coming next. When Minnie was hurt she lashed out at whoever and whatever was within arm's reach. "And Minnie went after her."

"Like those lions in the zoo at feeding time. It was ugly. Minnie laughed, then told Claire what a freak she was and how no one would ever love her. Gunner and I pulled her away, but it was too late. And everyone stood around watching. I think half the school was there. Claire's face turned bright red. I was going to say something, try and calm her down, but she just turned and ran." T.J. swallowed. "She was dead the next morning."

"Shit."

"But, Meg." T.J. knelt down next to her. "I'm the one to blame. I should have stopped her. Gone after her. But I didn't. I just stood there and stared like everyone else." T.J. hung his head. "So this, all of this, is my fault."

"It's not your fault." Meg reached up and caressed his cheek. "It's not your fault," she repeated. "Claire was depressed, and what happened to make her that way started long before she met you. This journal proves that. If it wasn't you, it would have been someone else."

"You think?"

"She fell in love with Nathan first. That alone would make me question her sanity."

T.J. laughed and grasped her hand. "No, I mean, do you think it could have been anyone?"

"Yeah. It was because you were nice to her. You noticed her. That's just . . ." Meg paused, searching for the right word. "Human. You didn't know she was going to make Prince Charming out of you."

"I guess not." T.J. fell silent for a moment, then took a sharp breath. "I can't believe it's one of us."

"I know." Meg had been mulling the list of survivors over in her mind. Five people, four of whom she'd known for years. It just didn't seem possible.

"I mean," T.J. continued. "I wouldn't have been surprised if it was Nathan. I know you're not supposed to speak ill of the dead, but the dude was an asshole."

Meg laughed despite herself.

"Kenny had an angry side to him."

Meg nodded. "And Vivian had the cold-bloodedness."

"But they're all . . ."

"Dead."

"Yeah." T.J. looked her straight in the eye. "So I guess all we really know is that *we're* innocent. We've been together almost the whole time."

Meg smiled, but something inside her twitched. Not quite the whole time. After Nathan and Kenny left, she hadn't seen him until Minnie screamed.

T.J. squeezed her hand and smiled back. If there was one person on the island she could trust, it was T.J.

They sat on the floor of the boathouse, hand in hand, staring at the journal in the fading light of the lantern. Meg wanted to say something, a word of comfort or hope, but she didn't really have either at her disposal. Instead she leaned her body into him. His arms crept around her waist and pulled her to his chest. She could hear the steady, strong beat of his heart as he held her, something normal, something alive. He rested his head against hers and they sat there, holding each other.

Meg closed her eyes and pretended they were somewhere else. A beach. Her bedroom. Smack dab on the fifty-yard line at the Kamiak High football field. Anywhere but the boathouse below White Rock House. She could almost imagine it all away. But not quite.

"They'll be waiting for us," she said.

T.J. took a deep breath. "I know."

"Do we tell them?"

"We have to."

"Then what?"

T.J. pulled away. "I don't know. I honestly don't. But whatever happens, I'm not leaving your side, okay? I'm going to be attached to you until the ferry arrives tomorrow."

"Promise?" Meg asked, using one of Minnie's favorite phrases.

He smiled. "You'll have to shoot me to get rid of me."

"Lucky for you I don't have a gun," Meg laughed.

"Isn't it?"

She picked up the journal and handed the waning lantern to T.J. "Okay, Prince Charming. After you."

THIRTY

"THE WAY I SEE IT," T.J. SAID. HE SWALLOWED hard and gripped Meg's hand tightly under the table. "The way *we* see it, whoever wrote the diary is behind everything."

They'd decided on the walk back up to the house not to mention that the journal might have belonged to a dead girl. Meg was worried that the news might put Minnie over the edge, but in the end, it wasn't like it really mattered.

What they had to do now was figure out a way to survive until morning.

No one reacted, just continued to stare at the diary, which sat in the middle of the table. It was as if the shock of all the deaths had numbed their senses, slowed down their reactions. Meg felt it herself. When she and T.J. finally returned to the house, the two additional red slashes on the wall somehow didn't hold the same terror they had earlier in the day. Meg distinctly remembered staring at them, marveling at the fifth slash with complete concentration, like it was a Picasso she needed to interpret. It perfectly cut through the other four on the diagonal, centered and without a single drip of red paint to mar its symmetry. It had been made carefully. Precisely. Whoever did it wasn't concerned about getting caught. They'd taken their time.

T.J. called Gunner, Minnie, and Kumiko downstairs to the foyer and they each reacted much the same. No hysterics. No panic. Meg could see the same dull look in their eyes as they marched through the foyer. Acceptance.

Death was the new normal.

Kumiko was the first to break the silence. "Really?" She folded her arms across her chest and narrowed her eyes. "Isn't the most logical explanation that one of us is the killer?"

Meg flinched. Well, of course it was the logical explanation. The first thought that popped into everyone's mind. But considering the five individuals who were currently huddled around a dining room table, lit only by a battery-operated lantern and a half-dozen candles, the idea sounded ludicrous.

T.J. remained calm. "We've been over this."

"Doesn't mean it's not true."

"Who then?" T.J. asked. "My best friend? Meg's best friend? You?"

Kumiko didn't answer.

"I've known Gunner since I was ten. Meg, when did you and Minnie meet?"

"Seventh grade." Meg smiled at Minnie, but she wasn't looking.

Kumiko pursed her lips. She clearly wasn't buying T.J's argument. "Just for kicks, I want to point out that any of us could have committed these murders." She glanced around the table, taking in each person. "*Any* of us."

"But I was with you," Gunner said. "For, um, most of them."

Meg caught a slight roll of Kumiko's eyes. "Yeah, but logically speaking, no one else can confirm that."

"Well, Meg and I were together when Vivian was killed," T.J. said. He squeezed Meg's knee under the table. "You may not believe us, but I know for a fact *we* didn't do it."

Meg opened her mouth to back up T.J., then paused. Yeah, they'd been together most of that morning. The perilous trek down to the boathouse in the storm of the century and all. But there had been a moment. Just a few minutes when T.J. had run back up to the house to get the flashlights. It would have been enough time. . . .

T.J. caught Meg staring at him. His eyes were so trusting, so soft. Meg shook off her doubts. She was being ridiculous. The stress of the day had made her paranoid.

"Bottom line," T.J. said, still looking at Meg, "*we* all trust each other."

"Speak for yourself."

It took Meg a few seconds to realize that it wasn't Kumiko who had spoken.

It was Minnie.

Gunner was the first to react. "Huh?"

"You heard me, Gun Show." Minnie's voice was razor-sharp. "I trust you about as far as I can throw you. And that goes for the rest of you, too." Minnie pushed her chair away from the table and stood up.

"Minnie!" Meg said.

"What?" Minnie laughed. It was cold and barking. "You think I trust you?"

Meg straightened herself. "Yes, of course."

Minnie looked unconvinced. "Why?"

Gee, I don't know. Maybe because I'm the only one who knows your secrets? "I'm your best friend."

"Really? *You're* my best friend?"

"Of course."

Minnie leaned across the table. "Then why have you been trying to *steal my boyfriend*?"

Had Minnie lost her mind?

Kumiko leaned into Gunner. "*She's* into you too?" she muttered.

Gunner slipped his arm around her back. "Um . . . er . . . Wait, are you?"

"No," Meg said. She may not be sure about many things in her life anymore, but her disinterest in the Gun Show was not one of them. "No, I'm not."

"Not that one," Minnie said. She pointed to T.J. without looking at him. "That one."

Meg felt the color drain out of her face. She thought of the make-out session she and T.J. had just shared and felt a pang of guilt. She'd known for years that Minnie was in love with T.J. She'd pushed him away. Without any luck.

"Boyfriend?" T.J. asked.

"Yeah," Minnie said.

"Minnie, I was never your boyfriend."

Minnie crossed behind the table and caressed his shoulder with the tips of her fingers. "You should have been."

T.J. flinched away from her touch. "Minnie, I was never going to be your boyfriend." His voice was harsh. "Ever."

"See?" Minnie said. "You're angry. That means you care." She laid a hand on his chest.

"Get away from me," T.J. said. He pushed her arm away. "You're fucking crazy."

"She's not crazy." Meg said it on reflex. She was so used to defending Minnie she didn't even realize she'd done it again.

"Don't defend her!" T.J. barked. "Why are you always defending her? She does nothing but treat you like dirt."

"It's not her fault, okay?" There she was, sticking up for Minnie again. Why was it never the other way around?

T.J. stormed across the room. "For chrissakes." He leaned his back against the wall and folded his arms across his chest.

Minnie mimicked his stance, folding her arms across her chest as well. "She was only nice to me so she could steal you. She sabotaged me."

T.J. laughed. "That's the stupidest thing I've ever heard."

"Is it?" Minnie said, her voice shrill and tense. "Then why did she start a rumor saying that you asked her to the Homecoming dance?"

"Hey!" Meg said. "I didn't start any rumor."

T.J. looked straight at Minnie. "Maybe because I *did* ask her to the Homecoming dance?"

Minnie's eyes grew wide. She swung around and faced Meg.

"I knew it. I knew you were lying to me. You told me he didn't ask you."

Now all the blood rushed back into Meg's face with a vengeance. Turning T.J. down was one of the hardest things she'd ever done, but Minnie would never have forgiven her.

"I didn't want to hurt you," Meg said lamely.

Minnie glared at her. "You should have told me the truth."

"She canceled on me that morning," T.J. said.

"Yeah, but she didn't want to." Minnie's eyes never left Meg's face. "She wanted to go with you. She cried her eyes out over that."

T.J. turned to Meg. "You did?"

"How did you . . ." Meg froze. She hadn't told Minnie that. She hadn't told anyone. She only wrote about it in her . . .

"Oh, no." Meg felt as if someone had punched her in the stomach. She was dizzy as reality dawned on her. "Minnie, you didn't."

THIRTY ONE

MINNIE JUTTED OUT HER CHIN. "SO WHAT IF I did?"

"Did what?" T.J. asked.

Meg exploded. "YOU READ MY DIARY???"

"Oh, shit," Kumiko whispered.

Meg had spent years of her life taking care of Minnie. Protecting her. Sacrificing for her. Writing was the only escape she really had, the only thing she did for herself. Minnie knew exactly what Meg's journals meant to her.

"How could you, Minnie? How could you?"

A flash of shame and regret passed over Minnie's face and for a moment, her eyes faltered. Then she caught sight of T.J. standing just behind Meg and it seemed to harden her.

"You've always been jealous of me," Minnie said, spitting out every word as fast as she could. "Always. Boys, clothes—you always had to have what was mine."

T.J. threw up his hands. "I was never yours!"

"And you tried to bring me down, to undermine my confidence.

I was fine before I met you. I wasn't depressed. I didn't have to take all these medications." Minnie was on a roll now. "That was you. That was *all your fault*. You did this to me. But you didn't break me, Meg Pritchard. You will never break me."

"You're crazy." Meg couldn't believe what she was hearing. Minnie sounded almost delusional, like some of the entries in Claire's diary. So similar it was almost spooky.

"I'm crazy?" Minnie screeched. "*I'm* crazy? Who's the one who has to sing Pink songs to herself in the mirror just to psych herself up to go to dances? Who's the one who copies lines of old poems in her diary and dedicates them to boys she doesn't even have the guts to talk to? It's pathetic."

Meg's face burned. Her most intimate secrets, feelings and fears and desires she'd shared with no one, were now on display. She wanted to tell Minnie that she hated her, but the words choked off in her throat. All she could feel were the tears welling up in her eyes. She desperately hoped no one noticed.

Minnie certainly didn't. "All you ever do is remind me to take my meds. 'Mins, did you take your meds? Did you remember your pills? You have to take them every day, remember?' Yeah. I remember. I remember that I was happy before I met you. I was normal. I was popular. The pills made me think I was crazy. You made me think that I wasn't normal when really it was just you being—"

"Stop it, Minnie." T.J. stepped between them. "Just stop it. You need to calm down, okay?"

Meg sunk her head against his back and gulped for air as if she was drowning.

"Calm down?" Minnie said. Her voice cracked. "Calm down? This *is* calm, Thomas Jefferson Fletcher. THIS IS CALM!"

Meg felt T.J.'s body flinch. "Look, I just meant—"

"I think I've been totally calm while she tried to steal you from me." Minnie turned her back and stomped around the table. "I think I've been perfectly calm while my best friend tried to steal my boyfriend."

"I AM NOT YOUR BOYFRIEND!"

T.J.'s yell echoed through the room. It caught everyone off guard, judging from the gasps that came from Gunner and Kumiko. Meg slowly backed away from T.J. He grabbed Minnie by the shoulders and shook her.

Minnie threw her head back in defiance. "Not my boyfriend?" she said. "Then what do you call the night we hooked up?"

"Delusional." T.J. tossed Minnie away from him in disgust. "I know what you've been saying. I've heard the gossip. I don't know what the hell you think happened at that party but I didn't sleep with you." He turned his back on her. "I was drunk, but not that drunk."

"What do you . . ." The words froze on her tongue as Minnie's face turned red. She stammered, but T.J. ignored her. He turned to Meg and took her hands in his.

"Is this why you wouldn't go out with me? Is this why you kept turning me down? Because you thought I slept with Minnie?"

Meg dropped her eyes.

He gripped her hands tighter. "I swear to God, Meg. I swear to God I never had sex with her. Not with anyone in months.

All I've been able to think about is you. I tried to forget you, but I couldn't. It's always been you. Only you."

"Liar!" Minnie screeched. She pried T.J.'s hands away from Meg. "He's lying. We totally hooked up at that party." Minnie wheeled on Gunner. "You saw me after. You know."

Gunner glanced at T.J., then Kumiko, and shrugged. "I . . . I don't remember."

Minnie sneered, then turned to Meg. "You know," she said. "You believe me."

Meg felt all of her facial muscles contract. Her eyebrows pulled together, her cheeks pinched, her lips hardened. That party was a bit of a blur; it was the first time in Meg's life that she'd been shit-faced drunk. She remembered Minnie draping herself over T.J. in the stairwell. She remembered that suddenly they weren't by her side anymore. And she remembered the empty, sick feeling at the idea that T.J. was having sex with her best friend just upstairs. But she never saw them enter the bedroom together, and the Tullamore Dew that she'd imbibed in the interim ensured she wouldn't remember anything more than imprints of the evening.

Meg looked from Minnie to T.J. and back. Both of their eyes pleaded with her. Whatever happened that night, they both believed they were telling the truth.

"I don't know," Meg stuttered.

"Liars!" Minnie plopped back down into her chair. "You're all liars."

"I didn't, Meg," T.J. said under his breath. She could feel his fingers digging into the flesh of her arm. "I swear I didn't."

"I believe you," she whispered. After months of living with her own version of what happened that night, she wasn't sure if T.J.'s words were the truth, but she wanted them to be.

"Well, this is just perfect!" Minnie said with a dramatic sigh. "Always thinking of yourself, Meg. Never of me."

Meg had had enough. "Really? Really, Mins? Are we even on the same planet? I do *nothing* but think of your feelings. All the time."

Minnie laughed. "Bullshit."

"It's not."

"That's not what you wrote in your diary."

Meg wondered how much of it Minnie had read. "You weren't supposed to read that."

"Oh, yeah? Then why did you leave it on my bed?"

"What?"

"You left it out, lying open on my bed. When I went upstairs today. You wanted me to find it and read it. Just like you wanted me to find the photo of that psychopath Claire Hicks."

Kumiko flinched at the name. "Who?"

"This freaktastic girl that went to school with us." Minnie tossed her white-blonde hair out of her face. "Meg left a photo of her in our room to scare me."

Meg threw up her hands and collapsed back into her chair. "I didn't put it there!"

Kumiko was still interested. "You said her name was Claire?"

"Yeah."

"Claire Hicks?"

Minnie tilted her head. "You knew her?"

Meg and T.J. exchanged a look. How did Kumiko fit in?

"Yeah," Kumiko said, her voice hushed. "Yeah, I knew her. She went to Roosevelt with me sophomore year." Meg caught the tremor in her voice.

"Wait, so she went to school with you, too?" There was the connection. Three schools, just like the journal said. Roosevelt, Mariner, and Kamiak. That covered all of the guests on the island.

Kumiko nodded. "She was in my physics class sophomore year. We were lab partners on our electricity midterm. She totally screwed up our project and almost got me a failing grade. I had to go to the teacher and beg him to let me take it again by myself."

T.J. gripped Meg's arm. "Did you say electricity?"

"Yeah. Why?"

Meg reached across the table and pulled the diary toward her. She didn't really want to read the entry to Kumiko—it felt too much like reading a death sentence to a convicted criminal. She glanced at T.J. for support and he gave her a tight smile.

Ugh. Meg swallowed and read the second-to-last entry out loud.

When she looked up again, Kumiko was trembling. "But . . . but that's impossible. No one else could know . . ."

"Exactly," T.J. said. "They're all like that."

"Wait," Minnie said. "You think Claire wrote that diary?"

"But she's dead!" Gunner said, as if the concept clearly ruled out all other possibilities.

"Are you sure about that?" T.J. asked.

Gunner's brow scrunched up. "But . . . there was a funeral."

"Are you saying that freak's not really dead?" Minnie asked.

"It's a possibility." T.J. sat down next to Meg. "Or someone else who's read the diary is using it to hunt us down."

Minnie threw up her hands. "But why? I never did anything to her."

Gunner and T.J. looked at each other, then at Minnie. "Don't you remember?" Gunner asked.

"Remember what?"

"Look," T.J. said firmly. "It doesn't matter. What *does* matter is that we've got two options."

"That many?" Kumiko said.

T.J. ignored her. "Either one of us is the killer or there's someone else in the house."

Minnie caught her breath. "Someone else?"

Kumiko sighed. "Obviously."

"So we either lock ourselves in a room and pray we all survive until morning when the ferry's supposed to return . . ."

"Or?"

"Or we search the house and find out whether or not we're really alone."

Silence again. Only this time there was less aggression in the atmosphere. Something about T.J.'s argument had struck a chord, though it was the part he never spoke out loud. They could search the house. And if they found no one, at least they'd know the truth: one of them was the killer.

"We all agree? We'll search the house?"

No one spoke, but four heads slowly nodded.

"Good." T.J. pushed his chair back from the table. "We should split up. It'll go faster."

"Yeah, 'cause that always ends so well," Kumiko said.

"I think we should stick together," Meg said.

T.J. turned and looked at her. "Yeah?"

Meg shrugged. "Safety in numbers." And easier to keep an eye on everyone.

"Okay," T.J. said. "Let's start at the bottom and move up."

THIRTY TWO

MEG WAS SCARED, TERRIFIED BEYOND THE POINT where she could even process her fear, and she felt as if all the familiar things in her life, the very relationships by which she defined herself, were toppling one by one.

The mood was somber as the five of them moved through the ground floor. T.J. and Gunner took a quick walk through the covered patio with the lantern. The blue glow of its light danced through the dining room windows as the boys trudged down both sides of the patio. Meg heard the sucking sound of the cooler opening and crashing closed, then the light bounced back in through the door.

"Clear," Gunner said.

No one spoke.

They shuffled through the kitchen, taking cursory glances into the pantry and broom closets before moving into the living room. Meg and Kumiko carried the candlesticks from the dining room table. There were only two that were still burning, and their flickering, changeable light was barely strong enough to illuminate the length of the room, merely an eight-foot radius around them. They all bunched together as they examined the bookcases and entertainment center slowly, like it was some kind of screwed-up ten-legged race. They examined every corner, and even though there wasn't a feasible hiding place in the L-shaped room, someone glanced under every table and behind every sofa . . . just in case.

The girls lingered outside in the hallway as T.J. and Gunner did a once-around of the study. It was incredibly creepy standing in that big, white house lit only by a pair of candles. Meg could see walls and floor, but the high ceilings were invisible in the blackness. Anyone could have been lurking and Meg wouldn't see them. A sudden image flashed before Meg's eyes. Claire Hicks, with her stringy black hair hanging lank in front of her face, those dark eyes staring out at you, just daring you to come closer.

Yeah, maybe the lack of visibility was a good thing. If she caught sight of a dead girl squatting in the corner of the foyer she'd probably die of fright. And with a body wrapped in a sheet lying just feet from them, and the once pristine walls of the foyer now marred with five red slash marks, it wasn't as if Meg was dying for a front-row view of any of it.

"All clear," Gunner said, as he and T.J. emerged from the study. The lantern illuminated more of the hall, though Meg still refused to turn her eyes toward the foyer.

"Then it's just the upper floors," T.J. said. He moved to the foot of the stairs and gazed up into the black abyss of the tower.

As the five of them stared into the still darkness, Meg almost regretted her decision to search the house. She wanted to find a room, lock the door, and not leave until morning. At least in the light of day she could see what might be coming for her, instead of the gloominess of that strange, isolated house.

At the second-floor landing, T.J. turned and faced them. "Maybe we should do the garret first? It'll only take a minute and then we can concentrate on the second floor."

Kumiko pursed her lips. "But if someone's hiding on the second floor they could sneak out."

"We'll leave someone on the stairs," T.J. suggested. "To keep watch."

"Fine."

"I'll stay." Minnie grabbed the lantern from T.J.'s hand. "I don't want to go up there."

Meg and T.J. glanced at each other. Was Minnie really the best choice to keep watch? "Guns," T.J. said, nudging his friend. "Stay here with her, okay?"

Gunner looked to Kumiko for approval. She gave a slight nod of her head. "Cool," he said.

It was funny how much Meg's feelings about that room had changed in just twenty-four hours. When T.J. had led her and Minnie up there the first time, she'd felt such a thrill of anticipation. It was a storybook moment, the princess's tower room, all dripping with romance and white gauze curtains. Now ascending the stairs made her sick to her stomach, and the garret with its single staircase felt more like a prison than an escape.

The room looked much as Meg remembered. If Minnie had

actually spent any time up there "sleeping" she certainly hadn't bothered to put either of the mattresses back on their frames first. Their clothes and personal belongings were still strewn everywhere, blanketing the room like oversized confetti. But Meg's eye was immediately drawn to two things that were completely out of place. On the chair in the corner sat her diary, which she knew damn well hadn't been there the last time she was in the room. And on the dresser, Claire's photo stood upright on its kickstand, not flat against the wood as Meg had left it.

"What the hell happened here?" Kumiko said. She was the last to poke her head through the floor.

Meg dropped her voice. "Minnie was looking for something."

"Her personality?"

Meg bristled. "Hey. She's my friend."

Even in the candlelight, Meg could see Kumiko roll her eyes. "Could have fooled me."

Kumiko's constant snark was finally getting on Meg's nerves. "Not that I need to defend her, but Minnie's usually not like this, okay? You can go ask your new boyfriend. He was in love with her, in case you've forgotten."

"Whatever. That girl is off the rails."

"You might be too if someone stole your meds."

T.J. opened the door of the wardrobe, then checked behind the floor-length mirror. "Look, we're all under a lot of stress, okay? Nobody's exactly at their best right now." He moved to one of the beds and checked beneath its displaced mattress. "Let's just finish the search."

Meg and Kumiko waited in silence as T.J. checked under the other bed. Finding nothing, they slowly tramped back down the stairs.

"All clear?" Gunner asked. He was standing as far away from Minnie as the landing would allow.

"Yep." T.J. started down the stairs, lifting the lantern from Minnie's hand as he passed her. "Just the second floor now."

It was like a choose-your-own-adventure book. Six doors opened onto the landing: five bedrooms and a bathroom. On the left, the master suite, which took up one whole corner of the second floor. Then three doors that opened straight onto the landing—south-facing bedrooms, one with Ben's body and one that Nathan and Kenny had shared, with an adjoining bathroom between them. And at the far end of the hall, two more rooms that faced the west and north sides of the house, respectively.

"How should we do this?" Meg asked.

"Same as upstairs," T.J. said. "Someone can wait on the stairs, the rest will check the rooms. Sound good?"

Everyone murmured their assent.

"Good," T.J. said. He started toward the master suite. "Why don't I start—"

"I'll do Ben's room," Minnie interrupted. Without looking Meg in the eye, Minnie shoved the lantern in her hand and marched through the door.

"Guess we'll start here," Kumiko said.

Meg had a moment of shock when she realized Minnie was volunteering to go back into the room where her new crush was lying dead. She handed the lantern to T.J., then she hurried after her. "Minnie, wait."

Minnie stood on the other side of the bed at the spot where they'd left Ben's body. Meg's eye drifted to the floor. She saw Ben's feet lying where he'd been for hours. Meg imagined how she'd feel if it was T.J. lying there, and shuddered.

"There's no one here," Minnie said without being asked.

Meg bent down to check under the bed. "Did you check—"

"Yes!" Minnie snapped.

"Sorry, I just thought . . ."

"I can think too, you know. You don't always have to be the smart one."

"All right, all right." Meg straightened up. "How about the closet?"

"Go ahead."

Minnie stood still while Meg turned to the closet. She opened the door slowly, not quite sure what she expected to see. But all she found was Ben's duffel bag on the floor. The rest was empty.

Minnie grabbed her by the arm before she even had a chance to close the door. "Let's get out of here."

Kumiko and Gunner came through the adjoining bathroom door.

"All clear?" Gunner asked.

"Yeah," Meg said. Except for the dead body on the floor, of course.

They filed back into the hallway.

"Okay," T.J. said, trading the lantern for the candle Gunner held. "Meg and I will search the master bedroom, K and Minnie can check the other two, and Guns, you watch the stairs." He didn't wait for approval this time but grabbed Meg's free hand and ushered her into the master suite.

"Whose room is this?" she asked.

T.J. walked across the room to the dresser. "Vivian's."

"Shocking." It figured that Vivian would requisition the biggest, nicest room in the house, and probably feel as though she deserved it. Pain-in-the-ass know-it-all.

Meg caught her breath. Vivian was dead. She'd slept in that bed last night and now she was lying under a tarp on a rocky beach with a branch sticking through her chest. And Meg could be next. Or Minnie. Or T.J. The panic welled up in her again. They had to get out of there. Had to.

"You okay?" T.J. asked.

Meg shook herself. "Yeah. Yeah, I'm fine."

"You sure? Did you hear what I said?"

"Um . . . no."

T.J. turned to the dresser, then the room was suddenly awash in orange light. "More candles," he said. He lifted a small, three-tiered candelabra and handed it to her, flashing his dimpled smile. "At least we can see now."

If White Rock House hadn't held such horror for Meg, she might actually have liked the master bedroom. It had a cozy, lived-in, bed-and-breakfast feel about it. Large windows on two walls were covered in heavy damask curtains, tied back with braided tassels. The king-size bed was about the biggest Meg had ever seen, with a fully draped canopy and quilted headboard.

A large fireplace took up most of the northern wall, with a duo of overstuffed, heavily pillowed armchairs in front of it. Meg could picture herself curled up before a roaring fire, book in hand, while the storm lashed at the windows outside. It was a lovely picture, marred by the memory of five red slash marks on the wall downstairs and the corresponding body count.

T.J. started with the wall of closets on the far side of the room, so Meg headed for the bathroom, which opened onto the bedroom through wide double doors. She swore it was bigger than her bedroom at home. An enormous spa tub sat in the middle of the tiled floor, with actual steps built around it. The shower was a huge glass cage, big enough for a whole family to shower together. And there were his and hers sinks on either side of the entry. Ah, rich people.

"Anything?" T.J. called out from the other room.

Meg swept her candelabra around. "Nope." Not that there was anywhere to hide in the open, tiled space. She had just turned to leave when something shiny caught her eye.

Normally she wouldn't have thought twice about a shiny, metallic object in a bathroom, except this was in the garbage bin. Just a small, plastic can with some wadded-up paper shoved into it, but something had glistened in the candlelight as Meg swept past. She set the candelabra on the counter, crouched down, and pulled away the crumpled paper.

Beneath it was a pair of keys.

The paper in one hand, Meg carefully lifted the metal key ring out of the garbage. She recognized the emblem on the key right away. It matched the markings on the pilot's wheel. A Grand Alaskan Trawler.

For the first time in hours, Meg felt a spark of hope. They had a way off the island.

The killer must have stashed the keys someplace where he thought no one would find them—in the garbage can in the room of a dead girl. The keys had clearly been hidden in the garbage can, and if it hadn't been for the fact that Meg was carrying a bunch of candles with dancing, flickering light, she might never have caught sight of them under the wadded-up paper.

Paper. Not toilet paper, but thick, lined parchment.

It took Meg a moment realize what it was. She carefully uncrinkled the page and immediate saw the familiar handwriting.

The missing page from Claire's diary.

"T.J.!" she yelled. "T.J., I found—"

But her words were lost as the blast of a gunshot rang out from the hall.

THIRTY THREE

MEG SHOVED THE KEYS AND DIARY PAGE INTO her pocket and dashed into the bedroom. T.J. stood blocking the door.

"Oh my God," he said.

"What?" She pushed his arm aside, then dug her fingers into his sweater as she saw the body crumpled on the floor. Gunner. His eyes wide open, a single gunshot wound to the forehead, with a thick trail of blood oozing down, arching slightly over his nose.

"Oh my God." Meg's voice was barely more than a whisper. Beneath her hand, she could feel T.J. trembling.

"Gunner!" Kumiko ran down the hall and collapsed at the side of the body. She had the presence of mind to feel for a pulse, and judging by the sob, Meg guessed he was already dead.

"Dammit," T.J. said, his voice barely above a whisper. Meg looked up at him and saw a wave of pain wash over his face. His best friend was dead.

Meg pulled her eyes away from T.J., desperately searching for Minnie. There was a killer in the house, someone who was hunting them down, and Meg needed to protect Minnie as best she could.

Minnie stood at the end of the hall. She held her candle below her face and Meg could see her features clearly enough. No pain, no fear. Just nothing.

Did she do it? Did she kill Gunner?

Meg shook herself. She'd known Minnie since they were thirteen. With or without her meds, Minnie was not a killer. Meg couldn't even entertain the idea.

Meg glanced back at T.J., but he was staring at the floor in the darkness, squinting as if he was trying to make sense of something. She followed his gaze and saw what he was looking at. A dark shape. A familiar shape.

Meg caught her breath. "The gun."

Kumiko's head snapped up. She stared Meg straight in the eye. "You did this."

"Me?"

Kumiko's eye flew from Meg to T.J., then she turned toward Minnie. "One of you."

"No," Meg said. She couldn't believe that one of them was a murderer. "There's someone else in the house. There has to be."

"There's no one else here," Kumiko said. "Don't you get it? It's one of us."

Meg backed away. "No. No, I don't believe it."

Kumiko's eyes darted back and forth between the three of them. "Any of you could have shot him and slid the gun into the hall."

T.J. took a step toward her. "Any of *us*."

Kumiko sobbed and passed a hand over Gunner's face, closing his eyes. "Right," she said slowly. "Any of us."

Without warning, Kumiko lunged at the gun on the floor. Before T.J. could get to her, she was on her feet, gun pointed directly at him. "Any of us could have done it. Only I know it wasn't me." She swung the gun to Minnie, then back to T.J. as she slowly backed her way toward the stairs. "There's nobody else on this floor, so it must have been one of you."

Meg stood slightly behind T.J., one hand in her pocket tightly grasping the boat keys.

"Why would we believe you?" he asked.

Kumiko laughed. "I don't give a flaming shit if you believe me. But I know I didn't do it, so I'm getting the hell out of here before I'm the next slash on the wall."

"It's dangerous out there," T.J. said. He slowly crept toward the stairs as Kumiko backed down them.

"It's dangerous *in here*."

T.J. took another couple of steps. "It's dark and the storm could pick up at any moment."

"I'll take my chances against Mother Nature over you guys any day."

Minnie stood farther up the stairs. "They'll find you, you know. The police. You won't get away with this."

"Get away with this?" Kumiko reached the landing. She eyed the foyer, then T.J. and Meg, who were slowly following her down the stairs. "You think I did this? You people are fucking crazy. I'm out of here." She spun around and made a dash for the front door.

Meg ran down the stairs. "Kumiko, wait!"

T.J. grabbed her arm. "Let her go."

Minnie followed behind. "Good riddance."

"But the killer's still out there. He could have climbed out through one of the bedroom windows. She's not safe."

T.J. shrugged. "She's the one with the gun."

"And how do we know she's not the killer?" Minnie added.

"The killer could still be in here," Meg argued. She stubbornly clung to her theory that the killer wasn't one of them but was hiding in the house somewhere. "Look, I don't think . . ." She paused.

"What?" T.J. asked.

Meg turned back toward the foyer. She had expected to hear the door open and slam shut when Kumiko ran out. Expected to, but didn't. "Did you hear the door?"

T.J. tilted his head. "No. I didn't." His candle almost extinguished, he picked up the lantern and Meg matched his quick pace through the open hall to the foyer.

She heard it first. A noise that sounded like a cross between chattering teeth and an electric toothbrush. Then as she moved into the foyer, the smell hit her. Burning hair, like when a flyaway strand gets caught in the hair dryer. Tangy and sharp, it made her gag.

As the light from T.J.'s lantern filled the room, Meg saw Kumiko by the front door. She had her hand on the door handle, the gun discarded on the ground, but she seemed frozen. Her body taunt and rigid.

And vibrating.

"Kumiko?" Meg said, and started toward her.

T.J. grabbed her shoulder. "Don't." He pulled her back, then dashed into the study.

"What's going on?" Minnie said. Her candle had practically burned itself out.

"I—I don't know," Meg said.

T.J. ran back into the foyer and shoved the lantern in Meg's hand as he passed her carrying some sort of wooden stick. He went straight for Kumiko. Meg held the light up and watched in horror as T.J. used a wooden broom to pry Kumiko's hand off the door. It took a few seconds, but when she was finally free of it, her body instantly crumpled to the ground, and instead of the sharp odor of burning hair, the significantly more disturbing smell of burnt flesh filled the air.

"What happened?" Minnie asked.

"Electrocuted," T.J. panted. He dropped the broom to the ground then bent down next to Kumiko's body. "I . . . I don't think she made it."

Judging by the steam literally rising off Kumiko's body in the frigid house, Meg wasn't surprised.

"It's just like the diary," Minnie said. Her voice cracked. "It's true. We're being hunted. Just like you said."

"How?" Meg said. "All she did was grab the door."

T.J. reached over his head and pulled off his sweater. He wrapped it around his hand and tapped it against the door handle, once, twice. Then he gingerly turned the handle and gave it a jerk. The door swung open about halfway, then bounced as if it was tethered to something on the other side and had reached the end of its leash.

Meg slowly approached the door, holding the weakening lantern before her with a shaky hand. On the porch sat a large black box encased in a bright orange trailer, complete with wheels for easy transport. It churned and hummed like an engine. A long orange cable snaked from the machine to the door handle, where it had been stripped of its protective outer layer and the interior wires separated out and secured to the metal handle with some sort of steel clamp.

"A generator," T.J. said. "Hooked up to the door. It must have electrocuted her as soon as she touched the handle."

Meg began to tremble. The house was booby-trapped? Perfect. What was next? What was waiting for them? They had to get out of there.

Meg whipped the keys out of her pocket. "I found these upstairs."

T.J.'s eyes lit up. "The keys to the trawler?"

"What's that?" Minnie said. Meg assumed she meant the boat, but no time to explain that now. They had to move.

"Can you drive it?" Meg asked T.J. "Can you get us out of here?"

"I can try. It's got to be better than standing around waiting for one of us to be next."

"'And he didn't hesitate,'" Minnie said. "'He pushed her aside and stormed up to me. He didn't want Meg, he didn't want Minnie. He wanted me.'"

Meg slowly turned. Minnie stood behind her. She held the missing diary page in her hands.

"What did you say?" Meg asked.

"'He told me to go home,'" Minnie continued. "'He told me he would call me. He'd come to me tonight. He should be here any moment. Tom loves me. And together we'll make them all pay.'"

"What are you reading?" T.J. snapped. "Where did you find it?"

"On the floor," Minnie said. "It fell out of Meg's pocket."

The missing page from Claire's diary. But it wasn't the story T.J. told her earlier in the boathouse.

Tom. She called him Tom.

A horrible realization dawned on Meg.

T.J. was the one who spoke to Mr. Lawrence on the phone. He could have been lying.

T.J. had suggested they go down to the boathouse. He'd disappeared for ten minutes around the time Vivian was killed.

T.J. had been to the house before. He knew it better than anyone.

T.J., who knew enough about boats to have stolen the radio.

T.J. was unaccounted for during the time Nathan and Kenny must have been murdered. He was strong enough to kill them both, and athletic enough to get there and back without anyone knowing.

T.J., who carried the salad to the table that night. T.J., who conveniently slept on the sofa. T.J., who suggested they search the house and who made sure he was separated from Meg when Gunner was shot.

T. J. Fletcher. Thomas Jefferson Fletcher, as Minnie had mentioned earlier.

"Tom," Meg said out loud.

T.J.'s head snapped toward her. "Huh?"

"Thomas Jefferson." Meg backed away from him. "That's your full name, isn't it?"

"Yeah. But no one's called me Tom since I was like six."

"Oh my God."

"What? What's wrong?" T.J.'s brows pinched together over his nose. He looked utterly confused. "What is Minnie reading?"

"Meg," Minnie said, her voice breathless. "What is this?"

"The missing page from Claire's diary." Meg took a few steps toward the still smoldering body of Kumiko, facing T.J., keeping the discarded gun in her line of sight. "It was you," she said. Her voice pounded in her chest. "It was you all along."

T.J. spread his hands out. "Meg, I have no idea what you're talking about."

She swallowed hard and tried to calm herself. She was going to need all of her wits if she was going to get out of the current situation. She had the keys in her hand—a means of escape. All she and Minnie had to do was get to the boathouse and she'd figure out a way to get the boat moving. They could make it to Roche Harbor, she knew they could. She just needed to get to the gun. . . .

"Meg?" T.J. looked genuinely confused.

"You lied to me about what happened that night," Meg said. "That's the missing page from Claire's diary. I found it upstairs in the garbage with the keys. Where you put them."

"Meg," T.J. said with a shake of his head. "I didn't. I swear to God I didn't."

"You lied."

"Baby, listen to me. You know me. You know I didn't do this."

Meg ignored him. "You tore out the last page of the diary so no one would know the truth. Maybe you killed her, too."

Meg's eyes locked onto his. She saw a moment of confusion pass over his face, as if he couldn't quite get what she was implying. Then his eyes shifted. It was just an instant. A flit of his pupils away from Meg's face. But she knew immediately what he was looking at.

The gun.

Meg was closer. She dropped the lantern, letting it clank across the tiled floor, then spun around and plucked the gun off the ground. She whipped her arm around and held the gun extended, pointed straight at T.J.

He'd taken a few steps toward her, but froze as soon as she aimed the gun at him.

"Meg," he said. "Don't do this. You have to trust me."

"Uh-huh," Meg said. She shuffled back toward Minnie. "Sure."

"What are you doing?" Minnie squeaked. "Meg, what are you doing?"

Meg set her jaw. She felt hurt, betrayed. T.J. had been playing her all along. "It's him, Minnie. Don't you get it?"

"T.J.?"

"No, the guy standing behind him." Was she really that dumb?

"That's not possible," Minnie said.

T.J.'s eyes were pleading. "Minnie, tell her. Tell her what happened on Homecoming night."

"I—" Minnie stopped. "I don't remember."

"Goddammit, Meg," T.J. said. "That diary page is a fake. I swear I told you the truth."

Meg wasn't buying it. He'd been playing her since the beginning. "Do I look stupid to you?"

"Not even a little."

Meg nodded at Minnie. "Mins, pick up the lantern."

"But—"

"Do it!" She was tired of Minnie's arguing. This wasn't the time. Minnie jumped and scurried across the foyer to retrieve the lantern. "Good, now get behind me."

"Meg," T.J. said. "You know me. You know me better than anyone." He took a step closer to them.

"Don't move!" Meg barked. She cupped the handle of the gun with both hands. She was shaking. *Come on, Meg.* She needed to focus on keeping her hands steady.

T.J. was stronger and faster than the two of them combined, but she had the weapon. Could she use it?

This wasn't the T.J. she knew, or thought she knew. He'd killed nine people, maybe more. And he'd kill Minnie and her, too, if Meg didn't stop him. She'd do whatever she had to do to protect herself and Minnie. In her heart, she knew what that meant.

T.J. shook his head. "Someone's manipulating us. I think you were right. There's someone else in the house."

"I don't believe you."

"Think about it," he said. "Why would I be killing people? I had no connection to Claire. Nothing."

Meg started to move backward down the hall. "Minnie, head for the kitchen. Stay behind me."

"I'm in the diary too, remember? Why would I be in there if I was behind all this?"

"You could have planted it. Written it yourself to throw us off."

"That barely makes sense."

"Then who, T.J., huh?" She couldn't think logically. All she could focus on was saving herself and Minnie. "Kumiko was right. There's no one else in the house."

"Meg," Minnie started. She stood right at Meg's shoulder.

"What?"

"Meg, I need to tell you something."

Minnie's voice was so calm, so serious. That was a rarity. Meg glanced at her, taking her eyes off T.J. for an instant.

Only an instant, but T.J. took the opportunity to lunge for the gun.

Minnie screamed.

Meg could just hear her over the gunshot.

THIRTY FOUR

T.J. WHIRLED. HIS BODY SEEMED TO PIVOT OF ITS own accord, as if the force of the bullet striking him in the chest swung his entire being around. He staggered away from Meg, just a few limping steps, with his back to her. She heard him groan, then he collapsed to his knees and flopped face-first onto the white tile floor.

Meg stood frozen. She still held the gun in both hands, her arms outstretched. Her whole body felt tense, like every single muscle was engaged. Minnie's shrieks seemed to come from far away, muffled and dampened. All Meg could hear was the pounding of her own heart.

She'd shot him. She'd shot the boy she'd been in love with for as long as she could remember.

You had to, Meg told herself. *He killed everyone. He would have killed you, too.*

Meg forced herself to believe it. She had no choice.

"You . . . ," Minnie panted. "You shot him."

"Yeah."

"Why did you shoot him?"

"I had to." She did, didn't she? She was protecting Minnie, protecting herself. She *had* to shoot T.J. She didn't have a choice. Right?

"But . . ." Minnie let the lantern drop to the floor. "But . . ." She took several steps toward T.J.'s motionless body before Meg stopped her.

"We have to get out of here."

Minnie's eyes never left T.J.'s body. "Why did you shoot him?"

"Minnie!" Meg grabbed her by the shoulders and turned her away from T.J. "We have to get off this island. Now."

Minnie's eyes were huge, disbelieving. "You killed him. You killed Teej."

Meg glanced at T.J.'s body. She'd closed her eyes the instant she squeezed the trigger and had no idea where she'd shot him. If he was dead, then they didn't have anything to worry about. If he wasn't and was just lying there playing possum, they needed to get down to the boathouse as fast as they could. Whatever Minnie's damage, it could wait until they were safely off the island.

"Come on." Meg grabbed the lantern off the floor and shoved it in Minnie's hands. "We need to get out of here. Now."

"But . . ."

Meg didn't wait for Minnie to argue, just grabbed her hand and dragged her out of the foyer. Meg rushed through the living room and kitchen to the back door. She wasn't going to risk getting barbecued like Kumiko, so she kicked at the door with her foot TV-cop-style, until the aging frame splintered and the door swung open.

Once outside, the night seemed even darker. In the black woods behind White Rock House, there were no white walls for the feeble light of the lantern to bounce off. Meg felt small and alone. And paranoid. Every noise sent a wave of panic through her. A crackling twig, the rustling of leaves as the wind gusted through the trees. She was positive someone was following them.

Meg pushed the panic away. T.J. wasn't going to be following them, and there was no one else on the island. She just had to get to the boat and figure out how to get the engine started. She'd deal with piloting the thing later. Even being adrift in the channel was better than being stuck on that island.

At least the rain had stopped. As the trees thinned out at the bottom of the hill, Meg could see a dozen stars in the sky between gaps in the thinning cloud cover. It was the first time she'd seen a light in the sky since before they'd boarded the ferry in Mukilteo. It gave her hope.

The wooden walkways that led to the boathouse were still damp, but the slippery layer of water that coated their surfaces earlier in the day had evaporated. Even in the darkness, Meg felt more confident. One hand on Minnie, one hand grasping the set of keys. They were going to make it. They were going to survive.

She kept forcing images of T.J. out of her mind. His dimples when he smiled at her. His excitement when he told her they'd both be going to college in LA. The feeling of his callused hands holding hers, his strong arm around her back pulling her body into his, his full, soft lips pressed desperately against her own.

"STOP IT!" Meg said out loud.

Minnie stopped. "What?"

"Nothing." Meg nudged her on. "Almost there."

The last thing she wanted to do right now was think about what a complete and total idiot she'd been. T.J. Fletcher in love with her? Hell no. He'd just been using her, and she'd been pathetic enough to fall for it because he'd told her exactly what she wanted to hear. Now she was his accomplice. He used her feelings for him to forward his own plans for murder.

His plans. And what were they exactly? Meg winced. T.J. had been right: it was the only part that didn't make sense. Why? Why had he killed all those people? Was there some relationship between him and Claire that no one knew about? She found that hard to believe, and yet it had to be something personal. These murders and the way they'd been brought about were absolutely 100 percent personal.

Meg felt the tears well up in her eyes. She'd loved him and he'd just been using her.

Once again, she forced herself to focus. It had to make sense somehow, she was just missing something. Not that it mattered. All she needed to think about now was getting them off the damn island.

With the exception of the tarp that now covered Vivian's body, the boathouse was exactly as she'd left it. The lantern illuminated enough of the wooden structure to show her that the boat seemed to be there and intact. A good sign, since T.J. had managed to sabotage everything else in the house. The boarding gate was still open, and Meg hopped on board, then grabbed the lantern from Minnie's hand and helped her step across the gap onto the deck.

"Okay," Meg said. "This way." She ducked into the pilothouse and rested the lantern and the gun on the wooden console next to the helm. "We just need to figure out where the ignition is and we'll be home free."

Minnie stood silently in the doorway, her arms wrapped tightly across her body—one up around her shoulder, one around her waist. Meg couldn't tell if she was cold or in shock.

"Don't worry, Mins," she said, trying to sound confident. "We're almost out of here." Meg fished the keys out of her pocket. They clattered in her hand as she scanned the control panel for anything that looked like a key ignition. She kept talking, more to calm her own nerves than Minnie's, but anything was better than the wretched silence. "We'll be home before you know it. And the police will take care of everything. We're going to make it, Mins. We're going to be—"

"He said it was you."

Meg looked up from the control panel. Minnie stood in the doorway of the pilothouse, the gun grasped in both hands, pointed straight at Meg. She shook visibly, and even in the dim light, Meg could see that Minnie had broken out in a full sweat.

"He said it was you," Minnie repeated. "That you'd killed everyone."

"T.J.?"

"He said you were jealous of me. That's why you pretended to be my friend. That's why you were leaving me to go to LA."

Meg was exasperated. Totally not the time for this conversation. "Minnie, we've talked about this."

"He said you'd try to kill me."

"Minnie!" Meg wasn't sure if the adrenaline of firing a gun had gone to her head or not, but suddenly her anger trumped the weapon pointed directly at her chest. "Minnie, when have I ever done anything but help you? Always. I've been there. Usually the only one there."

Minnie wasn't listening. "Then he made me read your diary. And I saw . . ." Her voice choked off with a sob.

"T.J. and me," Meg said, completing the thought. "I know. I should have told you the truth but I didn't want to hurt you."

"You loved him," Minnie said simply.

"Yes."

"And you shot him."

The pain of that reality hit Meg afresh. Her body tensed and her heart ached. "Yes."

Minnie sucked in an erratic breath. "I'm so sorry," she sobbed. "I'm so sorry."

A creepy feeling trickled down Meg's neck, a cross between fear and disbelief. "Sorry because you're about to shoot me?"

"This is all my fault. I shouldn't have made us come here. And I shouldn't have listened to him."

"Mins, it's okay. T.J. had us all fooled."

Minnie lowered the gun. "Not T.J."

Meg's mouth went dry. Not T.J.? "Minnie, what the hell are you talking about?"

"It wasn't T.J.," Minnie said, her voice calm and even. "The killer is—"

There was a click, followed by a rush of air. Then a crunch, like a knife passing through bone, a flash of metal followed by a splattering of blood as something ripped through the pale white skin of Minnie's throat.

Minnie's eyes bulged. She dropped the gun and both of her hands flew to her throat, clawing at the object that protruded from her neck.

"Mins!"

Meg could see it clear as day, glistening wet and lethal in the dying light. It was an arrow, thick and metallic, just like the one that had killed Nathan. Minnie's eyes met Meg's; Meg could see the disbelief reflected there. Minnie opened her mouth to scream, but no sound came out, only a thick stream of blood that gushed over her lips and down her chin.

Minnie staggered toward Meg before her feet gave way and she lost all control, pitching forward into Meg's arms. Meg tried to ease her onto the floor as Minnie's body shuddered, her eyes wild with fear and horror.

"Mins, oh my God. It's okay. It's going to be okay." What was she supposed to do? Pull the arrow out? Mouth-to-mouth?

Minnie sputtered and gagged, spitting blood as she tried to form words. Her arms flailed, pulling at Meg. Her eyes pleaded for help.

"Minnie? Minnie?" Oh my God, what could she do? Tears welled up in her eyes. There was no one to call, no one to save them. They were so close to safety. Too close for it to all end now. "Mins, stay with me!"

Then Minnie's entire body seized up. She made a deep gurgling sound, as if her lungs were inhaling a gallon of blood. Her eyes rolled back in her head and blood poured out of her mouth. Minnie's limbs went stiff and her body convulsed so violently Meg could barely keep her hands on Minnie's shoulders. She kicked at the deck of the ship, arching her body forward, then she shuddered and fell lifeless in Meg's arms.

Meg choked back a sob, but she barely had time to process the fact that her best friend was dead.

"Sad way to go," a voice said. "Drowning in your own blood can't be pleasant."

Meg swallowed her grief as she rose to her feet. She knew that voice. But it was impossible. It couldn't be.

She turned and saw a bleached-blond head standing on the floor of the boathouse, smiling at her.

Ben.

THIRTY FIVE

"YOU?"

Ben smiled. "Me."

"That's impossible. You're—"

"Dead?"

Meg nodded, her throat suddenly dry.

"Yeah, not so much."

He seemed so easygoing, so matter-of-fact, as if he were telling her about the latest X-Men movie he'd seen, or recapping last night's Seahawks game. He stood on the wooden floor of the boathouse, dressed all in black—long-sleeved shirt, gloves, skinny jeans, and boots. He cradled a crossbow on his left forearm, and in the dim glow of the lantern, Meg could just see a flash of metal in his right hand. Another arrow. He was rearming.

"It was you all along," Meg said.

Ben shrugged. "Damn, you got me!"

The pieces began to fall into place. He'd faked his own death. After that, he could have killed everyone else totally undetected. He'd removed the radio and the paint from the *Nemesis*. He'd sabotaged the handrail and maybe even convinced Vivian to go down to the boathouse after them. He was the one she heard on the patio. It was the perfect plan.

Her face must have registered the realization. "Awesome, right?" He beamed at her.

Meg was horrified. He looked positively proud.

"You're smarter than I gave you credit for. You almost caught me twice. Once with your little internet stunt. I'd cut the cable wire but missed the internet. Leave it to the writer to have a laptop with her. Had to tell Minnie I was running to the bathroom, then hung out Lori's bedroom window to cut the internet cable. Just in time, apparently."

If only Ben hadn't been up there with Minnie when Meg went to get her laptop, maybe no one else would have died. The thought made her sick.

"Then after I killed Nathan and Kenny," Ben continued, "you almost caught me coming back into the house. I made it into the study just in time. Hid under Lori's body, which was less than pleasant, I'm not ashamed to say. Then while Minnie was screaming, I slipped out the back and climbed up the side of the patio to my bedroom window." He wagged a finger at her. "Not easy, because of you. Still." Ben smiled. "I won."

His tone made her skin crawl.

Ben heaved the crossbow over his shoulder and rested his other hand on his hip. "But I'm disappointed. I was really hoping for a murder-suicide. You offing Minnie, Minnie offing you. Either or." His eyes lowered to Minnie's body. "In the end she proved slightly more attached to you than I had anticipated, even with the jealousy and lack of meds."

Meg caught her breath. "You stole them."

Ben cocked his head. "Of course! I was hoping for a super-off-the-reservation meltdown so I stole them a week ago. Snuck into the house while Minnie and her parents were at church and replaced them with sugar pills so she'd be a total train wreck by the time she got here. Stealing the bottle from her luggage was just for effect. And, you know, so I could blame it on you."

Meg clenched her teeth. Poor Minnie. No wonder she'd been so on edge, so snippy and impatient all week.

"Watching her downward spiral into paranoia has been one of my favorite things about this weekend. And I just want you to know," he continued, the mock concern returning to his voice, "that you shooting your little boyfriend back there *totally* made up for not getting to watch Minnie kill you both. It was epic."

Meg felt a wave of cold panic sweep over her. T.J. was completely innocent and she'd killed him. She thought of the look on his face when she was pointing the gun at him. He was begging with her, pleading with her to trust him. But she was so sure it was him, and so scared. She should have listened to him. Because of her, both T.J. and Minnie were dead.

And Ben had done it all.

Panic gave way to rage. She wanted to launch herself at him, gouge his eyes out, throttle him with her bare hands. She gripped the rail so tightly she thought she might snap the metal in half, but she just stood there. Unable to move, unable to act. Just like always.

Ben laughed. "You *want* do to something, but you can't. You never can. You're the thinker, but actually *doing* things, not so much. You leave that to everyone else."

Meg tried to control the flush she knew was racing up her neck to her face. She didn't want him to know he was right.

"See?" he laughed.

Dammit.

The cool collectedness in his voice made her blood run cold. He'd been manipulating them the whole time. What was he going to do next? She had to think. Try to get a step ahead of it. It was her only chance.

"Which brings me back to my first point—I'm *so* glad you're Number Nine," Ben said.

Meg needed to find her voice. Ben wanted to talk, wanted to show what a sick genius he was? Fine. As long as he was still talking, she was still alive. And suddenly, she wanted to stay alive more than anything. Like she owed it to Minnie and T.J. and everyone else to win this game.

She had to.

Ben couldn't get away with it.

"W-why?" she asked, stumbling over her words. "Why us?"

"Well, ideally, I mean, in my fantasies about this weekend, it was you and Minnie left as Eight and Nine. You having figured out what was going on based on the clues I left you. . . ."

Clues. Meg caught her breath. The diary.

"Yes, Claire's diary. I kind of hoped it would look enough like yours. That was just luck."

"You planted it with my stuff."

He smirked.

"And you forged the last page so I'd think . . . I'd think . . ."

"You'd think your boyfriend was the killer? Brilliant, right?"

"You're sick."

"It makes you more comfortable to think so, doesn't it? That I'd have to be insane to do all this? Not true. I'm saner than your little friend down there."

Meg's eye drifted down to Minnie's face, contorted, bloody, lifeless. Heavy tears cascaded down Meg's cheeks. Her best friend was gone.

"I had this glorious scene in mind," Ben continued, "where you figure out that I was the one knocking everybody off and try to tell Minnie, but she's so far over the edge with paranoia and insanity that she kills you anyway, then kills herself." He sighed and shook his head. "Leaving me, Number Ten, the winner. I had her almost completely convinced you were the killer. Right until the very end, I think. Oh well. No murder-suicide, but it *was* fun to watch her pull the gun on you."

Meg wiped the tears from her cheeks with the back of her hand. She was disgusted at the idea that Ben had been fantasizing about all these deaths for God only knows how long. Her stomach clenched and she had to fight back the urge to vomit.

"Like I said, you surprised me. But in the end, you didn't quite figure it all out, did you?"

"I figured out enough." *Keep him talking, Meg.* Keep him talking then figure out an escape route. "That everyone here was connected to Claire Hicks somehow. That you were killing us off in the same ways you thought we'd wronged her."

"*Thought* you'd wronged her? *Thought?*" Ben roared. The ferocity came out of nowhere, and Meg involuntarily took a step back. "The nine of you killed her. You're all murderers."

"Look who's talking."

Ben's dark brows lowered. "I'm not a murderer. I'm a vigilante. I'm bringing down the swift sword of justice."

"Justice?" Meg couldn't believe what she was hearing. "Really? What, because Kumiko blamed Claire for a failed science experiment and Lori beat her out for a choir solo?"

"Kumiko went to the science teacher and asked permission to do the experiment again, this time without a partner. She got an A while Claire still got a failing grade. She was stuck in the remedial class the next semester, with a bunch of freaks and morons. And Lori didn't beat Claire out for anything. She stole that solo by lying to my sis—"

Ben caught himself but it was too late. Meg had heard what he started to say. "Sister. Oh my God."

Ben didn't say a word, but he didn't need to. Meg's brain whirled. She looked him directly in the eye: those bright blue eyes, pale skin, sharp jaw. Of course. How could she not have seen it? The hair had thrown her off, but if you took away Ben's bleached-blond hair and made it dark, practically black . . . just like Claire.

"You're Tom," she said. It wasn't a question. "You're Claire's brother."

He flinched.

"It was you who caused those accidents at school, Bobby's car brakes and Tiffany's infection." Another realization dawned on Meg. "But . . . the real Ben. The blond guy in the diary. Who was—"

"She sent me that diary the night she killed herself." Tom's voice had lost the false lightness. It was lower now, raspy and tight. "I realized then that she had to be avenged. She wasn't that girl. She was happy. She just wanted to fit in at Roosevelt, Mariner, even at Kamiak. She was kind and sweet, but you guys beat that out of her."

"And you killed Ben." Meg recalled Ben's taunts from Claire's diary. *Burn*. The body in the locker room at Mariner. Burned. "You killed him and took his place."

"Don't worry, I made sure he suffered appropriately, just like the rest of you."

"How is any of this appropriate?"

Tom shrugged. "Claire sent her diary with a note. *Make them understand what they did, Tom. All of them*. So that's what I'm doing. Making you understand."

"It's not our fault she killed herself."

"YOU KILLED HER!" he roared. "Understand that. You killed my sister. She was special, sensitive, and trusting, and you killed her. All of you."

"You can't really believe that."

"I *know it.*" His voice was shaky now. The emotion creeping in. At least something she was saying had gotten to him. "She was better than all of you and you never understood her."

"I never even knew her!" Meg's eyes darted around the boat, looking for a way to escape. She caught sight of the gun Minnie had dropped when she was shot, lying in a pool of Minnie's blood by the stairs that led down to the main deck. She squeezed her eyes shut, holding back another wave of tears. Minnie had died for nothing, and Meg was the only one left to tell the authorities what really happened on Henry Island. Meg opened her eyes and glanced back at the gun. If she could just get . . .

"Don't move," Tom snarled. He unshouldered his crossbow and pointed it straight at her. "Don't even think about reaching for that gun."

Meg felt the hope drain from her. This was it. This was the end. But she wasn't going to give him the satisfaction of seeing her fear.

She thrust out her chin in defiance. "You won't get away with it."

"Meg," he said. "I already have."

THIRTY SIX

MEG WASN'T A PSYCHIC. THERE WASN'T AN intuitive or supernatural bone in her body. But somehow she picked up on Tom's intention, saw it in his eyes or his movements. Even as his finger pulled the trigger, her body was in motion. No time to think about it, no time for a logical plan of action. She threw herself to the right, diving into the wheelhouse. She could actually feel the force of the arrow. It missed her head by inches. As she rolled on her side, she heard it puncture the wooden frame.

Thank God he was going for a kill shot. If he hadn't aimed for her head, she might have been hit.

Tom swore.

She heard him toss the crossbow onto the ground. He must be out of arrows. Well, that was something. Time to move.

She leaped to her feet and ran to the captain's chair. The keys were still in the ignition, and as she frantically tried to turn the engine over, she said a silent prayer promising to go to church with her mom every day for the rest of her life if only the damn engine would start.

"The harder you make it," Tom said, "the worse you'll suffer, I promise. Just come out and let me shoot you."

She felt the boat shift.

Oh my God. He was climbing aboard.

Meg spun around, frantically searching for a place to hide just as a gunshot rang out. She instinctively hit the floor as the port window of the wheelhouse shattered. Broken glass sprinkled across the cabin floor. Shit. She'd forgotten about the gun.

Meg huddled behind the captain's chair and forced herself to think as rationally as possible. Forget the crazy maniac trying to kill you. Her eyes drifted to the dark outline of Minnie, lying lifeless on the deck outside the wheelhouse. She wanted to give up. To give in.

No! She shook herself, trying desperately to clear her head. *Focus, Meg.*

She had two choices. There was the staircase leading belowdecks from the wheelhouse. It was the fastest and surest escape, but also the one Tom would probably follow. And once he had her below deck in the dark, she'd pretty much be trapped. The second option was the door on the starboard side of the wheelhouse. As best as Meg could remember, it led to a balcony that stretched around the front of the boat. Maybe if Tom went below she could lower herself to the main deck and escape before he even realized she was gone? It was worth a shot.

Meg cringed. Bad choice of words.

As quickly and quietly as she could, Meg crawled across the floor of the boathouse. She had to bite her lip to keep from crying out as shards of broken glass cut into her palms and knees, digging deep into her flesh. The three feet across the wheelhouse felt like three miles, and her hands and legs were bloody by the time she reached the starboard door. She silently unlatched it, then pushed the metal door open a fraction of an inch. By some stroke of luck, the hinges swung open silently. Without a second thought, Meg slipped out onto the balcony, then carefully closed the door behind her.

Just in time. She barely got the door completely closed when she heard a crunching sound. Boots on broken glass.

Meg hardly dared to breathe. She crouched on the far side of the door, her hand still gripping the handle. Had he seen her? Had he seen the door close? Her heart thundered so loudly in her ears she was positive he could hear it. She waited, half expecting a bullet to shatter the window above her head, or for the door she leaned against to come crashing open as Tom barreled through. Her legs burned. Her palms stung with a mixture of sweat and blood.

Crunch, crunch, crunch. Then his footsteps sounded more hollow. *Thud, thud, thud.*

He was going downstairs.

Yes!

As soon as Tom's muffled footsteps faded from earshot, Meg sprang to her feet.

She tiptoed around to the front of the pilothouse, crouching low and trying to keep her head below the cockpit windows. If she could just make it to the port side of the yacht, she was pretty sure she could jump onto the floor of the boathouse. And then she'd run. And keep running. That was the extent of her plan.

She had just rounded the front of the pilothouse when gunshots erupted from the darkness. The window above her shattered. Meg screamed and ducked back behind the pilothouse, covering her head with her arms as broken glass rained down on her. She wasn't sure how many shots he fired, but the next sound Meg heard was a shallow clicking.

No more bullets.

Finally. Finally something was going her way.

"Shit," Tom swore from somewhere near the back of the boat. He was between her and the safety of the darkened boathouse.

She climbed over the rail of the pilothouse and lowered herself onto the foredeck below. At the bow of the boat, there was a small inverted dinghy mounted on a rack. She crawled beneath it, then wedged herself behind the winch that lowered the anchor, right in the pointed bow. It was an obvious hiding place and it wouldn't take him long to find her. She needed to think.

Meg felt around her in the darkness. Was there anything she could use as a weapon? A coil of thick rope, the taut chain attached to the anchor, a life preserver hanging from the bulwark. So unless she was roping sheep or going overboard, she was out of luck. Perfect.

But instead of footsteps pounding toward her hiding place, she felt the weight of the boat shift again. Tom was climbing off.

She heard a clanging sound and a groan, before Tom spoke. "I meant what I said, Meg." He sounded out of breath. "I'm going to make you suffer. After your little friend over there, you deserve it most of all."

Meg poked her head around the dinghy and squinted into the darkness. What was he doing? "How do you figure?"

"You were there. You know."

She heard a splashing noise, like he was throwing water onto the deck of the boat. Then the smell hit her. Gasoline.

He was going to burn her alive.

For one sick moment, she almost wished she was Minnie, lying there dead on the deck of the boat. *No, don't think that*. She had to stay calm. She could figure a way out. She just had to think.

And keep Tom talking.

"Look, I don't know what game you're playing," she said, mustering up as much false bravado as she could manage. "But I have no idea what you're talking about."

Meg crawled out from her hiding place. There was just enough light from the failing lantern in the pilothouse for her to see over the side of the boat. There were only a few inches of clearance between the starboard rail and the side of the boathouse, but up where the bow curved inward there was a little bit more space, especially between heaves of the waves. If she timed it right, she could probably jump into the water without being crushed between the boat and wall, and maybe she could swim beneath the boathouse and get back onshore. Maybe.

It was the only chance she had.

"Fine," Tom said. She could hear the impatience in his voice. "Let me refresh your faulty memory. Homecoming night."

Homecoming. There it was again. Maybe this was all her fault after all? If she'd just gone to the dance with T.J., maybe Minnie wouldn't have attacked Claire? And now they were all dead: Claire, Minnie, T.J., and most likely Meg too. All because she'd been afraid to confront her best friend.

She heard Tom flicking a lighter, then the entire boathouse was aglow in orange light. She peeked around the side of the dinghy and saw him standing with a homemade torch in hand, his shirt tied around an oar, doused in gasoline, she guessed. She was running out of time.

"I'm sure to you and Minnie and your intellectually challenged dates, what you did that night barely registered on your scale of importance, but it was an arrow through my sister's heart. Pardon the pun."

"That's not a pun," Meg said. She couldn't stop herself; the words just flew out of her mouth. Even though she was about to go up in flames Joan of Arc–style, she was tired of feeling like a victim. If she was going out, she was going out swinging.

"SHUT UP!" he roared.

Way to go, Meg. Poke the angry man-eating lion with a stick, why don't you. But he was still talking, which gave her more time to try and read the timing of the heaving boat. The more she stalled, the better her chances.

"I don't know," she said, trying to sound unimpressed. "I mean, killing a bunch of us idiots off shouldn't be that hard."

Tom laughed. "Not hard. But brilliant. Do you have any idea the months of planning that went into this? Preparing the house, luring you all here, dealing with the Taylors . . . All for justice."

"Not for the Taylors," Meg said. "Unless they stole a choir solo from Claire too?"

"Collateral damage," Tom said.

"I'm sure their family won't see it that way."

"Had to be done. It was the only way the plan worked. Every detail, every contingency had to be prepared for. By me. Who pretended to be Mr. Lawrence on the phone? I did. No one even knew I'd left the house. Climbed out my bedroom window and was across the isthmus and back in fifteen minutes. And who made sure that Jessica and her friends were all invited to a different party this weekend? Yeah, I thought of that, too, so if any of you brought it up to her, she'd think that's what you were talking about. Hacking into Jessica's Facebook account, dummying Tara's cell phone to invite Kumiko, drugging the beers so you'd all sleep through Lori's murder."

"What?"

"Exactly," Tom laughed. "Brilliant, right?" It was. "I couldn't have one of you waking up while I was hauling her carcass up to the rafters, could I? I thought of everything."

Meg saw an opening. A chink in Tom's thick bullshit coat of armor. "Not everything."

"I'm sorry?"

"You didn't think of everything. You missed one really, really big thing."

"Impossible."

"Nope." Meg laughed. "I wasn't there Homecoming night."

"Yes, you were."

"Nope. Sorry."

"Claire said you were." For the first time, Tom sounded less than confident. "She told me she was going to confront you and T.J."

"Maybe she meant to, but I canceled on T.J. that morning. I stayed home. *I wasn't there.*"

Silence. Clearly this was the one outcome Tom hadn't accounted for. Still, it wasn't like it mattered. He couldn't exactly let her go, and he'd already shown with the Taylors that he was willing to kill innocent people in order to avenge his sister. Meg concentrated on the motion of the boat. It was now or never.

"Whatever," Tom said. "You're guilty by association."

Great logic, crazy. Meg threw a leg over the rail. She wasn't sure this was going to work but it was better to smash her head on the side of the boat than go up in flames. She took a breath, trying to brace herself for the cold water.

Tom cleared his throat. "Enough. Meg Pritchard, it's time to say good—"

A roar interrupted him. "Get away from her!"

THIRTY SEVEN

MEG SPRINTED TO THE PORT SIDE OF THE BOAT in time to see T.J. launch himself at Tom, hitting him square in the stomach with his shoulder, like a defensive end taking out the quarterback.

"T.J.!" Meg cried, her heart thundering in her chest. She couldn't believe it. He was alive.

Tom was just as surprised, clearly not expecting there to be anyone else on the island. The force of the blow knocked the wind out of him. He dropped the torch as he flew through the air, and Meg heard them both grunt as they careened into the pile of gas cans.

T.J. rolled off the side of the pile into a puddle of pooling gasoline on the floor. He pushed himself up to his knees, using just one arm. The other was tucked up by his chest. Meg could see a large dark spot on his sweater near the collarbone and thanked God she had absolutely no aim. She'd managed to shoot him in the shoulder, wounding him but not killing him.

Tom leaped to his feet and ran at T.J. Meg barely had time to react.

"Look out!"

But T.J. must have been weakened by his injury. He barely raised his head at Meg's warning, and Tom kicked him in the stomach with such force that T.J.'s whole body lifted off the ground.

"I knew I should have checked for a pulse," Tom snarled.

T.J. staggered to his feet. "I was playing possum," he panted. He turned his head and spat. "Wanted to see who was still alive in the house. Wanted to know whose ass I was going to kick."

T.J. swung his fist, but Tom easily avoided it. Whatever strength T.J. had mustered for the initial attack had drained out of him. He struggled to maintain his balance as his blow missed Tom's face. Then Tom retaliated with a vicious punch to T.J.'s jaw.

T.J. reeled and fell back against the wall of the boathouse, then crumpled to his knees. Tom was on him in a flash. He pounded on the side of T.J.'s head with his fist. Over and over.

"Not so tough now, huh? Not the big man anymore?"

T.J. tried to fight back but his strength had abandoned him. Tom straightened up and in the flickering light of the dying torch Meg could see him smile. "I wish my sister could see you now. Pathetic."

Get up, Meg wished with all her heart. *Get up, T.J. Please.*

But he didn't. Tom shoved his hand into his pocket, and Meg heard the clicking of his lighter. He held the flame in front of his face. "Good-bye, Mr. Football."

They say there are moments when time seems to slow down.

Suddenly you can see things clearly, a moment of unobstructed understanding. Meg saw Tom standing there over T.J., the lighter poised in his hand. Tom, who had killed her best friend before her very eyes, who had destroyed so many lives, who had manipulated her into trying to kill the boy she loved. He'd taken enough. She was not going to stand there and let him win.

Something in her snapped.

Meg heard a roar, a scream that was at once primal and terrifying. It must have come from her own throat, though she was never quite sure about that. In the same moment, she hiked her foot up on the bulwark and pushed off with a strength she didn't know she possessed, launching herself at Tom. All the fury and rage that had been bubbling beneath the surface erupted. She landed square on his back, knocking them both to the floor.

Meg's hand locked onto Tom's wrist. The lighter was still aflame, and all Meg could focus on was keeping it away from T.J. They rolled across the wooden deck of the boathouse, and as they spun she managed to knock the lighter from his hand. It flew through the air and landed on the deck of the boat.

It took half a second for the gasoline-drenched aft deck to burst into flames. The fire raced up the port side walkway, up the short ladder to the pilothouse, and down the curved lines of the bow.

Meg started to get up, but Tom was faster. He was on top of her before she could get to her feet, his hands wrapped around her neck. "I told you I'd make you suffer." His long fingers dug into her throat, cutting off her air.

Meg tried to pry his fingers away, but he was too strong. She reached out with her arms, searching for anything she could use as a weapon. Her lungs burned and she felt as if Tom was going to squeeze her head off as she stretched her fingers, praying for a miracle.

Then she felt it. Something cool and metallic. A gas can.

With all the strength she had left, Meg lunged to her right, wrapped her hand around the handle of the can, and swung it at Tom's head.

He grunted, and his grip on her throat lessened enough for her to catch her breath. She swung again, harder this time, and he ducked, pulling his body away from her. That was what she needed. Meg wedged a knee up between their bodies and kicked Tom square in the stomach.

He flew off her, staggering backward toward the boat. It was engulfed in flames. The heat was intense, and the roof of the boathouse was already ablaze. Burning roof tiles fell to the wooden dock on which they stood, igniting the spilled gasoline that sprang to life with dancing flames. They raced across the dock, following the trail of fuel from Tom's mad frenzy to douse the boat. Before Meg knew it, Tom was surrounded by the flames, trapping him between her and the burning shell of the boat.

Meg backed away. Tom tried to dart through the wall of fire, but he must have gotten a significant amount of gasoline on his clothes. The sleeve of his shirt caught fire first, then the leg of his jeans. He tried to pat the fire out with his gloved hand but that only spread it faster.

In a moment of horror, Tom's eyes locked onto Meg's. She could see in his face the realization, a man coming to terms with his own death. But there was no fear. In fact, Tom smiled at her, then calmly walked through the wall of flames, his arms outstretched toward her.

He was going to take her with him.

Meg backed up, desperate for an escape, and kicked something with her foot. The oar Tom had rigged up as a torch. She snatched it off the ground and ran at Tom. She jabbed the oar into his chest so fiercely she heard him gasp as the air was sucked out of his lungs, then, with a final effort, heaved him back into the middle of the flames.

Tom stumbled, flailing his arms as fire consumed his body. Then he tripped and fell back into the conflagration that was the boat. Meg heard a high-pitched scream—more of rage than of pain—and then Tom Hicks disappeared into a wall of flame.

She'd done it. She'd saved T.J. and herself. She'd won.

As the fire swallowed the whole of the boathouse, Meg heaved T.J. off the floor and half dragged, half carried him out into the night.

THIRTY EIGHT

MEG SHIVERED AND PULLED THE THIN BLANKET up around her ears.

"Cold?" T.J. asked.

"Nope," Meg lied. She looked down at him even though she could barely see his face. "Just tired."

"You're a horrible liar."

It was true, and Meg made no attempt to refute it. She was freezing cold and fighting desperately to hide any sign of it. Meg lifted her head and stared out into the darkness of the night. Right now they needed to keep a positive attitude. Plus number one, they were still alive, though T.J. had a bullet lodged in his shoulder and had lost a lot of blood. *No, stay positive,* Meg said to herself. Right. Still alive.

Plus number two, it had stopped raining. They sat on a soggy wooden dock with nothing but flimsy blankets to protect them from the cold of night, but it was true—no more rain. Yay.

She tried to hold on to those two positives in a vain attempt to keep her mind off the horror of what had happened. Her best friend, dead. Violently. Pointlessly. Meg couldn't save her. In the end, she'd only been able to save T.J., and even then, just barely.

They'd sat on the rocks near the pyre that had been the boathouse until the last embers died. At least it was warm, and besides, neither of them wanted to go back up to the house. Eventually, though, Meg had to. T.J. needed to stay warm if he was going to survive the night. She didn't stay in the house a second longer than she had to, grabbing a few blankets from the living room and a bottle of Advil from the kitchen.

Oh, and the longest, sharpest knife she could find. She'd seen Tom go up in flames as the boathouse collapsed around her. But it didn't mean she totally and completely believed he was dead.

Then she and T.J. slowly made their way to the dock. He was getting weaker by the moment, leaning the bulk of his weight on Meg for support, and by the time they reached the landing dock, she was practically carrying him.

T.J. shifted his head in her lap. She heard him suck in a breath at the pain that must have ripped through his shoulder every time he moved.

"How's the pain?" she asked. It wasn't as if he'd answer truthfully, and it wasn't as if she really wanted to hear that every breath, every moment was agony.

"Not bad," he said through gritted teeth. She wondered if the Advil helped at all.

"Now who's the liar?"

She stroked his forehead with her hand. He flinched under her touch and she quickly pulled her hand away. But he was clammy, and his body felt unnaturally hot, like he was running a fever. That couldn't be good.

"Now we just have to hope the ferry comes back," T.J. said.

"Screw the ferry," Meg said as she caressed his cheek. "I'm guessing our little bonfire was like a Coast Guard beacon. All of Roche Harbor must have seen it. I bet the helicopters will be up as soon as the sun rises." Actually, she prayed that was the case. If the Coast Guard showed up, T.J. could get medical attention right away.

He shivered. "Good."

Meg checked the horizon for the twentieth time that hour. Was the sky lightening at all? She wasn't sure. She'd been staring into the darkness for so long, she couldn't tell anymore if she'd willed her eyes to see a faint blush of dawn. But the blackness of the sky seemed to have a purplish hue. Was the night finally over?

"Sun's rising," T.J. said. He didn't open his eyes.

"We made it." Meg tucked a blanket around his good shoulder, careful not to touch the side where she'd shot him. It was no trick of the eye now. The purple sky gave way to a deep blue before streaks of pale yellow crept across the horizon.

"We'll be home soon," Meg said. She'd spent most of the dark night jabbering away about nonsense. What they'd do when they got back to the mainland. College in the fall. Los Angeles. And beaches. And celebrities. Anything to keep their minds off reality.

"Yeah," he said. His eyes squinted open just a sliver. "But part of us will always be here."

Meg couldn't help but smile. "Are you sure you're not the writer?"

That warranted a pair of dimples as a slight grin appeared on T.J.'s face. She bent down and kissed him lightly on the lips. "I'm glad you can still smile," she said as she pulled away.

"Oh, you know. What's not to smile about? A bunch of my friends are dead and you shot me."

The reminder that Minnie was dead made her stomach drop. Her best friend was gone, murdered right before her eyes. Their last hours together had been a nightmare and so much had been left unsaid between them. Meg had tried so hard to save them both, and now she felt guilty that she had survived while Minnie had not.

T.J. must have felt the same way about Gunner. How would they ever get past the survivor's guilt? Not to mention the fact that Meg had shot him. Would he ever be able to forgive her? Would she ever be able to forgive herself?

Meg could have tried to explain away her actions, but she wanted to make sure she got it all on the table. "I was shooting to kill. I thought you were the murderer."

"We were all suspects."

"Yeah? Did you think I did it?"

"No." T.J. laughed, which turned immediately into a weak, dry cough that racked his body.

"See? So that means I'm the worst person on the planet."

"Meg, he *made* you believe that. He was one step ahead of us the whole way."

"I guess." Meg couldn't shake the fact that she'd tried to kill T.J. It seemed like an insurmountable obstacle. "But I fell for it. And it was partly out of anger. I didn't believe that you really liked me, especially not after what I did to you. I mean, you've been avoiding me for months, and it was easy to believe you were just using my feelings for you to accomplish all the murders. It made me feel . . . pathetic."

"I'm sorry. About avoiding you. I was really angry at first. Hurt, you know? I couldn't even look at you."

Meg winced. She thought she'd only been hurting herself. She never realized she'd wounded him as well. "I . . . I didn't know."

"It's done now. Besides . . ." T.J. reached his good arm back and squeezed her leg. "You saved my life. Tom would have killed me. You could have gotten away once I distracted him. Saved yourself. But you didn't." He grinned again, looking more like the old flirtatious T.J. "I think that sort of cancels out Homecoming."

"What about the bullet in your shoulder?"

T.J. smiled. "I'm sure we can think of another way for you to make that up to me."

Meg recalled the panic she'd felt at losing T.J.—once when she shot him, and once when he tried to save her from Tom. If only she'd trusted him and her own feelings, perhaps he wouldn't be lying there wounded. Perhaps Minnie wouldn't be dead.

A heavy tear rolled down Meg's cheek.

"Hey." T.J.'s voice was strong and forceful. "Don't be so hard on yourself." There he went, reading her mind again. "We're still here. We made it."

She looked down into those sparkly brown eyes and the dimples that dotted each cheek. "Yeah. Yeah, we did."

"Now it looks like you're stuck with me."

Meg smiled despite herself. "And if it doesn't work out, I can always shoot you again."

T.J.'s eyes twinkled. "See? Gold."

A sound broke the monotony of lapping waves. Something rhythmic. Something man-made. Like a fan turned on full blast.

Meg and T.J. both looked up at the same time. A tiny dot appeared in the sky—orange against the growing light of dawn, and getting larger by the second.

The Coast Guard.

"Can you handle me?" T.J.'s hand grasped hers, tight and firm. "Can you? Because after all of this, I just . . . I can't imagine being without you."

Ten bodies. Ten lives cut short. Meg could see them all in her mind, from Lori's purple face to the sleeping death of the Taylors, to Tom's mask of hatred as the flames consumed the boat. Ten people who would never live their lives, never feel love or hate or fear or anything ever again. How much time had she wasted living in fear? Living for others? How much of her life would she continue to let slip away without enjoying a single moment?

That ended. Here and now.

"I love you, Thomas Jefferson Fletcher." Meg couldn't believe how easy the words came. "I've loved you for as long as I can remember."

The helicopter was closer now, circling the smoldering ruins of the boathouse. Then someone on board spotted them and the helicopter turned toward the dock, so close the force of its blades sucked the air right out of Meg's lungs.

"When you texted me the day of Homecoming . . ." T.J.'s voice trailed off. "I thought you really didn't care about me."

"I know," Meg said. She so desperately wanted him to understand. "I—"

He held up his hand. "I get it. I get it now. You and Minnie . . . it was complicated." The chopper hovered right above them. Meg looked up and saw the side door open and a stretcher swing out on the crane.

"Meg!" T.J. shouted against the noise.

She looked down at T.J. His face was serious again. Tight and worn.

"Don't let her come between us again, okay? It's done."

Done. Done and dead. But as nightmarish as the whole weekend had been, as horrifying and painful and life-altering in a way that even years of therapy wouldn't be able to cure her of, it had done one beautiful thing. It had brought her and T.J. together.

She bent her head to his and kissed him. Whatever they'd become after the weekend at White Rock House, they'd become it together.

There was no going back.

ACKNOWLEDGMENTS

TO MY EDITOR, KRISTIN DALY RENS, WHO inspired this book. More than just an editor, she's a muse.

To my agent, Ginger Clark, without whom I'd be curled up under my desk in the fetal position half the time. She's a friend and a warrior, and I'm so lucky to have her.

To my fabulous team at Balzer + Bray—Alessandra Balzer, Donna Bray, and Sara Sargent, who have been cheerleaders and rock stars all around. And to the extended HarperCollins family, specifically copy editor Amy Vinchesi, production editor Kathryn Silsand, Emilie Polster and Stefanie Hoffman in marketing, Caroline Sun and Olivia deLeon in publicity, and the amazing cover designer Ray Shappell.

To Holly Frederick and Dave Barbor at Curtis Brown, Ltd., who have, once again, worked tirelessly on behalf of this book.

To the greatest group of readers the world has ever known: Carrie Harris, Jennifer Bosworth, Jennifer Donahue, Amy Bai, Lisa and Laura Roecker, Christine Fonseca, Roy Firestone, Mark Uhlemann, Rachel Hunter, Abby McDonald, LynDee Walker,

Nikki Katz, and especially Laurel Hoctor Jones.

To my network of supporters who keep me sane with a variety of phone calls, texts, chats, happy hours, and mental health days: Jessica Childress, Shannon Spencer, Amy McKenzie, Amy Dachtler, Tara Campomenosi, Rachanee Srisavasdi, Amy Romero, Eileen Tsai, Ellen Files, Bryn Greenwood, Leah Clifford, Jen Hayley, Jill Myles, Jessica Morgan, Juliette Dominguez, David Eilenberg, Kirsten Roeters, Suzanne Keilly, and Jake Gilchrist. Plus the denizens of Purgatory, the collected awesome of the Apocalypsies, and the YARebels old and new.

To Scott Tracey, who, when he heard the pitch for this novel, insisted I write it.

To Alpheus Fletcher Underhill IV, for technical expertise and an unlimited supply of story ideas, which I could never use but appreciate nonetheless.

To Yadira Taylor, one of my dearest friends, who will always be tied to this book. It's dedicated to her mom, whom I miss dearly.

To Roy Firestone, who made me cry several times during the writing of this book. I'm a better person (and friend) because of it.

To my mom, who did so much to facilitate my deadline I can't even list them all for fear it might make me sound like a dysfunctional twelve-year-old. She's the best mom ever. Enough said.

Much love.

TURN THE PAGE FOR A SNEAK PEEK
AT GRETCHEN'S NEWEST BOOK,

ONE

2:20 P.M.

JOSIE CROUCHED BEHIND THE PHOTON LASER module and aligned it with the beam splitter at the other end of the lab table. "Once we build the vacuum dome," she said, making a minor adjustment to the laser's trajectory, "this should work."

"Should?" Penelope said.

Josie glanced at her lab partner. "There's a reason no one's been able to prove the Penrose Interpretation."

Penelope snorted. "Because it's unprovable?"

"Thank you, Captain Obvious," Josie said, with an arch of her brow. "Would you also like to tell me why the sky is blue and the Earth is round?"

"Ha-ha." Penelope bumped Josie out of the way with her hip and took her place behind the laser. "I don't know how you talked me into doing *this* as our science-fair entry. What if it doesn't work? I'll never get into Stanford if I fail AP Physics."

Josie sighed. "We're not going to fail." She looked around the room at the array of textbook experiments their classmates were working on: balloons and static electricity, wave pools, concave mirrors. Total amateur hour, whereas she and Penelope were tackling Penrose's wave-collapse theory of quantum gravity. It was like bringing a major leaguer to a T-ball game. "Mr. Baines grades on a curve. We'll be fine."

"We'd better be." Penelope moved around the table. For the bazillionth time, she began carefully measuring out the positions of the one hundred or so mirrors they'd use in the experiment, noting their exact locations in her spiral notebook. Her straight black hair swished back and forth in front of her face as she scribbled furiously. "Are you sure you're not just doing this as an FU to your mom?"

Josie stiffened. "Of course not."

Penelope didn't look up. "I don't know. Seems like trying to prove an almost impossible theory that's in direct conflict with the hypothesis your mom's spent her entire career exploring is kind of a slap in the face."

It was, of course. Josie knew it. Penelope knew it. If Josie's mom had bothered to initiate an actual conversation with her daughter in the last six months, she'd probably know it too. But Josie wasn't about to admit that in fourth-period physics.

"I'm worried about the laser," she said, changing the subject. "I'm not sure it's strong enough."

Penelope calmly looked up at Josie with her almond-shaped eyes. A grin crept across her face. "We could always borrow the experimental laser your mom has up at her lab."

"No way," Josie said.

"Oh, come on! It's perfect."

Josie held firm. "We cannot use the hundred-kilovolt X-ray free-electron prototype from my mom's lab, okay? Get over it."

Penelope wasn't about to give up. "Maybe you could have your dad borrow it? For legitimate work purposes? And then if it just *happened* to end up in our demonstration the night of the science fair no one—"

"My dad moved out last weekend," Josie interrupted in a clipped tone.

She hadn't told anyone yet, except Nick, and only because he'd picked her up for a date ten minutes after Josie's dad had broken the news that he'd rented an apartment in Landover.

"Oh," Penelope said, her eyes wide. "Shit, I'm sorry."

"It's okay." It wasn't.

Penelope opened her mouth to say something, when the loud speaker in the classroom crackled to life.

"Attention, students," said the voice of the school secretary. *"We have a special announcement."*

"What now?" Penelope groaned.

"Quiet down, everyone," Mr. Baines said. The murmur in the classroom dulled.

Josie checked her watch. A special announcement five minutes before the end of the school day? That was weird.

"Good afternoon, this is Principal Meyers. As some of you may have heard, another body was found in the woods west of Crain Highway this afternoon."

The classroom erupted into excited whispers. "What?"

Penelope squeaked. "Another one?"

"Like the previous incidents, the victim was killed sometime between the hours of ten o'clock in the evening and four o'clock in the morning, from an apparent animal attack."

Josie arched an eyebrow. "Animal attack? In Bowie, Maryland?"

"Shh!" Penelope hissed.

"Therefore, students are asked to refrain from visiting the Patuxent River Watershed or other surrounding uninhabited areas after dark until the animal or . . ."

Principal Meyers paused and cleared his throat with that kind of dry, forced cough a kid makes when they're trying to convince Mom and Dad they're too sick to go to school.

"Until the animal," he continued, *"or other perpetrator responsible for the attacks is apprehended."*

"Other perpetrator?" Josie said out loud. "What the hell does that mean?"

But Principal Meyer offered no response to Josie's question. The loudspeaker popped once, twice, and fell silent.

TWO

2:35 P.M.

THE END-OF-DAY BELL PEALED THROUGH THE classroom, jarring everyone into action.

"Don't forget," Mr. Baines shouted above the commotion of screeching chairs, backpack zippers, and the almost choral musicality of thirty cell phones all being powered on at once. "Final review of your projects tomorrow. Be prepared to defend your hypotheses."

"How can I think about my science project after that?" Penelope clutched Josie's backpack as they slowly filed out of the room. "Other perpetrator. See? I knew the police were covering up for a serial killer."

Josie half turned around. "Who said anything about a serial killer?"

"Sixteen dead bodies in six months, their gruesome, dismembered, and half-eaten remains left in the woods in the dead of night?" Penelope almost sounded excited as she described the murder scenes. "Please, this is classic serial-killer territory."

Josie laughed. "Okay, CSI."

"Fine, don't believe me." Penelope trotted alongside her in the crowded hallway. "But it fits. The pattern, the escalation. And now we've had two murders in the last week alone." She paused and dropped her voice. "I'm sure this animal-attack crap is just a cover-up so the population won't panic and descend into martial law."

Ah, that was the Penelope Josie had known for years. The lovable conspiracy theorist who spent most of her free time combing antigovernment blogs and with each passing day became increasingly convinced that Big Brother was watching her. "Pen, you're blowing this way out of proportion."

"No, I'm not," Penelope said, sounding hurt. "I never blow anything out of proportion."

Josie planted her hands on her hips. "Remember that time you were convinced your eighty-year-old neighbor was a spy for the Venezuelan government? Or what about when you almost electrocuted yourself trying to find the hidden listening devices the NSA had installed in the walls of your house?"

Penelope pursed her lips. "Still no proof I was wrong about either, thank you very much."

"Hey!" a familiar voice called out through the postclass crush of bodies. Josie spun around and caught her breath as she spied the tall, black-haired figure of her boyfriend, Nick Fiorino, threading his way through the crowd.

"Hey, gorgeous," Nick said, planting a kiss on Josie's cheek. "Miss me?"

Nick pulled her close and Josie let out an audible sigh. Out of the corner of her eye, she could have sworn she saw Penelope roll her eyes.

"Can you believe they found another body?" Nick shook his head. "How many is that now? Like a dozen?"

"Sixteen," Penelope said quickly. "Although coverupcadet.com suggests the actual number may be more like two dozen, if you take into account the missing-persons reports of the last six months and cross-reference them against people known to be in the vicinity of a wooded area." She chuckled nervously. "This is why I don't leave the house."

"Wow, Pen," Nick said. "That's, um . . ." He glanced sidelong at Josie, grasping for words.

"Insane?" Josie suggested.

"Fine, don't believe me." Penelope narrowed her eyes. "But we'll see who's insane when the feds catch the serial killer. Later." Then she turned on her heel and marched off down the hall.

"I don't think she likes me," Nick half joked.

Josie smiled at him. "You know how Pen is with . . . people."

Madison's meticulously groomed head of curls popped up beside Nick. "Can you believe it?" she said, slightly out of breath. "Another body!"

"I know, right?" Josie said.

A look of concern passed over her best friend's face. "Don't take that shortcut through the woods anymore, okay, Josie? If there's an animal out there stalking people, I don't want you to be the next victim."

Josie smiled. It was sweet that Madison was concerned about her. "Don't worry," she said lightly. "Penelope thinks it's actually a serial killer, so it's cool."

Madison's eyes grew wide. "A serial killer?"

"Let's not go there," Nick said.

"Anyway," Madison said with a shake of her curls. "Josie, what are you doing after school?"

Josie sighed. "I have to drive to Landover before my shift at the Coffee Crush."

"Landover?" Madison said.

"Yeah." Josie dropped her eyes. "I have to go pick something up from my dad's new place."

"Your dad's new place . . ." Madison's voice trailed off as she processed Josie's words.

Josie sucked in a breath as she felt Nick's hand grip her shoulder. Ugh. Better to just get it all out in the open. "My dad moved out last weekend." The words tumbled on top of one another as they raced out of her mouth. "Movers accidentally took the old mirror my mom used to keep up in her lab. She's dispatched me to retrieve it. That's it."

"Oh," Madison said. Then her eyes widened as reality dawned on her. "Oh!" She paused. "Okay, well, I'm taking my demon little sister to dance class, but I'll be home by the time you're off work. So call me, okay? If you need to talk?"

Josie smiled weakly. "Will do."

Madison nodded, then turned and headed down the hall. Josie's smile lingered as she watched Madison go. Madison might be a bit of an airhead upon occasion, but she was also incredibly sweet and thoughtful. Two things Josie desperately needed in a best friend these days.

Nick leaned down and whispered in Josie's ear. "You okay?"

"Yeah." Josie took a deep breath, then let it out slowly. She *so* didn't want to drive all the way to her dad's new condo by herself. The thought was so depressing. "Any chance you can ditch track practice and come with me?"

"Sorry, gorgeous," Nick said with a shake of his head. "Regionals are in two weeks. Coach would kill me if I miss practice."

Josie tried to hide her disappointment. "Oh."

"Walk me to the gym, though?"

Josie nodded absently. "Yeah, okay."

They navigated the halls in silence, Josie wrapped up in her thoughts. Her parents' separation had hit hard. One day they seemed like their normal, happy selves, but seemingly overnight things had changed. Small fights at first, then before Josie knew it, her parents' nightly screaming matches were the new normal around the Byrne household. In less than six months, her dad had moved out. Now Josie's home life was a hot mess. Her dad was still in shock and, like a lovesick teen, spent most of his time trying to get Josie's mom to take him back. Her mom had thrown herself into her work, going so far as to have a home lab constructed in their basement to avoid charges of child abandonment while she worked twenty-four seven on her new experiment. Meanwhile, Josie could count on one hand the number of conversations they'd had in the last week that weren't about work or—

"Did you hear me?"

Josie's head snapped up. She and Nick were standing in front of the entrance to the boys' locker room. His hands were folded across his chest, and his dark eyebrows were pinched together.

"Huh?"

Nick sighed. "Josie, were you even listening to me?"

"I'm sorry," Josie said, with a shake of her head. "I was just . . . I don't know. Lost."

"You've been like that a lot lately," he said quietly. "Between your parents and your science project, it's like you don't have time for anything else." It wasn't an accusation so much as a statement of fact. "Do you even remember what today is?"

Josie caught her breath. Was it Nick's birthday? Had she forgotten Nick's birthday? No, that was in October. Josie relaxed. Forgetting her boyfriend's birthday would have been a disaster.

"Never mind." Nick shook his head and stepped toward her. "Look, there's something I need to talk to you about. Something important."

Josie looked up at him. There was an edge to his voice that made her heart beat faster. "Is everything okay?"

"Yeah, yeah," he said quickly. "I mean, there's just a lot going on and I needed to—"

Deep in Josie's purse, an alarm went off. Her cellphone reminder that she needed to be in the car on the way to her dad's if she was going to make it back to work on time. She'd already gotten a written warning because of her tardiness—usually because she was lingering at the track, watching Nick practice—so she needed to motor. "Crap," she said. "I have to go."

"Oh." The muscles around Nick's mouth sagged, reflecting more dejection and pain than his clipped, monosyllabic response. What was going on with him?

"Call me," Josie said. "After practice, okay? We'll talk tonight."

"Okay." Nick flashed his crooked half smile, the sadness of a moment before evaporated. He was his old, carefree self again. "Don't let any monsters attack you on the way back from Landover, okay?"

Josie snuggled her face to his chest. "I'll try."

THREE

3:45 P.M.

JOSIE'S ANCIENT HATCHBACK SHUDDERED IN protest as she stepped on the accelerator.

"Come on." She leaned forward in her seat, willing the old car to go faster. "If I'm late again I'm going to get fired."

As if in answer, the Ford Focus lurched forward. A hand-me-down from her cousin, it was almost as old as she was, and the engine screeched in protest as she held the pedal to the floor. The speedometer flickered, desperately grasping for forty-five miles per hour, and for a fleeting moment, Josie thought the Teal Monster, as Madison had dubbed the car, might actually have some kick left in her.

Or not. The engine sputtered, momentum slowed, and Josie had to downshift to third gear.

"I hate you," she said, slapping the steering wheel with the palm of her hand. "Just so you know."

From inside her purse, Josie's phone rang. Keeping one hand on the wheel, she fished out her cell and hit speakerphone.

"Hello?" she said loudly, over the roar of her car's engine.

"Did you get it?" Her mom's voice was crisp and businesslike.

Josie whizzed around a turn and hoped her mom couldn't hear the screech of tires on the other end of the line. "The mirror?"

"Of course."

She eyed the rearview mirror, sending a death stare bouncing to the back of her car, where the oversized rococo monstrosity sat covered in a fluffy blue blanket, wedged into the flattened backseat through a feat of advanced car yoga.

"Josie, are you there?"

"Yeah, sorry." Glancing right and left, Josie careened through a yellow light just as it turned red, praying there were no state troopers around as she barreled through the intersection. A speeding ticket was the last thing she needed. "I've got the mirror," she said, before her mom could ask again.

"Good." Her mom cleared her throat. "I just had a shipment delivered at the lab. So I'll—"

"Be home late," Josie said, finishing her thought. It was a conversation they had at least twice a week, whenever her mom got a shipment of materials delivered to her lab at Fort Meade. Top secret stuff, but Josie guessed it was the ultradense deuterium her mom used in most of her experiments. If so, it might be a few days before her mom surfaced from the lab.

"Right." Her mom paused. "Okay, well, drive safely. I'll call you later."

Josie clicked off her phone. Part of her was relieved when her mom worked late: the tension between them recently had been almost unbearable. But since her dad had moved out, the house was lonely, and the idea of spending another night there by herself was incredibly depressing.

Her mood sinking like lead in water, Josie flipped on the radio. It was programmed to the AM news station.

"From the evidence at the scene," a man said in a cool academic voice, "we have determined that the attacks were not caused by a bear. They appear to be the work of a predatory cat of some kind."

A reporter cut into the prerecorded statement. "When pressed for information, Captain Wherry stated that local investigators are targeting known collectors of exotic animals in hopes of finding the cause of the recent attacks. For WPTN, I'm Morgan Curón."

Josie rolled her eyes. A cat? Really? Sixteen dead bodies and all the authorities could come up with was an exotic cat?

Maybe Penelope was right: it *was* a cover-up.

"Time for weather on the nines," the news anchor said in his overly cheerful radio voice. "And we're looking at glorious weather for this April fifteenth."

Josie's stomach dropped. Today was April fifteenth?

Holy crap, no wonder Nick looked so sad when she left. Today was their anniversary.

And Josie had completely forgotten.

Shit, shit, shit. Major relationship screwup. How could she have forgotten? It was just a few weeks ago that she and Nick had been at the mall and he'd pointed out a necklace he thought she might like in the window of a chain jewelry store. Entwined hearts with little red stones at the apex of each. No wonder he'd been acting so weird that afternoon. He was waiting for her to wish him a happy anniversary so he could give her the necklace.

She reached for her phone; she needed to talk to him right that second. But he'd be in the middle of practice. Damn. She'd have to wait until after her shift and then maybe they could celebrate their one-year anniversary tomorrow?

She was the worst girlfriend ever.

Josie sped around a corner, tapping the brakes as lightly as possible so as not to lose momentum, and veered onto Leeland Road. Another glance at the time. 3:50 p.m. Ten minutes. She pushed Nick and her anniversary from her mind. There was nothing she could do about it, and at the moment she had to focus on getting to work. As long as she didn't get caught at the railroad crossing she was totally going to make it.

Wishful thinking. Josie heard the peal of bells before she even saw the flashing lights. Train coming.

Crap.

Option A: slam both feet onto the accelerator and pray her car had enough power to slip under the rapidly descending crossing arm. Option B: slow down and wait for the train. Option A: decent chance of a gruesome, fiery death. Option B: decent chance she'd get fired.

Kind of a close call, but after a moment's hesitation, Josie hit the brakes and screeched to a stop just as the railroad-crossing arm locked into place across Leeland Road.

It didn't take long for Josie to regret her sensible decision.

Immediately, she realized it was a government transport train leaving Fort Meade. Probably the same one that had just delivered the shipment to her mom.

Oh, the irony.

Josie counted the cars as they ambled by. *Seventeen, eighteen, nineteen*. She checked the clock. 3:57 p.m. "Come on!" she said through clenched teeth.

Twenty-two, twenty-three, twenty-four. Josie leaned over the steering wheel and craned her neck, trying to get a view of the rails stretching south through the thick greenery of forest that hugged both sides of the road. She could barely see twenty feet down the tracks. Was there an end in sight? She couldn't tell.

Twenty-six, twenty-seven, twenty-eight. Josie fished her cell phone out of her purse. She'd call work and explain. See? It wasn't her fault. She would have been on time if it hadn't been for the stupid train. How could she control that?

3:59. With a heavy sigh, Josie scrolled through her contacts to the coffeehouse's number and hit the green button.

Josie wasn't quite sure what happened next. The Teal Monster idled at the crossing, the occasional shudder of the strained engine rumbling beneath her. Then suddenly, the car lurched so violently that Josie's head smacked into the roof. She screamed—half from surprise, half from fear—and smashed her foot onto the brake pedal. Had someone hit her? She frantically looked into the rearview mirror, but saw only the barren expanse of Leeland Road twisting into the woods. Confused, she turned all the way around to make sure a deer hadn't accidentally rammed her.

That's when she noticed the mirror. It lay cockeyed in the back, and the blue blanket had slid to one side. The mirror must have moved in the backseat while she was stopped at the crossing.

Huh?

She reached back to see if the mirror had been damaged, when a light flashed—fierce, white, and so intense that a searing pain shot through her eyeballs to the back of her skull and left her irises screaming for mercy. It was a clear, sunny afternoon in the middle of April, but the light that filled Josie's car blinded her as if she'd been sitting for hours in utter darkness and someone had suddenly shone a spotlight in her face. She slapped a hand over her eyes, desperate to block out the blinding flash. Blood thundered through her temples, and her eyes ached against the piercing light. Josie buried her face in her hands, and felt the car shudder . . .

Then everything went dark.